Glass Houses

Anne Coombs

Anne Coombs was a journalist, author, political activist, and philanthropist. She authored five books, including *No Man's Land* (Simon & Schuster, 1993), *Sex and Anarchy: The life and death of the Sydney Push* (Viking, 1996) and *Broometime* (Hodder Headline, 2001), co-authored with Susan Varga.

Anne was one of the founders of Rural Australians for Refugees. She was a board member and chair of GetUp! She shared a passion with her partner for a fairer Australia, advocating for refugees and people seeking asylum.

In recent years Anne was a frequent essayist and commentator, and a regular contributor to the Griffith Review. She also wrote a feature film script set in Australia's far north, currently being developed for production.

Anne died at her Exeter home in December 2021.

Anne Coombs

Glass Houses

A Novel

UPSWELL

First published in Australia in 2023
by Upswell Publishing
Perth, Western Australia
upswellpublishing.com

ISBN: 978-0-6455368-3-6

A catalogue record for this book is available from the National Library of Australia

Cover design by Chil3, Fremantle
Typeset in Foundry Origin by Lasertype
Printed by McPherson's Printing Group

Upswell Publishing is assisted by the State of Western Australia through its funding program for arts and culture.

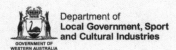

Department of
Local Government, Sport and Cultural Industries
GOVERNMENT OF
WESTERN AUSTRALIA

1.

Glaston had been in the doldrums for forty years when I arrived. Not so much dead or dying as undecided. Worn down by branch closures and businesses leaving, by farming changes and the fickleness of markets; held up by a solid past and the confidence of those who saw beauty in it. Its streets are lined with trees – pepper and jacaranda and flame. In November the explosions of purple and red, one after another into the distance, catches you in the throat. And in the summer the pepper trees lean down towards you as you walk beneath them, offering you their cool green tips.

It was once the most beautiful town in New South Wales and although now shabby its stone buildings and graceful awnings are a reminder of better days. There were once three banks along its main street, substantial edifices of sandstone topped by pediments and curlicues. One had an eagle above its iron-studded double doors. The town hall and the courthouse attest to the pride of those early civic fathers and to a colonial administration that, for the most part, did their bidding. This was a town where business ruled politics and where the emerging squattocracy were undecided whether they were part of the establishment or against it. A new land, new rules.

When Lt William Berge took up land near the crossroads and the coaching inn there was not much more to Glaston. It was just a small outpost on the River Glass. The river was said to have been named after a naval admiral who had been popular in London because of the decisive role he was said to have played in some battle, but who had then run off with a fellow officer's son. My friends in Glaston liked this story. But another version of where the Glass Valley got its name was that when Leichhardt first saw it on a still winter's morning the whole valley was covered in frost and shone like frosted glass.

To get to his land William Berge had to call the puntman from his shack and, if it was after dark, negotiate a price to get across the river. It was not a particularly broad river and slow-moving, but it was deep and there were dangerous snags. Once, when the puntman was too drunk to move, Berge was forced to swim his horse across, the mount plunging reluctantly from the bank, striking out desperately for the far side. Berge and his horse parted company midstream and both nearly drowned. So the first thing that Lt Berge did when he came into his fortune was to build the Glaston bridge. And the second thing he did was to lay the foundation stone for his mansion, Glastonbridge.

I stayed on in Glaston far longer than I intended; stayed on out of inertia or hope or sheer perversity. But long enough to develop a deep and irritated affection for the place. The people I met were unlike any I'd known before. I was amused and increasingly fascinated. And because I needed distraction it was easy to be swept up in their lives – easier than dealing with my own. I envied them their unquestioning acceptance of who they were and what mattered to them in life. After a time I realised it was not so simple. But by then I was too caught up with them to judge them. And by then I knew that they were not taking me away from my life at all, but towards it; that the stories I heard were part of my story. Raymond's most of all. I might postpone my life but his was drawing me onwards. And as his unfolded, so would mine. We can blind ourselves to our own motivations and sometimes we have to. Otherwise we can't live with ourselves.

*

The first time Raymond saw Glastonbridge was on a cold June day in 1989. A fateful day. A day for staying indoors, for the warmth of a fire; or for city streets, for brightly lit shops and the press of humanity. Not the sort of day to be standing on a neglected rural hillside in the drizzle. But Raymond didn't notice the drizzle. He didn't notice the way the raindrops were slowly soaking through the shoulders of his jacket, that his fingers were white-tipped and his toes numb. All his life he'd been looking for a house like this. Not in shape exactly. How could anyone even imagine such a shape? The length of windows, the pinnacle of roof, the tower and battlements and angles jutting everywhere. He had never known of this place's existence, yet seeing it now, it was so familiar to him. It was absurd, fantastic. Out of place, out of time.

Raymond looked up at the building. It's massive stone walls rose above him, defiant. He felt...what did he feel? Both insignificant and masterful. The house was like a beast to him, a living thing. Disregarding, defiant. He was a mere insect beside it. And yet, and yet...he put his hand out, tentatively at first, touching the stone wall as if it were a powerful stallion. He might be its keeper and it might be his refuge. A place away from this world that had always been such an uncomfortable fit.

He wandered one more time through the mansion's interior. In places the floor was wet where rain had come in through the broken panes. The cold stone walls accentuated the winter chill and afternoon gloom. But Raymond barely noticed. He was transfixed by the atmosphere of the house. Flag-stoned passageways led from room to room, the walls lined with timber panelling. The ceilings were so high they disappeared into the dimness but in one place a high window revealed the intricate plasterwork. The downstairs rooms all had massive stone fireplaces, the one in the great hall so large it could have been meant for a Scottish castle.

By the time he had climbed to the top of the house and back down the twists and turns of the servants' stairs, his heart was beating so loudly he thought he might have a heart attack. Could one die from excitement? Even though the place was a mess – it had been unlived in for twenty years and unloved far longer than that – he was struck by its austere integrity. Part of him quavered before it. Did he really dare to take on such a place? He knew he must. Sometimes, at the last moment before clasping something that he dearly wanted, he drew back. But this time he barely hesitated.

In the last remnants of light, he walked down what had once been the terrace steps and turned for a last look at the house. The steep pitch of the front gables loomed above him against the darkening sky. From the mock battlements on the tower came a chirping and fluttering of wings as birds settled for the night. A mist was rising from the river flats below him as he turned towards the car.

Three months later he moved in, even though there was no working kitchen, no bathroom and the roof leaked in multiple places.

The River Glass is these days a gentle, pebble-bottomed river lined with willows. Glastonbridge stands high above it on the leeside of the hill, behind a screen of pines and oaks, a vast neo-Gothic fantasy. By the time Raymond saw it, the local people seemed to have forgotten the house was there. It had been empty and boarded up for years. The hundred or so acres left from the original grant of five thousand were leased by a neighbouring farmer, who ran his steers and weaners on the neglected paddocks and rarely went near the house. Only occasionally, when a frisky calf got through the broken-down garden fence and had to be chased out, did it register with the farmer that the house was still there, behind a tangle of nettles and lantana.

When Raymond bought Glastonbridge, his sister Lillian was still living in New York. From that distance, Raymond's new project had seemed a typically eccentric undertaking but not one that greatly concerned her. It was three years later, when she came back to Australia for their mother's funeral, that she voiced an opinion.

'How could you bring Mother to live in this!' It was a statement, not a question. 'How *could* you!'

Raymond looked around him, at the stone-flagged floor, at the ladders against the wall where he was stripping wallpaper, at the grand staircase. True, the staircase was draped in drop sheets and had been for the past six months. But it was still grand. He was puzzled by Lillian's reaction. 'She wanted to. She could have stayed in Sydney but she wanted to live here. She told me once it was like going on an adventure, "a heroic adventure with a grand purpose" – that's what she said.'

'And who were you meant to be, Indiana Jones? I can't believe you, Raymond, I think you've gone completely mad.'

At breakfast the next morning in Raymond's makeshift kitchen, sombrely dressed in their funeral clothes, Lillian hissed: 'You killed her! Bringing her to live in this ruin! It's your fault.'

Raymond stared at the floor for a few moments, then sighed heavily and said: 'She was eighty-four, Lillian.'

'Exactly. You should have looked after her better.'

Raymond had loved his mother. He couldn't quite bring himself to put aside her ashes so he kept them in a small metal box on her favourite mantelpiece. As he moved around the house he often felt that she was there with him. And he was comforted by that. He knew others thought it strange – his friend William wouldn't even go into the room where the ashes were kept – but to Raymond this sense of his mother's presence was no odder than many other things in the world. The world was a perplexing place. What he'd said to Lillian was true – his mother had wanted to be part of the adventure of Glastonbridge. And he wasn't going to deprive her of that.

And sometimes he needed her presence, because sometimes it felt as if the adventure was turning into a maze, a tiresome journey with no end in sight. What was he trying to achieve here? And what was the point of it? These thoughts came to him in the middle of the night, when he lay awake listening to the old house creaking and groaning around him. Maybe it was too late for him, maybe he was too old to take on such a house.

*

Theo Roth came out of the restaurant into weak spring sunshine. It had been a good lunch. Baillieu's was a new place, run by a young French chef. Fashionable, despite being in East Redfern, which Theo still couldn't think of as anything but one of Sydney's slum suburbs. But you would never hear him say that. Theo had strong opinions but rarely voiced them. He was, after all, in real estate.

He made his way down the pavement towards his Rolls, a corpulent figure, dressed completely in white. A white linen suit over a white Fabergé T-shirt, topped by a white fedora. White was Theo's corporate uniform. He'd started wearing it as a young man, to give him confidence, to set himself apart. Now he wore nothing else. Even his car was white, with red leather upholstery.

He got into the car and took off his fedora, tossing it onto the seat beside him. His head was large and distinguished, with deep-set eyes behind wire-framed spectacles, a large, rather protruding nose and a small pointed beard. He smoothed his beard, a habitual gesture, and glanced at the clock set into the polished dashboard. He had fifty minutes before the auction began. He should get a move on – he had to find a park for the car and get a good seat – but he lingered. A scrawny yellow mutt was wandering down the street towards him. It made straight for the Rolls and looked as if it was going to piss on a tyre then thought better of it. The mutt eyed him slowly then walked leisurely away with a stiff-legged old-dog walk. Theo's eye followed the dog as it wandered down the street. The old animal had a kind of dignity. He hoped he'd have as much when he was old and unwanted.

He'd been feeling a bit unwanted lately, at a loose end. Stepping back from the daily burden of running the business was one thing, but what was he to do with himself? He was too young to retire, and he'd always had prodigious energy. Being a 'consultant' did not take up enough of it. He had thought he might spend more time down at the farm with the family, but it didn't suit him. He and Julia were accustomed to spending large slabs of each week apart.

He thought idly about what he'd heard at lunch: that Lillian Tyler-Watson might be in financial trouble and that her brother Raymond might have to bail her out. He liked Raymond, he really did. They'd known each other for years, back to the days when antique auctions were quiet and gentlemanly affairs. But these days he couldn't think about him without feeling sick to the stomach. How had Raymond managed to slip in and buy Glastonbridge before anyone – before he, Theo Roth – had even known it was on the market? That was six years ago but he squirmed every time he thought about it. He shouldn't think about it. He'd get an ulcer.

In part it was his professional pride that had been wounded. Somehow, his contacts had failed him. No, he mustn't think about it. But he had a vision of the day Raymond had invited him up to see the house, Raymond jigging around on the huge crumbling terrace like an excited schoolboy. It was then, standing under the towering parapet of the western wing, the wind roaring through the pine trees, that Theo realised Raymond had beaten him, that none of his dream houses would ever compare to this one.

'Shit!' He shook himself, put the Rolls into drive and headed gracefully down the road towards the harbour.

At about the same time, Philip Dexter was on his way to the same auction. He pulled the door of his Queen Street shop behind him then, noticing a few smudges, discreetly rubbed the brass plate and call button with the sleeve of his jacket. He stood a moment on the step. It was a Monday afternoon and Queen Street was quiet. Only two or three figures wandered down the pavement past the elegant windows of the antique shops. Dealers' names were embossed on the plate glass in gold and black, his own 'Philip Dexter – Fine Arts and Antiques' one of the most elegant among them. Almost directly opposite was the two-storey building where Raymond opened his first shop in 1961, the year Philip was born. That building was too small for the up-market dealers who now dominated the street. It housed a business dealing in reproduction Portuguese wall tiles. Too garish for Philip's taste but he was occasionally able to suggest it to clients who wanted something colourful and ethnic for the bathroom.

Philip was not particularly tall but the elegance of his bearing suggested otherwise. He always dressed well: today, a navy Zegna jacket over pale grey trousers, and a scrumptious yellow tie. With his wavy blond hair and light olive skin, he was considered handsome, but that was largely because of the way he carried himself and the ten laps he swam every morning at the Boy Charlton Pool.

Philip was in no hurry. He had already viewed the lots and knew which pieces he intended to bid for, for either himself or clients or friends. Raymond wanted Philip to bid on an elaborately carved oak mirror, under the illusion that others might not realise it was Raymond who was buying. One look at the monstrous mirror and most people would recognise that the only place it would suit was the hall at Glastonbridge, above the fireplace. Unheard of before Raymond bought it six years ago, Glastonbridge was now infamous.

When Philip reached the auction room at Darling Harbour, he registered at the front desk and made his way past the rows of seats to one at the front. He nodded and smiled at several people along the way but avoided being caught in conversation – people always wanted to ask advice. He sat down and opened the catalogue, pretending to study it closely. Most people were milling about the lots stacked around the sides and back wall of the room. But at least one familiar figure had taken a seat. Theo Roth was in his usual spot in the centre of the back row. Philip had only been sitting a minute when Raymond scrambled along the row of seats and perched nervously beside him.

'I don't know why you insist on sitting here – it's so conspicuous.'

Philip ignored the question and smiled at Raymond with genuine pleasure: 'How are you, Raymond?'

'Oh, not very good. Lillian had another go at me last night. I'm not going to stay with her any more. I was going to ask you a favour. Could I stay at your place, just for tonight? I'm going to head off for Glaston tomorrow.'

'Of course you can,' Philip said. He was familiar with Raymond's rows with his sister. 'But why don't you just tell her where to get off?'

'Oohh, you don't know Lillian.'

'So you still want the mirror?' Philip asked.

'Oh yes, but I wouldn't be surprised if Theo goes for it. He seems to go after everything I want lately.'

'I don't think he'll want the mirror,' Philip said firmly.

'Oh, I wouldn't be so sure,' Raymond grumbled.

Philip held out his hand. 'Give me your number, then, and go and find yourself a seat. There's nothing else you want?'

'Oh, if I had the money...' Raymond trailed off as he took his bidder's number from his pocket and handed it over.

Philip thought, you're probably the richest man here, Raymond. So why do I always feel I'm dealing with a child?

Raymond stood up and moved away, hunched and rather crab-like. Trying to look discreet, no doubt, Philip thought as he settled himself back in his chair. The reason he sat in the front row was very simple. Others sat further back so they could see who was bidding for what and how much they were prepared to pay. Philip sat at the front so everyone would see how much he was buying and how much it was costing and that he was getting the best lots. They would see, too, how many different buyers he was bidding for. He took the four bidders' numbers from his coat pocket and put them on the seat beside him. All this helped to confirm his pre-eminence among dealers and attracted new clients.

When the auction was finally under way, Philip began to enjoy himself, not that he gave any sign of it. Not a sliver of a smile passed his lips. He sat impassively as hour followed hour, rising once or twice to get himself a glass of soda water then resuming his seat. His quick circuits of the room on the way to the buffet gave him a chance to see who was in for the long haul, in other words, who was waiting for the big items.

In a quiet spell while the auctioneer was dealing with a large and uninteresting batch of colonial cedar, Philip thought about Raymond. It was strange how these days he took care of Raymond, whereas before – how long ago? Twelve, thirteen years? Not so very long – it had been the other way around. That first afternoon he went to visit Raymond, he'd been so fearful of him. Raymond was the most important dealer in Queen Street. What mattered even more was that his specialty was the seventeenth century, England and the Low Countries. Philip knew about Raymond's buying trips, that his house on the shore of Sydney Harbour was filled with Jacobean oak and tapestries and old Dutch masters. He had thought that Raymond Tyler, heir to the Tyler fortune, connoisseur of unimpeachable social standing, might well laugh at an upstart twenty-two year old from the western suburbs who thought he knew something about antiques. But Raymond hadn't laughed. He'd questioned and marvelled, questioned then marvelled some more. They'd talked for hours, only stopping when a customer came into the shop. At the end of the afternoon Raymond had offered him a job, almost apologetically. 'Not much of a job – just a shop assistant, really.'

But it had turned out to be much more than that. Raymond had given him a start and every day of his life Philip gave silent thanks. People said cruel things about Raymond sometimes, but he never would.

When bidding began on the mirror, he thought at first that he had the field to himself. A couple of cocky amateurs made premature bids then dropped out. One other dealer – he could guess who without looking around – helped push the price up to $32,000. There the bidding stopped, in Philip's favour, and he allowed himself to relax slightly. But suddenly the auctioneer said 'Thirty-four thousand, the gentleman at the back of the room.' Philip tensed. He couldn't believe it. 'It's against you sir,' the auctioneer said, looking hard at him. Philip sat up very straight and turned slowly around. The rows of chairs were two-thirds empty. Most people had given up and gone home. But in the middle of the back row sat Theo Roth. Philip stared at him intently for a second or two – Theo was sitting slightly forward, looking at the floor. Then Philip turned back to the auctioneer and said, very quietly and firmly, 'Thirty-five thousand.'

Then he did something he never normally did: he turned around again and watched Theo, but Theo still sat there looking at the floor. He made no more bids and a few seconds later the mirror was Philip's. Or rather, Raymond's.

'I told you, I told you,' Raymond said excitedly when they met at the buffet just as it was closing up. 'He did it just to make me pay more!'

'Now, now, Raymond,' Philip replied mildly, 'not here.' He smiled calmly for the benefit of those who might be watching. 'Are you going to Lady Regan's tonight?'

'Yes, can I get a lift with you? Brutus is still at the mechanics.'

Brutus, Raymond's ancient black Chrysler, was always at the mechanics but Raymond refused to part with it.

'Where are your things then?'

'They're still at Lillian's. We can slip in and get them on the way. She'll be out.'

'I thought Lady Regan had lent you a car?'

'She had but she needed it back. I'd had it a week. It was a nice car, too, an Alfa. She's a dear, Lady Regan. She's very misunderstood.'

'That must be why you get on so well.'

'What do you mean?' Raymond asked.

'You're always saying you're misunderstood.'

'Am I?'

'I'll go and settle up. Meet you outside in five minutes.'

At the desk, Philip found Theo Roth.

'Good evening, Theo,' he said smoothly, as if nothing had happened. Theo nodded a greeting in return. They stood side by side, waiting to pay for their lots.

'Are you doing extensions at your place?' Philip asked. 'I thought perhaps you must be if you wanted that mirror. Couldn't quite picture where you would put it otherwise.'

Theo was silent a moment then said, 'You're right. I liked it but then I realised it was too big.'

'Spur-of-the-moment bid, was it?'

'You could say that.'

Lillian lived in an apartment that took up the entire top floor of a modern block of units in Darling Point. She'd been there a couple of years since coming back to Australia from New York after her husband died. Raymond stayed with Lillian when he was in Sydney, most of the time, except for when they were fighting, which they did a lot.

Of course Raymond always said the fights were Lillian's fault. The night before, they'd been sitting having a drink – it was actually his birthday and had been a good day – when a familiar note entered Lillian's voice, a note of complaint. Almost immediately Raymond could feel himself shutting off. He knew he should concentrate on what she was saying but why did she have to spoil everything? Why did every conversation turn into an argument?

'Raymond, are you listening?' she said.

'Yes, yes. Of course.'

Anyone observing them would pick almost immediately that they were brother and sister. Both were below average height, of compact, almost nuggetty build. Both had short tightly curled hair that hugged the scalp like a skull cap. But Raymond's was iron-coloured while Lillian's was that indeterminate colour between light brown and grey. Raymond was only one year older than Lillian but looked much older.

'Raymond!' she said sharply.

'Mmm.'

When she was living in New York, they had exchanged fond letters, even occasional phone calls. They hardly ever argued then. He wondered whether her husband Harold had found Lillian a difficult woman.

Lillian Tyler-Watson looked at her brother in exasperation. He wasn't listening. That was typical of Raymond: he could be sharp enough when his interests were at stake then go off in a daze the moment you began talking about your own. 'It won't be good for you, either,' she said angrily, 'if your sister is declared bankrupt.'

'I'm sure it won't c...come to that,' Raymond said, stammering slightly. 'You're exaggerating, Lil, as usual.'

'How can you be sure? You seem totally unwilling to help. It's so unfair. I'm sure Daddy wouldn't have meant it to work like this.'

Raymond hated the way she still called their late father 'Daddy'. He found it hard to even think of him as 'Father'. Sir Anthony was the only form of address that suited him. A life devoted to service and sheep; public duty and private wealth. Tasmania had been precisely the right-sized field for Sir Anthony's ambitions.

Raymond touched his forehead, tired all of a sudden. 'Not all that again,' he said. 'I think I've been very fair. When I bought Glaston-bridge I made sure you got the same amount for your own use. It's not my fault that you went playing the market and lost the lot. The rest of our capital, and you notice I do call it OUR capital, is tied up.'

'Rubbish,' Lillian said, standing up. 'You never have any trouble finding the money when you spot something you want in an auction catalogue. Just two pieces from your collection would clear my debt.'

'Hardly,' he laughed nervously. Then saw her expression. 'Just what two pieces did you have in mind?'

'Well...the Sly bookcases, for example. You know Theo Roth would pay almost anything to get them for his place.'

There was nothing dazed about Raymond now. He sat very straight in his chair and said coldly: 'Don't be absurd, Lillian, those bookcases are meant for Glastonbridge.'

'Oh yes, when you finish restoring Glastonbridge,' she said sar-castically. 'That'll be the day. At least at Theo's they'd be shown to advantage, not left covered in dust and workman's tools.'

Raymond pushed himself out of the chair. 'If you've quite finished, I'm going to bed. Even if you haven't finished, I'm going to bed. Because you never finish, do you Lil?'

They stood facing one another. Neither said anything but both were overcome by alternating waves of stubbornness and something that was near panic. Lillian thought, I shouldn't have said that about the bookcases. Raymond thought, if only Harold hadn't died, she'd still be in America and we'd still be friends and there wouldn't be these constant wrangles over money. It was he who broke the tension. Wearily, he said again, 'I'm going to bed,' then turned towards the door.

'That's right. Use my home like a hotel.'

Raymond paused then decided to ignore her. He had almost reached the door when he heard her say, 'I'll see you in the morning then.' Her voice was cool but not cold, midway between dismissal and apology. He left the room without looking back.

Lillian stood with her back to the big picture window, behind her a sea of lights and the dark sheen of the harbour. She was trembling with anger and resentment. Why did Raymond always do this to her? If only Harold hadn't died. She remembered the first time she'd seen her future husband. In Venice, in the Piazza San Marco. A flock of pigeons had suddenly risen from the cobblestones into the air and there was Harold, standing alone, looking for all the world as though he'd been left there by the angels. That was how it had seemed to her then, and still did. She was a miserable twenty-four year old doing the grand European trip, lonely and melancholy, and he had rescued her. He'd rescued her, too, from Mother and from Raymond. She'd never thought of it like that before. Now Mother was gone but there was still Raymond to deal with.

Lillian looked out the window unhappily. In the dark you could hardly see the view. In the morning, in the sunlight, when the harbour sparkled blue, she'd be more cheerful. It was hard to be sad in the sunshine and in front of such a view – the best view in Sydney.

*

Society friends who knew Raymond in Sydney or Melbourne – at the Contessa's dinner table or on Lady Regan's arm – would not have recognised him in Glaston. His usual dress was a pair of grey tracksuit pants, the crotch hanging low between his legs, and an old green sloppy joe stained with paint and linseed oil. Each day he'd rise from the small single bed in what had been (and eventually would be again) the butler's pantry, don these clothes and make his bed. The house might be in chaos but the bed was always made. The rest of the day would be spent helping his workman, Bob, or pulling apart a piece of furniture, or popping into Glaston to the hardware shop or to visit William.

Clover had been working at Glastonbridge for a couple of years, restoring the woodwork. When she heard Brutus grunting up the driveway she went to put the kettle on for a cup of tea. She thought Raymond looked tired when he came in but he grinned at her, sheepishly.

'How's it going?'

'Good,' she said. 'I've finished the doors and architraves in the tower room.'

'Let me get out of these clothes,' he shook himself, as if suddenly uncomfortable in his city wear, 'and I'll come up and have a look.'

Clover smiled, her pale blue eyes filling with light. She had a complexion the colour of clear honey and wide cheekbones that made her look as if she was smiling even when she wasn't. Clover was in her thirties but looked younger. She was one of those people who come into themselves late. Only recently had she discovered that her calling was with wood. The feel and grain of it, the colours hidden deep within it. Her talent was to bring old timber back to life. Now she was settled in Glaston, a town full of the stuff.

Sometimes, as she worked along the dark-grained wood, her nostrils full of metho and linseed oil and shellac, Raymond would come to her and ask her to stop what she was doing and move to another part of the house that he was suddenly keen for her to work on, or to help him with a piece of furniture he was restoring. At first she agreed but she soon became so frustrated with this starting and stopping and jobs left half done that she put her foot down.

'Not till I finish here,' she'd say, 'then I'll do it', knowing that by then his desire to see the real colour of the timber in the second nursery, or whatever, would have faded.

He still asked but seemed to bear no grudge when she refused. 'Of course, of course, you're right,' he'd say, and wander off.

He did the same thing with Bob. More often than not, Bob complied. They were as bad as each other. Bob could turn his hand to anything – carpentry, bricklaying, plumbing – and he was just as prone as Raymond to leaving things half done.

Some people thought Raymond was frivolous, a dilettante, but Clover always defended him. 'They don't see how he loves every part of the house, or how much he knows about each thing he buys for it. Raymond is making a work of art,' she'd say. Nothing, not even the smallest item, was allowed to become part of his grand design unless it qualified. Furniture, houses, bore witness to human lives. Worn by use, they were the evidence of all that had gone before, a way of getting back into lives long since ended.

*

What is it about houses? Is it about shelter? Family? Comfort? Our castles don't have drawbridges but they are still our sanctuaries. Perhaps that is why 'home invasion' has such powerful resonance, much as ghost stories once did. Ghosts were an invasion of private space, too. Anything that crosses those boundaries, physical or metaphysical, shakes our blithe confidence. The known can suddenly become unknown. Love can be like that, too.

But back to drawbridges and walls ten-foot thick. That was what Raymond wanted. He didn't feel at home in the world, not the modern world anyway. He was born into this time that nothing in his make-up fitted him to be part of. Clover understood this, I think, because she was that way herself.

I once said to her, 'Why does it matter so much, this getting back into the past?'

She looked at me, puzzled. 'What else do we have to learn from?'

'How about the present?'

'The present is just the past moved on a bit,' she retorted.

I never did quite work out what she meant by that. But it was true that the friends I made in Glaston, although very contemporary in some respects, were also anchored firmly in times that had gone before. The things that interested them were perennials: music and good food, art and craftsmanship. And friendship.

2.

It must have been at the Austinmeers' that I first met Raymond. I can't even remember now how I came to be there, how I came to know Sally and Titus. Probably Sally just came across me one day, looking like a lost sheep, and took me home with her. The Austinmeers were – are – hospitable, gregarious people. I remember it was summer and the grape harvest was soon to begin. As I drove up towards their house the vines on either side were lush and heavy with ripening fruit, the sky blazing blue and it was hot, hot, hot as only Glaston can be on a summer's day. A dry baking heat that seems to suck the moisture out of you. In the front garden, amid masses of white and yellow daisies, was what must have been an old well with a stone lid on it. And on this was spread rows of tomatoes. I'd never before met anyone who actually made their own sun-dried tomatoes.

That's where Titus found me, looking at the tomatoes.

'Hello,' he said. 'You must take some home with you. We've got more than we'll ever eat.'

The instant generosity was the thing that got me. I soon learned that Titus and Sally were the centre of an intimate group of friends whom they kept supplied with food, wine and cheerful company. Certainly Raymond relied upon them for all three.

During lunch Raymond told stories. He had a way of picking on a chance remark to make an oblique reference to some absent person – usually someone who was very famous or very dead, often both – which led to questions from the others, and the beginnings of a story. Raymond's stories were like journeys, with digressions and delays that made you eager to reach the end. But once you did, you wanted to go back and do the journey all over again, savouring the good bits one more time. So many varieties of human weakness! Each different but recognisable. They made us laugh, but not in a cruel way. Then Raymond would look at each of us in turn, with a question in his eye: Did we, too, see the bizarreness of life?

After lunch that first day, Raymond's old friend William sat down neatly at the piano and started to play. Within moments Titus was on his feet. He stood with legs slightly apart, as if to brace his substantial weight, his barrel of a chest swelled and he broke into song, a strong bass-baritone.

William had been in Glaston the longest of any of them. He was probably about the same age, maybe sixty. His partner, Robbie, was much younger. Out of the five of them, Robbie was the only one with anything like a full-time job. He was a garden designer and spent part of each week working for clients in Sydney. Sally was also a designer – of interiors rather than exteriors – but she spent more time in her studio behind the house than in other people's homes. 'Trying to paint,' she told me with a rueful smile. There was a painting of hers above the sideboard. A strong, stylised still life. It was good, almost very good.

As I helped her carry empty plates to the kitchen, the others were talking about houses. 'Houses! Houses! Houses!' Sally exclaimed. She looked at me with a wry smile. 'You'd better get used to it, we're all obsessed with houses.'

*

When Lillian was at Glastonbridge for their mother's funeral, she met Raymond's friends. There were drinks afterwards at William and Robbie's. On the way there, Lillian sat in the passenger seat of Raymond's car, her knees clamped tightly together, her back and arms rigid, as though she was trying not to touch anything. Her highly polished black shoes shuffled among a mess of papers on the floor. She hated riding in Brutus.

'Almost there,' Raymond said, turning off the tarmac onto a dirt lane. 'William's place.'

They swung through the gateway, a magnificent blue plumbago hedge on either side. 'I suppose it's all right once you finally get here,' Lillian grumbled. Before them was the house, a severe Italianate mansion, painted deep ochre and cream. Around it was Robbie's creation: three acres of formal gardens.

In the eighteen months Lady Tyler had lived at Glaston, Raymond's friends had grown fond of her. The evening was spent swapping affectionate stories. Lillian looked on, grim faced. Her mother had got away from her without Lillian ever saying all the things she'd long meant to say, and she blamed Raymond.

'I remember,' Sally said, 'going over to Glastonbridge early last year. February, I think. It had been raining for days and days and I had to get out of the house because Titus was just pacing up and down lamenting his ruined harvest. I found Betty in bed, in the front room upstairs. Buckets around the bed to catch the drips. There was water *running* down the walls. And she just sat there, quite chirpy, wearing that brocade bed jacket of hers. I squeezed a chair in between the buckets and we sat like that until Raymond came home.

'That's when the roof wasn't finished,' Raymond said placidly.

Raymond accepted his mother's death with a calmness that to some looked like denial. It was Lillian who was distraught, and angry. She'd left Glaston the next day and flew back to New York the following week, without speaking to Raymond. There ensued one of those long stand-offs that were a regular feature of their relationship. After about a year, one or other of them broke the silence and they began, tentatively, communicating again by phone and fax and postcard.

Then, one winter's evening as he watched Sally setting the fire in the Austinmeers' sitting room, Raymond had announced, 'Lillian's coming home, for good.'

Sally said, looking up, 'Is that good news or bad news?'

Raymond shrugged. 'Oh, you know, she's family. There's that to be said.'

'So at the moment they're friends,' Titus said when he heard that Raymond was going down to Sydney to meet his sister at the airport. 'I wonder how long that will last.'

It lasted eighteen months. Now they were estranged again.

*

The driveway to Glastonbridge became almost impassable after heavy rain. In part this neglect was deliberate. Raymond wanted to discourage sightseers. He would have preferred it if Glastonbridge had sunk back into its former obscurity. Next to the gate he stuck a suitably discouraging letterbox, a rusty ten-gallon drum with the end cut out, nailed on its side to a post. He rarely got mail of any consequence in this letterbox. He stuck the drum there mainly to take the *Glaston Gazette* three times a week.

The letter from the National Trust was soggy when he picked it up, the letterhead slightly smudged. He threw it onto the seat and almost immediately forgot it. The glaziers were coming that day. He was eager to see how the new windows looked. So, with one thing and another, he forgot about the letter. By the next day it had fallen to the floor and it wasn't until three days later, when he was rummaging in the mess on the passenger side, trying to find the cause of the foul odour that was stinking out Brutus, that he came upon the letter under the seat, along with a bag of rotting oranges. It read:

Mr R. Tyler
"Glastonbridge"
Glaston
NSW

3 November 1995

Dear Mr Tyler,

At its recent meeting, the Trust's Authentic Restoration Advisory Committee discussed information that has come to its attention regarding work being undertaken by you at the William Berge designed house, Glastonbridge (circa 1841).

It is the Trust's opinion that Glastonbridge is an important national monument and should be registered with the National Trust, as a precursor to listing by the Heritage Council. That this has not occurred in the past is perhaps due to the failure of individuals to bring the house to the Trust's attention and the obscurity of its location.

The Authentic Restoration Advisory Committee is disappointed that you have apparently been working on the house for some years but have not seen fit to approach them for advice. Both professional and lay members of the committee have a fund of experience available to those undertaking major restorations. We should also point out that grants of $5,000 to $10,000 are available for specific projects of a difficult and demanding nature.

I have been authorised to arrange an inspection with you of Glastonbridge. The purpose would be to inspect and record the house for our register and to offer advice and direction on restoration methods and procedure. The party would consist of no more than 15 people and I am sure you would find it a valuable and worthwhile experience.

Please telephone me to arrange a time...

Raymond snorted when he read it, particularly the bit about the grants. Ten thousand dollars! He spent that in a week. He bet that Joan Beaverstoke was behind it. Those Trust types were only interested in snooping around other people's houses. Bloody busybodies! He tossed the letter into a dresser drawer in the kitchen. He'd worry about it later.

He was more worried about Lillian. Raymond wished that he could just walk away from his sister. But he never managed it for more than a few months at a time. And even then, although he might not speak to her, she was always invisibly there, like static. Sometimes he thought he hated his sister; rarely did he think he loved her.

Raymond sometimes wondered about love, about what it was. Other people seemed to have it in their lives almost effortlessly. They forged alliances. Like Sally and Titus, and William and Robbie. He'd never had that. It occurred to him that he loved Philip, although he'd never say such a thing, and although they often argued and Philip was often impatient with him. Dear boy.

It was nearly a fortnight since the last argument with Lillian and still there was no phone call from her. In the past it had been almost peaceful when they were not communicating. She had been so far away, in New York, that it was easier to put aside thoughts of her. But now she was in Sydney, too close at hand for peace of mind. What was she doing? What was she saying to mutual acquaintances? What plan was she hatching?

For as long as he could remember, his mother and his sister had been the counterpoints to his life. His mother, solid and knowable, and always at his elbow, even when she was a thousand miles away. And Lillian, although troublesome and for many years physically removed, always at the other elbow. Each of them seemed to carry something of Bamford with them.

He still grieved for his childhood home. His father always thought he had left willingly. How could he tell him that he'd had no real option?

That he couldn't fit his allotted role. But he should never have sold Bamford. A quiet voice said that to him sometimes, in the dead of night, when he most despaired over the task he faced at Glastonbridge. He would not have admitted his regrets or his fears to anyone, not even to Philip, least of all to Lillian. But because he knew she felt the same about Bamford, knew that she remembered the same green slopes, the same garden, the same secret corners of the house, he could never entirely cut off from her. At times when they were not speaking, he would seek solace in the few pieces of Georgian furniture from Bamford, in his mother's silver, in the stately gilt Empire clock that had sat on the mantelpiece in his father's study. Occasionally he would drag out from the back of a stack of pictures a large painting, swathed in an old sheet, uncover it and set it against the wall opposite his narrow bed. It was of Bamford, painted in 1835 when the house was still quite new, when the bones of the garden were still evident and the trees only half grown, when the orchard was neat and tidy and the vegetables grew in serried rows. The lines of the old house were so different from Glastonbridge, so simple and elegant. He'd look at the painting for a long time, then wrap it up and put it back behind the others. He wondered if he would ever be able to hang the picture of Bamford, ever be able to put it up on a wall and walk past it every day.

Growing up there surrounded by servants, gardeners, shepherds and herdsmen had been like living inside a feudal village. Because they had a telephone and cars and electricity, most people assumed Bamford belonged to the twentieth century. But he had realised quite early that in its essentials Bamford was still a medieval country estate – in the intimate interconnectedness but strict hierarchy of the half a dozen families that lived there, in the rhythms of country life, in its self-sufficiency. When his father set off to take his seat in state parliament, he could just as easily have been leaving on the Crusades. The sense of destiny was much the same. That was meant to be Raymond's destiny, too.

Was he sentimental about Bamford? Or was it simply essential to him – or at least his idea of it? His thoughts turned from Bamford to his sister, and immediately his insides knotted in apprehension.

*

William and Raymond had developed the habit of washing their dogs together, William's pair of King Charles spaniels and Raymond's poodle, Miffy. Miffy was the first pet Raymond had ever owned. She was given to him by Philip as a companion after Lady Tyler died.

William once complained: 'He hasn't a clue how to look after an animal. You'd never know he grew up on a farm. If Bob wasn't out at Glastonbridge every day, the poor dog would starve.'

There was not much opportunity for talking while actually washing the dogs, but afterwards, to stop the dogs rolling in a garden bed, they always put the three of them on leads and went for a walk along the lane that ran beside William's house and stopped a mile down at the railway line.

Once the leads were untangled and the dogs were walking relatively calmly, Raymond said, 'I wanted to ask your advice. About Lil. I don't know what to do about her. It's so difficult now she's back in Sydney.'

William said nothing at first. He didn't have a sister himself, and he had very little experience of women. Eventually he asked, 'Is it money again?'

'Lil always wants money, but that's not it really. Whatever I do it would never be enough. If I give in on one thing, she'll start harping on something else.'

'Family,' William said, and laughed nervously. The dogs had wound themselves around him so he did a small pirouette to untangle himself. His slight frame was trim and dainty for a man of sixty.

'Not all families,' grumbled Raymond. 'What about Robbie's? Some of them are hard up, but they don't take it out on one another. Lil's greedy. I wish she'd just piss off back to New York.'

'Well,' said William hesitantly, 'have you suggested that?'

Raymond scowled at him.

'Maybe you should just give her the money.'

'I can't just give her what she wants. If I did that, we'd both be broke in no time,' Raymond said, kicking a stone. There was a hardness in Raymond's tone when talking of money. If only his father had known the Tyler fortune would be in good hands with Raymond. He was a canny bastard. 'I wish she'd trust me,' he continued. 'She always thinks I'm going to cheat her.'

William didn't know what else to advise. He was glad when Raymond suddenly took another tack.

'Had a letter from the National Trust the other day,' Raymond said.

'Oh?' This sort of news was always interesting. 'From the local branch?'

'Nah. Head office wrote it, but I bet that Joan Beaverstoke is behind it.' Raymond looked off into the distance and it appeared he wasn't going to continue.

'Well, what did it say?'

'Huh. They want to come and have a look. Bloody hide! Do you know what the idiot said? That there might be a grant in it – five to ten thousand dollars. And they expect me to let them tramp all over the house for that.' He paused, then added, 'If it was twenty, I might.'

'What are you going to do?' William asked.

'Ignore it.'

William wasn't sure that was wise but said nothing. As they neared the house, they heard music blasting through the open drawing room windows – Kiri singing *Un bel di velremo* at high volume. Robbie was working on the iris bed beside the lily pond. He was wearing only shorts and a battered hat, his taut brown back glistening in the sun. When he saw that back, William felt a twinge of nostalgia.

After seeing Raymond off, he wandered into the garden. Robbie was standing in front of the lily pond, surveying his work and swinging his arms gracefully in time with the music. He looked like an opera conductor in front of a grand set. Years ago Robbie had said, 'I want to make gardens that are like stage sets'. And here he was, a working-class boy from Granville, doing it! Such drive. William admired that. He'd never had it, not really. Robbie was the true artist. All William had now was his hobbies.

Which reminded him that he had planned to wash his Staffordshire porcelain that afternoon. He'd have to turn down the music if he went inside, and that would spoil Robbie's fun. Undecided, he paused on the verandah and sat on the edge of a cane peacock chair that had been Lady Tyler's. He should probably go into town and get some chops for dinner, but he was distracted by a memory that came to him of the last conversation he'd had with Betty Tyler.

She'd said to him, 'That boy of yours has a natural gift and passion. You need both.'

'Yes,' William had agreed. He was accustomed to people saying 'that boy of yours' when referring to Robbie. There was a time when the age difference rankled, but he was over that. 'I never had the passion, not really.' It had been almost a relief when repetitive strain injury had forced him to give up performing.

'But you need something else as well,' Lady Tyler had continued. 'Judgement. He's got that, too. Raymond hasn't.'

'Raymond's pretty cunning, though.'

'Oh that,' she waved her hand dismissively. 'You know the trouble with my children?' She hadn't waited for him to respond. 'One has all the taste and the other all the pretence of it. And neither has any judgement or any sense of moderation. For that I blame myself and Tony. Well, Bamford really. What sort of place was that for rearing children!'

*

Taste, passion and judgement were the three pins on which Philip balanced his harmonious life. As he fitted his cufflinks he looked out the window, through the tree tops. The lights were coming on along Queen Street. He pulled down the shirt sleeve and slipped his arm into the jacket of his suit. Sometimes he thought it would be very pleasant to work as Sally did, spending three or four days at a time in Sydney, consulting with clients and suppliers and overseeing workmen, then disappearing back to Glaston, back to her studio. He'd told her several times it was almost enough to make him swap dealing for designing. But he wasn't serious. Nothing compared to the thrill of the deal – the chase, the seduction, the triumph.

These days the hunt could take him to any corner of the world. It was then he needed judgement, to be sure that a piece was real and not fake, not to get carried away with excitement because he *wanted* it to be real. Check the provenance, he always told his staff, and check it thoroughly. Raymond had taught him that lesson when they were looking for Queen Anne pieces to furnish his mother's Sydney house. 'Far more "Queen Anne" furniture has been exported from England than could ever have been made while the dear Queen was alive,' Raymond had said.

Philip was unusually nervous about the coming evening. He and Jules had been lovers for six months but it had been a quiet and inconspicuous affair, as his affairs always were. They hadn't gone anywhere together where they were likely to meet any of Philip's clients. Not that there was anything to be ashamed of. He simply liked to keep people guessing. He liked to flatter, charm and even flirt a little with his women clients. And they loved it. More than one was a little in love with him. And he had almost been a little in love with one or two of them. But not really. Not if he were honest.

Although it was a Monday night, the restaurant was already crowded when he arrived. Le Carion was the place of the moment; Jules had wanted to check out the competition. Philip spotted half a dozen familiar faces the moment he walked in the door. And there was Jules, seated at a table halfway down the room, behind a column. He was sitting very straight, his pale, elegant face deliberately expressionless but with an eagerness behind his eyes. As soon as he spotted Philip his gaze held unwaveringly. His hair was swept back from his face, making his cheekbones seem even higher. Philip was so affected by the sight of him that he walked straight past two of his best clients without so much as a wave of acknowledgement.

They sat opposite one another, perusing their menus. Both were immaculately dressed. Their suits were creased only where creases were meant to be, not a spot of fluff was to be seen, and their discreet but stylish ties were perfectly knotted. Jules's long dark hair was tied back with a thin ribbon of black leather. Philip was acutely aware of him. But aware, too, of all the people around them. Perhaps this had been a mistake.

Then Jules looked up from his menu and said, with his delicious French accent: 'I cannot believe the things they do with duck in this country. They 'ave stuffed them with snails, and on a bed of *couscous!* Is it not crazy? And the sauce. Pistachio. *Merde!*'

Philip laughed. He forgot everyone else in the room. 'Perhaps you should put it on the menu at Baillieu's.'

'Per'aps,' Jules said doubtfully. He was learning fast that bizarre combinations were the pathway to success in Sydney cooking. Looking around the crowded restaurant, he said, 'People like it.'

'This month they do,' Philip said drily. A good review had recently transformed Le Carion from obscure eatery to epicurean icon. 'I hope Oscar is celebrating,' he went on. 'It's best to celebrate these things while they last.'

Philip wished someone would take their order. Most of the other diners had finished their meal before they had even begun. A waiter was approaching, a blond youth with tousled hair and high cheek-bones. Philip raised an eyebrow in appreciation.

After they had ordered, Philip said, surprising even himself, 'Sally and Titus have asked us to Glaston for Christmas.' Did he want Jules at Glaston for Christmas?

'Oh? How nice of them.' Hesitantly, Jules went on, 'You know, I am closing the restaurant for January. I must go and visit my family.' He paused. 'I thought…would you like to come with me…per'aps? To France. For a few weeks. You said you must go soon anyway. It would be good. You could visit your dealers. I could visit my family. We could spend some weeks together…in the Alps…in Paris?'

A smile spread from Philip's lips across his face, through his chest and limbs, suffusing his whole body. He sat there in a warm glow. 'Yes, let's do it.'

Jules clapped his hands together and held them clasped in front of him, beaming. Philip put his hands down by his sides to prevent him-self from reaching across the table. They sat grinning at each other until their meals were placed before them.

'Who is that man over there?' Jules asked some time later. 'He has been watching us. Now he is eating his soup. You should see how he is eating his soup!'

Philip glanced across the room. 'It's Theo Roth.'

Theo's lap was covered in several large napkins and he was attacking a bowl of clam gazpacho.

'Tell me about him. I have seen him in my restaurant.'

Philip told him. He loved to entertain his friends with gossip. Philip's gossip was always piquant but never vicious. It was how he got away with telling so much of it.

'I've kept the best till last,' he said, after relaying stories about half the diners in the restaurant. He picked up the bill. 'Behind me, at the table in the corner. A big guy with dark hair and a woman, fairish.'

Jules nodded.

'The Duracks,' said Philip.

Jules gasped: 'The food writers! How did you know? Are your eyes behind your head?'

Philip laughed. 'Come along,' he said. 'Time for us to go. We can pay them a visit on the way. Have they finished their meal?'

Jules looked over Philip's shoulder and nodded. 'He is drinking his *café.*'

'Perfect.' He pushed back his chair.

They skirted several tables on their way out so as to pass by the Duracks. Philip hailed the culinary couple, paused, praised the critic's recent book, then gallantly introduced Jules: 'Chef/proprietor of Baillieu's. In East Redfern. You don't know it? Modern French cuisine. Doing very well.'

After dinner, they went back to Philip's place. But a couple of hours later Jules got up and dressed. He said he wouldn't stay the night because he wanted to go to the markets early in the morning and 'would not steal your sleep for the world'. So at one in the morning Philip was awake and thinking about the coming trip to Europe. Travelling together could be a mistake. He realised he had very definite ideas about what he did and did not like to do while travelling. He liked to sleep in and breakfast late and lightly; eat one truly fantastic meal a day; walk a lot; be selective about art museums but study those he did go to carefully and slowly. He remembered the way Raymond was in museums, almost running through the rooms, his eyes darting this way and that. Then rushing back to Philip to tell him what he'd found, urging him to hurry. Amazingly, Raymond hardly ever missed a thing of worth. The one piece that he was so eager for Philip to see was usually the pick of the place. Of course, Raymond had often been there before, whereas it was always Philip's first time, back in those days when he and Raymond went overseas together on buying trips.

As so often in quiet moments, his thoughts turned to Raymond. He wondered what Raymond would make of Jules. Not that he would say anything directly. He had a strange coyness about love relationships. Not about sex relationships, though. Philip remembered the time he'd come upon a cupboard full of leather magazines when he was staying at Glastonbridge. Raymond had looked at him in that blank, challenging way he had sometimes, daring him to make some remark.

He wished occasionally that Raymond would find someone, although the idea was absurd. Who? Still, he wished there was someone in Raymond's life, someone to whom he could pass some of the burden. The burden of this man who had been his teacher, his employer, surrogate father, most loyal friend.

*

I used to think that Philip was too good to be true. Handsome, successful, clever (brilliant really, he could have done anything he wanted) and NICE. The arrogance and snobbery were just surface stuff, the way he felt he had to be in his line of business. Away from it he was anything but. He was only too aware of where he'd come from – worse than the wrong side of the tracks. The sticks. If Raymond was born out of his time then Philip was certainly born out of his place. But what other place could there have been for him? Where else but Australia at the end of the twentieth century could such a creature have existed? He had not only become affluent and clever, but also classy. The class that comes from genuine taste and refinement.

I don't mean he didn't like a raunchy joke. With friends he could be deliciously wicked, irreverent. But he had that rare thing, a fine-tuned sensibility and a mind to match.

I've often asked myself whether there wasn't something that Philip could have done to somehow defuse things. He was the closest Raymond had to family given that his sister was no use. But there was that wicked streak in Philip. He liked to stir things up, just for the heck of it. Between Raymond and Theo, for example. I saw him do it once with Theo. It was clear Theo was a bit fascinated by Philip – by Philip Dexter, the product.

*

Theo couldn't work out what it was about Philip Dexter that always drew people's attention. It wasn't that he was so very good looking. It was more to do with presentation. He was so damned refined! But not queeny, not at all. Maybe he'd just settled on a style of dress and manner that suited his business. Theo had no argument with that; he'd done the same thing himself. The white suits, the white hat, the white Rolls Royce with the red leather upholstery; all this made him instantly recognisable around the streets of Sydney. Theo liked to knock the socks off people at first appearance then assiduously undermine all their preconceptions about property dealers by being as disinterested and restrained as a parson.

From the time he first set up as a real estate agent he had a particular way of working. When approached by a prospective buyer, he always said he'd pick them up at their home before taking them on an inspection. By seeing their house he could tell almost immediately if the place they were going to look at would suit them. The style of house, the internal decor, the furnishings would give him a feel for the sort of people they were. It was not unusual for him to say, 'That place you want to look at probably won't suit you, but I have another house...' By the time he delivered them back home after seeing several properties, usually somewhat dearer than they had originally wanted, he was discussing with them the best way to sell their own property. He'd go inside with them, inspect their house and make suggestions about inexpensive ways of improving it for sale: a little less furniture here, a big print on that wall there, some paint on the doors, a rug over the worn carpet. Offering it all in a quiet, melodious voice. Not insisting, just suggesting. More like a friend than a real estate agent.

The neighbours, too, would know that Theo Roth was in the street. No sooner had his white sign with the scarlet lettering gone up in a front garden than he would get two or three calls from other people in the street who were considering selling. And so from the early 1970s his business had grown from a trickle to a flood. By the time he decided to semi-retire he had offices in almost every suburb. He trained his people to work as he had worked, but none were quite so successful. To keep in touch, he still went on house calls, and not just to the ritzy suburbs where the big houses and big money were. He didn't think that would be fair. The Lebanese family in Auburn or the grunge dykes from Enmore deserved his attention as much as anyone else. This was how Theo's social conscience expressed itself.

Not long after he had started out in the late sixties, when he was a sensitive and somewhat unworldly young man, he'd gone to look at a house in Lewisham. He wasn't expecting much, just another deceased estate. It was a gloomy, two-storey place, once grand but much neglected. The old woman who lived there had been a Russian émigré. She'd lived in the house for forty years.

Inside, it was a museum piece. The owner had tried to re-create in Lewisham something of the home she'd once known back in Moscow or St Petersburg or Minsk. The main room had a huge and heavy crystal chandelier, so dusty and greasy that it barely gleamed when the lights were switched on. There were faded velvet drapes, delicate gilt chairs, and around the walls hung dark oils: family portraits. Alexandre Astomov, Dmitry Stepanovich, Sophia Alexandrovna, Maria Stepanovna. Some bell within him rang as he walked around the perimeter, repeating the names. He'd always thought of himself as Australian. Australian first then maybe Jewish, and, only distantly, Russian. But now the Russian in him swelled up and caught him in the throat. The music of the names, like bells in snow. He walked from room to room, dazed by the power of the atmosphere that Irena Astomov had created here in a Sydney suburb.

It was in a small room upstairs, off the main bedroom, that he found them. The room was windowless and lined with red baize. There was no centre light, just small candle-like wall fittings above each icon. It was like a private chapel and his first thought was 'she must have been religious'. But when he looked around there was no altar, no cross, no prayer book. Only a chair, placed so as to best view the icons. He sat on it and looked at them.

He got up and did a circuit of the room, stopping in front of each small picture. He had to look closely. The figures were dark and the light poor. Only the gold leaf glinted through the gloom. There was Christ in several manifestations – serious, lugubrious, enigmatic. The Virgin. A knight mounted on a horse – St George, he thought. Another Christ, more Virgins, the Trinity, then a couple of female figures that he couldn't identify. There were ten icons in all. He stood in the centre of the room and turned to survey them. Then something strange happened. Maybe it was because he was young and fanciful, but suddenly it was as if he'd had a memory lapse. The identity of the figures in the icons disappeared and all he was aware of was an outpouring of sympathy from the row of dark eyes, a lament for all sadness, a sharing of grief.

Shaken, he hurriedly left the room. But two weeks later when the contents of the house went up for auction, he went and bought the icons, at a ridiculously low price. It was the beginning of his collection. A few of his friends teased him about a Jew owning icons. He didn't try to explain. His icon collection came to dominate his life.

But the week before Christmas it was family, not icons, on his mind. His family had never acknowledged Christmas, let alone celebrated it, but marrying and mixing with non-Jews, he'd picked up the habit. He was on good terms with his ex-wives and always bought them both something for Christmas. In fact, he usually bought them the same thing for Christmas. Last year it had been brooches, slightly different in design but the same price. This year he thought he'd get them something for their houses. He had chosen both the houses and knew what would suit each: a coloured glass fruit bowl for Stella – it would look good on the stainless steel benchtops; and for Marie, a ceramic platter brightly painted with farmhouse hens, to go with her country-style kitchen and lime-washed walls. He had promised Martin, his son with Stella, a guitar. Jody, Marie's daughter, had asked for a pony. But as she and her mother lived in Dover Heights she would have to settle for a dog. He'd arranged with his current wife, Julia, that Jody could have one of the pups from Yarralong Bounty's litter. He'd bring it down for her on Christmas Eve.

Since they'd bought Yarralong five years ago, Julia had taken to raising cattle dogs. She was so devoted to them and to country life that she could rarely be persuaded to come up to town. He sometimes wondered if he would ever again see her in a dress. She said that a year as Miss Australia had cured her of charity balls and gala concerts and she'd be happy to never go to another party. It suited Theo really; he liked his bachelor life in Sydney during the week and the brief transformation to family man at Yarralong on weekends. The kids, four-year-old Sasha and the baby, Alexander, were delightful in small doses. And Julia was as happy as a pig wallowing in shit at Yarralong. This Christmas he'd bought her a three-wheeled cross-country bike so she could ride around the property with the kids on the back.

He was still looking for Marie's ceramic platter and drove over to Queen Street, thinking he'd try the Portuguese place opposite Philip Dexter's. Did he want to run into Philip or should he park the Rolls around the corner? There was a parking space right in front of the shop, so he took it. As he got out of the car, Philip was farewelling a customer at his door. He saw Theo and waved. Theo waved back and, after a moment's hesitation, crossed the street to speak to him. They hadn't spoken since the exchange at that auction.

'Good afternoon, Theo,' Philip said.

Theo held out his hand – his left hand – and Philip took it. He'd long since become accustomed to Theo's idiosyncratic handshake.

'I was wondering if you were still looking for a pair of bookcases?' Philip asked mischievously.

'Possibly…do you know of anything?'

'Not specifically, but I'm going to Paris after Christmas and there's a dealer there who sometimes comes across that sort of thing. Would you like me to put a few feelers out?'

'If you hear of anything, I'd be interested.' Theo paused then asked, 'How does that mirror look at Raymond's?'

'I'm not sure if he's got it up yet. I haven't been to Glastonbridge for a while.'

They stood a moment on the pavement then Philip said, 'Okay then, I'll keep an eye out. Have a Merry Christmas, and give my love to Julia.'

He had his hand on the door when Theo said, 'Do you think Raymond might sell those bookcases of his?'

Philip thought he detected a slight note of entreaty. 'I don't think so, Theo. I've looked into it and it's clear Sly built them specifically for Glastonbridge. Raymond was very lucky to get them back.'

'Luck seems to run Raymond's way.'

'We all have our ups and downs.' Philip paused but decided not to say more. 'Bye Theo.'

'Yes, Merry Christmas,' Theo said automatically. He turned away. He usually enjoyed shopping but now he had lost all interest.

*

I only once heard Raymond talk about Bamford, his family home, about the life they'd had there. After a few drinks, around a dinner table, he often spoke of the grand old Tasmanian families, the bastard sons and runaway daughters, the fortunes lost or stolen – 'I once knew a woman who accidentally married her sister's son' was the beginning of one such. But he hardly ever talked about Bamford. My most enduring memory is of him in the Austinmeer dining room. Lounging with one elbow on the table, a glass of red held loosely in his hand, regaling his friends with some stranger-than-fiction story. The gossip was picked up more often than not from Philip. Philip, who was like their own private email on the doings of the Sydney glitterati. And the way they each reacted to the latest salacious slur: Titus's gleeful yodel; William saying, 'Oh no, no, Raymond, you shouldn't. It isn't nice.' Sweet man. And Robbie, Robbie with his mop of brilliant red hair, tossing it back, trying to look bored but not missing a syllable. In the background, Sally calling from the kitchen, egging Raymond on.

'No, no!' he'd say at some point. 'I won't say another word.' And suddenly he'd become subdued, withdrawn. And immediately, the focus moved away from him like a receding tide, as if there was some unspoken pact to protect him. He was so contradictory – the diffidence and stubbornness, the shyness and arrogance, the ribaldry and coyness. The way he was so careless of people one day, so caring the next.

One day he turned up at the cottage I was renting.

'Sally said you might be lonely,' he said.

He perched on my sofa and I looked at him and wondered if I was expected to explain myself.

'Funny how we've all washed up here,' he said.

I blurted, 'I spent a summer here once when I was a kid. With a great-aunt.'

He just nodded.

'No one left now,' I said lamely.

In the ensuing silence he gazed away from me, across the room: 'It's a good place to try out a fantasy. Or at least that's how it seems to me.' He looked back at me. 'Everyone's mad here!'

We both laughed. 'Must be the heat,' I said.

'Can we have a cuppa?' he asked.

3.

Whenever Raymond and Lil weren't speaking, which was quite often, Raymond was obliged to find somewhere else to stay when he was in Sydney. If it was only overnight, he stayed with Philip. But Philip's flat wasn't big enough for an extended visit. So he had taken to staying at the Contessa's at Vaucluse. Everyone called her 'the Contessa' or sometimes, informally, 'Tessa'.

Raymond liked it at the Contessa's. He liked the gardens running down to the harbour, the attentive but unobtrusive staff, the well-appointed rooms. And she was a charming hostess. But then two things occurred that worried him. More than that, they terrified him. The Contessa was often startling in her behaviour – it was part of her charm – but this time she'd gone too far.

One evening he went out onto the verandah before going to bed. It was too hot to sleep but a perfect night to be outside. Strolling past the line of French doors, he heard his name called. He looked towards the voice and saw, through an open door, the Contessa reclining on a huge pink bed and wearing a transparent negligee. She supported herself on one elbow and gestured towards him. Raymond stopped in his tracks. 'Oh! Good evening, Contessa,' he said, dropping his chin to his chest so as not to look at her. He muttered hurriedly, 'I hope you sleep well' and turned and scuttled back to his room.

He could barely believe what he had just witnessed. The Contessa was often frisky but never brazen. Was she unaware how provocative she appeared or how transparent were her nightclothes? The next morning he was in the bathroom, shaving, when he heard a noise at the door. Before he had a chance to turn around, the Contessa slipped through the door. Giggling, she threw something sheer and perfumed over his head and wrapped her arms around his middle. Raymond, a towel around his waist, lather on his face and his razor in one hand, did not know where to look. On top of that, he was ticklish. 'Tessa, you mustn't! Oh no, no!'

He could feel her naked breasts against his back and recoiled instinctively. The thing over his head, which he now recognised as her nighty, had shaving cream all over it and was getting in his mouth. He got it off his head, dropped the razor in the basin and pushed past her, almost losing the towel.

'Contessa, you mustn't,' he said, with his back half-turned.

'Oh Raymie,' she crooned, holding out her hands.

'No! Behave yourself,' he said, in just the same tone he'd heard William use with the dog. Then he opened the door and fled.

At breakfast the Contessa was contrite but said nothing about what had happened. They both read the newspapers. After they had finished the pot of coffee, he stood up formally and said to her, 'Under the circumstances, I think it best if I don't stay here tonight.'

She nodded penitently and looked up at him with a small guilty grimace. She even went with him to the front steps and waved as he drove away. That was the nice thing about the Contessa: she didn't hold a grudge.

So it wasn't entirely sentimentality that drove Raymond to seek a rapprochement with Lillian. He needed somewhere else to stay in Sydney.

When he rang her after six weeks silence and suggested lunch, Lillian was not surprised. Yet she was pleased it was him making the first move, not her. She resolved to be particularly sweet to him, not to chastise him and not to talk about money. That could wait.

They arranged to meet on neutral territory, at Zigolini's in Woollahra. She thought he looked quite smart. Had he made an effort for her? She was always a little embarrassed at reconciliations, but Raymond never was.

'What have you been doing, Lil?' he asked, as if he'd seen her last week.

'I'm still doing that fine arts and architecture course I told you about. We're looking at sixteenth-century Florence. Palazzos, gardens – that sort of thing. I never realised so much was going on back then.'

Raymond grunted, as if his mind was on something else.

'Have you been staying at Philip's?' Lillian asked.

'A bit. There and at the Contessa's.' Lillian felt resentment rising. It was months since she'd been invited even for a drink at the Contessa's. 'You like her, don't you?' she asked, trying to sound neutral.

'She's all right. She can be a bit much. I was thinking, Lil, why don't you come up to Glastonbridge for Christmas? The front windows are in now and I can make that room below the tower really nice for you. That room never gets hot. I know you hate the heat but really the house is quite cool. And if it does get really hot we can always go down to the cellar.'

'With the bats,' Lillian said, but she was touched. It had been years since she and Raymond had spent a Christmas together. 'All right,

I'll come. How will I get up there?' Lillian hated driving long distances alone.

'I could stay in town a few more days and you could come back with me if you like. I'll just have to organise somewhere to stay.'

'Don't be silly,' Lillian said, 'stay with me.'

Lillian, too, sometimes thought about their childhood at Bamford, but she would not have recognised the Bamford that Raymond remembered. Her memories held nothing medieval. Hers was a wartime Bamford: her father somewhere north, they thought New Guinea, her mother endlessly organising. There were only two men left on the farm; the women did the rest and bickered constantly, except when Mother was around. She was seven when her longed-for father came home. He was stiff and formal and unused to children. But he was kind to her on the rare occasions when they were alone. Sometimes he let her go with him when he rode out to inspect the farm. She'd follow behind him on Brandy. They didn't talk much. What she remembered most was the soft stillness of the air, the drone of insects, the tops of the long grass brushing Brandy's belly, and the rump of her father's grey rolling rhythmically before her like an ocean liner.

She and Raymond were close without ever being really friendly. They knew each other's moods but not each other's minds. In her early teens Lillian spent most of her time around the stables, grooming the succession of horses that followed Brandy. She and Raymond saw less and less of each other and she gradually became aware of a change in him. A hardening, a remove. He began to fight with Mother, who was often tearful, while relations with their father deteriorated beyond mere fighting.

When Raymond left to go to art school in Sydney, it was almost a relief, at first. At least Mother took more notice of her. She took her shopping and bought her clothes and made plans for her. She was Sir Anthony and Lady Tyler's daughter – she'd never realised before what that meant. Within two years she'd had three proposals of marriage, but she wouldn't consider any of them. Her parents didn't know what to do with her. When she turned twenty-three they packed her off on the grand European tour.

Coming back to Australia in her late fifties, widowed, was not easy for Lillian. Everything was changed. Bamford was gone – Raymond had sold it and she would never forgive him. But Raymond was all she had. Him and a few old and almost forgotten friends. Her monthly remittance from the Tyler investments only just covered her expenses. In thirty-three years of marriage, she and Harold had rarely exchanged a cross word, but sometimes now she howled at him and cursed him for leaving her in this predicament. Harold's sons from his first marriage sometimes rang her. Once or twice the younger one, Ben, thinking she sounded depressed, urged her to go back to New York so she could live near him. Her face softened when she thought of Ben.

But she couldn't go back to New York. It was a big decision to come and live in Sydney. To go back to the States now would be like defeat. She told herself she was doing it as much for Raymond as for herself. He needed her. After lunch together she felt more content than she had in a long time. She was even looking forward to seeing Glastonbridge. She wondered who would be up there for Christmas. Perhaps Philip?

Lillian was barely out of the car before Raymond began pointing out all the work done since her last visit. He sauntered off in the direction of the front terrace – expecting her to follow – to show her the new windows. Then he took her around to inspect the western wing. Lillian tried to look genuinely interested. She looked where he pointed, nodded sagely, was even occasionally admiring. It was an hour before she even got inside the house – and then it was through the former servants entrance.

'Can't open the front door at the moment,' Raymond said. 'Waiting for hinges.'

Lillian was hoping for a cup of tea but Raymond trotted ahead, beckoning. He wanted to show her his most recent project, the ceiling of the upstairs hallway. Lillian followed him along the arcade, with its line of pointed timber arches on one side and linenfold panelling on the other, to the staircase. He was chattering away to her about the difficulties he'd had. How he'd had to make two trips to Sydney to get the right sort of paint, because the first time he wasn't happy with the texture. How they'd had trouble getting scaffolding tall enough to reach the cornices; how it was costing him a fortune. At this comment, Lillian went very quiet and still.

He didn't notice. He led the way upstairs, dodging ladders and buckets and stepping over pieces of timber. 'Oh yes, watch that,' he said, indicating where part of the handrail had been taken out to be repaired. In its place was a flimsy rope. The staircase wainscot was topped by carved beak-head moulding and as she climbed the stairs Lillian compared each evil little gnome-like face with the one next to it, concentrating on the extraordinary detail of the work so as not to shudder in revulsion at the mess in which Raymond lived. None of the rooms in the house were used for the function for which they had been designed. The dining room housed a very makeshift kitchen, while the sitting room was a storeroom for his collection of perpendicular and Jacobean clocks.

Upstairs, the hallway was covered in drop sheets and scaffolding. She demurred when Raymond offered to help her up onto it. 'So you can get a closer look,' he said. As a compromise, she climbed a few rungs up the ladder. She didn't need to get closer – the colours on the cornice were so garish as to be unmissable. She stepped down off the ladder and looked up again. From the floor the effect was striking and, she had to admit, absolutely right.

'Very nice,' she said, 'quite unusual.'

'Not really. They always did have multicoloured cornices. The neo-Gothics that is, not the originals. I'm going to do the upstairs drawing room next,' he said, walking towards that door. 'But more subtle colours in here. What do you think?'

'Marvellous,' she said faintly, brushing some plaster dust from her sleeve.

'You're lucky to have something that so involves you,' Lillian said later, when they were drinking tea in the second nursery, the room Raymond used as a sort of sitting room. She stood up from the edge of the settle and looked out the window to the terrace below. Raymond made a noncommittal grunt.

'Do you remember the nursery at Bamford?' she said suddenly, brightly turning to face him. 'I can still picture the wallpaper.'

'Never liked that room,' he said.

'Oh, I did.' After a pause, she said, 'But you were always downstairs, with Mummy and Daddy. I spent a lot of time in that room. With Miss James.'

Here we go, thought Raymond. The old complaints of favouritism. To head her off, he said, 'Are things okay with you now, Lil? Did that accountant chap I recommended fix things up for you?'

'Oh...' she was dying to speak but she feigned reluctance. 'I'm going to have to do something drastic soon – maybe sell the New York place. Only I'm not certain yet...if things will work out for me here.'

'Oh yes, you must keep your apartment in New York,' Raymond said hurriedly.

'If only we still had Bamford...'

'Actually Lil, if you are short at the moment, maybe I could help out. If I reorganise things a bit. I might be able to lend you something.'

'I thought I could get some money from Tyler Holdings.'

'No, no, no,' Raymond said quickly. 'It would be too much trouble. Better to leave the company out of it. Just between ourselves.'

'Really? You'll really lend it to me? I need about eight hundred thousand.'

'Oh...oh well,' Raymond said, reluctant, but also relieved. Money really was the easiest way with Lil.

*

That Christmas in Glaston had a particular atmosphere. It was the best I'd had in a long time and my memories of Glaston are all coloured by it, by how we were then. It reminded me of the Christmases of my childhood, although of course it was nothing like them. Maybe it was the sheer comfortableness of it. It began with Christmas Eve drinks at William and Robbie's, on the verandah overlooking the garden, and the next day, Christmas dinner at Sally and Titus's. Then it just seemed to go on from there – picnics by the river, a barbecue at Glastonbridge, with Raymond fussing about ineffectually while everyone else did the actual work. I met Lillian, and Sally's sister Rosemary, that Christmas. I got the message that neither sibling relationship was all that good.

'What do you do here?' Lillian asked me the first day. 'I always wonder what people in country towns actually do. You work?'

Before I had a chance to say anything, Raymond answered for me. 'She's between engagements, as they say. Taking some time out,' and he gave me another of his quick conspiratorial smiles.

'Oh, you're an actress! I've always been so interested in the theatre...'
So I let her think that.

A week or so later everyone went their separate ways and life entered
a not unpleasant lull. Glaston dozed. Summer heat settled on the
town. Miles from the coast, no sea breeze gave respite and day after
day blue skies blanketed the horizons. Dust gathered in the gutters
and the only activity was in the pubs, where drinkers tried to wash
the dryness from their throats.

Business slowed. At the supermarket end of High Street there was
a small rush at eight in the morning, but by nine most people had
retreated back indoors. Half the businesses in town were shut, their
owners gone down the coast. There was a magical quietness to the
town on those afternoons. A quietness that the occasional truck starting up or motorbike roaring through seemed only to accentuate.

One of the few places that remained open was Hogarth's, the
bookshop. Walking there of an afternoon, the heat was so intense I
sometimes thought that if I stopped walking and stood still I might
melt into the pavement, meld with the soft sticky black tar.

The bookshop was owned by two women, Norma Sells and Joan
Beaverstoke, friends of Clover's. I suppose it was because of Clover,
really, that I started going there. She often called in on her way home
from Glastonbridge. You could get a cup of coffee and browse and
have a chat.

Of the two women, it was Norma I liked best. She was sharp and could
be supercilious. But kind, too. I got the feeling I was forgiven a lot
because she felt sorry for me. Sometimes I'd catch her eyes resting on
me then she'd look away quickly. Norma was not someone who liked
to lock eyes. Not like Joan. Joan had made an art form of it.

Joan was older than me but quite a bit younger than Norma. She ran
the business side of the bookshop – the new books and the coffee
machine. Norma looked after the old books. They were her passion

and she knew each one on the shelves. She sat in the back room surrounded by them. Often there'd be an elderly gentleman or two sitting across the desk from Norma, talking, discussing what they'd read. There was a quiet and steady stream of people to Norma's room. I sometimes ran into William there. He'd spend hours sitting with Norma, their murmuring voices breaking into chuckles. Norma would come out and fetch a couple of coffees and take them back, Joan watching her retreating back disapprovingly. Probably because the coffees never got paid for.

It was in the front section that I usually sat and where Clover often could be found. She and Joan were close. I don't know why – they were so unalike. But Clover seemed to somehow depend on Joan, to depend on her approval. Joan was a large, robust woman in her mid-forties, soft of flesh, firm of eye. I don't think she cared that much for books, but she had realised that Glaston needed a bookshop and that Norma would agree to this sort of business when she wouldn't agree to any other.

If Joan had been the type to plan her life in advance, I doubt if Glaston would ever have figured in her plans. But each stage of her life had been a going forward in an open-armed, steady-eyed kind of way. She rarely looked back, or even to the side, but took on whatever was before her with a calm and interested gaze. Clover said that the one big decision of Joan's life had been going into the Navy when she was seventeen. Joan liked the Navy, the calm order, the uniforms that meant you never had to worry about what to wear, the way there was a system for everything. The bookshop – her part of it, anyway – was always as neat and ordered as an officer's kit.

'So living with Norma, that wasn't a decision?'

'Oh no,' said Clover, guileless. 'That was fate.'

'I'd rather be down the coast,' Norma said to me one day. 'Always spent Januarys at the coast, at Hawks Nest. Every year of my life till Joan turned up.' It was clear that Norma didn't like her routines being broken – and that it still amazed her she had let Joan break so many of them.

Joan's abiding interest was houses. Old houses. She was very active in the National Trust. The window displays at Hogarth's were invariably full of books about historic homes or pioneering families. She was always pushing these books onto people. If some tourists came in and got talking, she'd start on about Glaston's colonial architecture. At some point she would drop in, 'My partner, Norma Sells, is from one of the old families. The Sells have been in Glaston since the beginning.'

Convenient word that word 'partner'. Multi-interpretable, safe.

The Austinmeer dining room was a window to one world. But Hogarth's was a window to another. At the Austinmeers I could have been almost anywhere. The Cote d'Azur in 1937, I sometimes thought. At Hogarth's you were well and truly in the main street of Glaston. And part of me was almost relieved to be there, to have come to rest amid such ordinariness. It was comfortable to merge into the patina of this half-forgotten place.

Yet it wasn't always comfortable at Hogarth's. Joan did not entirely trust me and it was mutual. Joan was only really interested in people she could influence, like Clover. And Duane Smith. But Duane was more than a match for her.

*

Duane's arms, as brown and beautiful as a girl's, were casually draped over the back of the chair he was straddling. He was wearing shorts that had been cut down from jeans, the edges fraying dangerously close to his crotch, and a T-shirt that had been similarly denuded of its sleeves.

'Heard something about Glastonbridge,' he said to Joan, who was standing behind the counter going through some figures. He didn't wait for her to respond. 'Heard that Raymond Tyler's sister is broke. He might have to bail her out.'

'I didn't even know he had a sister,' Joan said, pretending indifference.

'Thought you'd be interested,' he went on. 'Could slow things down a bit out there.'

Joan, Duane knew, was becoming increasingly fascinated by Glastonbridge, largely because she no longer got invited out to see it – not since she'd become so involved with the National Trust. Joan looked up at him.

'I'm restoring for Raymond now,' Duane said, preening ever so slightly.

Joan raised her eyebrows, impressed despite herself.

Duane said, 'The more I see of what goes on with these old properties, the more I realise how important the Trust is.'

Joan just nodded and said, 'We've got a vacancy on the committee. Why don't you stand for it?'

'Well, I don't know. I suppose if you were to nominate me I wouldn't say no.'

Joan liked to think of her feelings for Duane as maternal. She saw such potential in him. Not yet thirty and already so attuned to the importance of the past! He would help her fulfil her dream of turning Glaston into a heritage town.

That night as Joan and Norma were getting ready for bed, Joan said: 'That Duane's going to go a long way. I wouldn't be surprised if he ends up in Sydney with the Heritage Council. It's nice to see someone so young being concerned about history.'

'You mean, making a nice living out of those concerned with history,' Norma retorted. 'I don't trust that boy.'

'Darling, you're such a cynic.' Joan gave Norma's arm an affectionate rub.

*

The circulation of the *Glaston Gazette* was not wide. It did not extend much beyond the middle reaches of the River Glass, which meant it covered two medium-sized towns and a scattering of hamlets. The biggest circulation day was Monday, when it published the results of the weekend sports competitions. On Wednesdays the only interesting reading were the court reports: youths had up for stealing cars on Saturday night or fined for being drunk and disorderly. On Fridays the *Gazette* was read for the classifieds and the weekly specials at Coles. It was a good way to advertise a garage sale, or a litter of kittens, or a secondhand car, as long as you weren't in a hurry to sell.

Brenda Watkins had worked for the *Glaston Gazette* since she was fifteen, when it was owned by her uncle. He gave her a job as a copy girl. For Brenda, the choice was either the *Gazette* or Fryer's fish shop. It wasn't a hard decision. She didn't exactly discover a talent for journalism but she progressed to writing for the paper. First, when she was sixteen, doing the sporting results then, at seventeen, the weddings and social notes. At eighteen, she was allowed to do news reports. She wasn't allowed to cover the local court until she was nineteen. She had shorthand by then, studied at evening college, one night a week for two years. This progression had nothing to do with ambition. Either she did it or she would lose her job: there was no such thing as a twenty-year-old copy girl.

Brenda was a big girl, inclined to fat. She had a sweet face and when her mousy hair was newly washed she could look quite pretty. In due course she got married, to a rather taciturn youth, all surly shoulders and rock-hard calves. They met at the Football Club. Brenda kept on working, had to. Needed the money. She kept on working after each of the two children, too.

At thirty-seven, Brenda was little changed from the girl she'd been at twenty. She was still genial and unambitious. But now she brought out the *Gazette* almost single-handed. The paper no longer belonged to her uncle. When he retired he sold it to Pemberton Publications, the big chain of country papers owned by Jamie Stoker. Instead of eight staff there were now three: Brenda, her cadet offsider Tim, and the woman who sold the advertising.

Brenda had met Duane Smith at a clearance sale at one of the home-steads outside town. He was the auctioneer's assistant and had given her the details so she could write her story. She thought he'd come up to Glaston with Dalgety's just for the auction. But a few days later she saw him again, at the service station on the edge of town.

'Are you just heading off?' she asked.

He looked at her, uncomprehending.

'Heading home?' she repeated.

He shook his head. 'No. No, I live here.'

'Oh.'

She finished filling the petrol tank, and he did the same.

'Can you tell me,' he said, 'that two-storey place down there, behind the big hedge, who does that belong to?'

'That place? William Ansell.'

'And who's he?'

'He's a musician. Retired. Been here eight years or so. Lovely house, isn't it? And you should see the garden. The fella he lives with is a garden designer.'

She looked at Duane to see if he got the inference. But Duane was looking at the house. Then he turned to her with a smile so soft and sweet it was like a gentle wave washing across her.

'I should introduce myself properly,' Duane said, holding out his hand. 'Duane Smith.' He pronounced it Du-arne.

'Duane.' Brenda turned the name over on her tongue. 'How do you spell that?'

Brenda had never known anyone like Duane. When he opened a small shop not far from the *Gazette* office, selling bits and pieces of second-hand furniture, doing repairs and restoration, she got into the habit of dropping in there a couple of times a week. Sometimes she went with him when he went on a run to pick up furniture. She went with him to auctions, too. She liked watching the quiet way he went about his business. Quiet but effective.

Duane let her prattle on while he worked. She knew everyone in the town and everything about it. In public, having her beside him gave him confidence. Everyone chatted to Brenda and because he was with her, they chatted to him, too. There was no better way for him to get to know the town, or for him to get known.

When Duane first arrived in Glaston, he latched on to those who presented themselves. Brenda because she wanted to be helpful and could do him no harm. And Joan because she knew the people who were likely to be his clients – the renovators of old homes, the collectors of bric-a-brac. He even joined the National Trust and went to the local meetings, hoping to make contacts. They sat around him in a circle, rheumy old men and innocent wide-eyed women. They looked at him, delighted. The only other person there under fifty was Joan (and her not by much).

Brenda liked the women who ran the bookshop but was shy with them. They were well read and she was not. She felt it was too late to start. If she'd been Duane's age...well, she could've done anything. But, really, she was lucky. She had the hubby and her kids but she still had her own life. Not like most of the women she knew.

She was flattered when Duane took her along to Hogarth's one hot Friday evening. Flattered and nervous. She'd never before dared to go into the back room, to Norma's domain, where the secondhand books and first editions were kept. To Brenda it was an Aladdin's cave. She could have roamed those shelves for hours. She didn't because everyone else was sitting out the back, under the pepper tree, hoping for a breeze. Brenda stood nearby, listening to the conversations but not taking part, conscious of Joan watching her with a steady gaze.

Clover was familiar with that gaze of Joan's. It made one feel important. When they first met, Joan fixed her eyes on her and Clover's confidence blossomed. Joan exuded a sense of steadiness, a calm port in a storm. She had the knack of making people feel valued. While Brenda hovered uncertainly on the edge of this merry group, Clover was at the centre of it, seated between June and Norma, laughing at a joke. Norma and Joan and – increasingly – Raymond were the closest thing Clover had to family in Glaston.

Not long after they met, Joan had asked her, 'Have you ever been in love?'

Clover, embarrassed, had said, 'Once I think. I suppose. She was a friend from school.'

Joan nodded, in a knowing kind of way that made Clover want to beg to be told what it was that Joan could see in her past, or her future. But Joan had a position to uphold in Glaston and would say nothing that might compromise her. It would not do to be accused of corrupting the young. So Clover went away feeling that some secret had been revealed to her uncertain heart, yet unsure of what that secret was.

Maybe that's what kept drawing her back. This atmosphere of suggestion, an atmosphere not everyone was sensitive to. Some felt it. Others did not.

4.

Houses – buying them, restoring them, furnishing them – were the focal point in the lives of most of Glaston's newcomers. As if each of them was striving towards their own little piece of heaven, here on earth. Raymond and Glastonbridge, Clover and her exquisite little Georgian cottage, William and Robbie's Italianate mansion. And it wasn't just the houses they lived in but those they dreamed of and read about and planned for. English country houses and French chateaux; the houses of *Country Life* and *Architectural Digest*; harbourside apartments from *Vogue* and *Belle*; derelict Sydney terraces awaiting their touch; solid old Glaston buildings, shuttered and closed and crying out to be reborn.

Each weekend everyone scanned the real estate columns; each had their favourite section. Sally eyed the flats for sale in Sydney's eastern suburbs and made noises to Titus about buying a tiny pied-à-terre. Titus would grunt noncommittedly and turn to *Country Life*, where he could lust after Elizabethan manor houses and Shropshire thatched cottages.

Robbie read about houses in Woollahra and Rose Bay and Edgecliff, places big enough for a garden. 'Secret gardens', 'magic hideaways' with four bedrooms, two bathrooms, off-street parking and room for the dogs. He toyed with the idea of persuading William to move back to Sydney but was never entirely sure if he himself really wanted to.

So he just kept on looking, and talking to Sally about maybe buying that pied-à-terre together.

William liked to compare the country houses that came up for sale with his own home, gauging his house's worth against comparable homes in Launceston and Lismore, Molong and Maitland.

Raymond read the commercial columns. He looked for run-down shopping centres or old picture theatres, then he'd disappear for days at a time, gone off to inspect some prospect in a distant country town or outlying city suburb in Adelaide or Geelong. Every now and then his friends heard about a purchase but the details were never clear.

Joan Beaverstoke was interested in any house built before 1890. She liked to know who owned what in the district, the condition of the property and any proposed renovations. She went to look at every old house that came on the market. The real estate agents knew her well and groaned when they saw her approaching. Everywhere Joan looked she saw places pleading to be saved. Norma listened to her laments but made no response. Norma was the only one who didn't give a fig for houses: 'They're only bricks and mortar.'

And wood. Clover liked old houses because of the joinery. She prowled around properties for sale inspecting the windows and skirting boards and architraves, some of which had been painted over with layers of paint – blue, brown, grey. Sometimes even red. 'It's terrible,' she'd say, 'the things people do to wood.'

And Duane, well Duane was interested in houses because he liked to know the value of the things that were in them.

When the Glastonians were not looking at houses they were talking about them. What was for sale, what had sold, how much for and who to, what might come up for sale, what terrific buy had been missed. What the next step in their renovations would entail, what colour the walls should be, what shape the windows. What was authentic and what was not. Who had done a botched job and what tradesman was to be trusted. Where curtains could be made and fabric bought, where to get cheap tiles and wholesale paint.

Glastonbridge was the monolith against which all other restoration efforts paled. They discussed the house's problems with Raymond and encouraged him, and dreamed sometimes what the house would be like when and if it were ever finished. They lusted after Raymond's furniture and sometimes resented his resources, but after each visit to Glastonbridge they went home thankful for the more modest scale of their own enterprise.

*

Of all those who knew Raymond, only Theo truly envied him. It began that day years before when Raymond first showed him the house. Like an extreme case of sibling rivalry. It didn't seem right to Theo that Raymond should have the place. Raymond who never finished anything, who was so disorganised, who had creative flair – yes, one had to give him that – but expended it in such an undisciplined fashion.

Shortly after New Year, when Theo knew that Lillian was back in town after her visit to Glaston, he invited her to lunch. Lillian wondered about the propriety of it. He was somewhat younger than her and he had a wife or de facto or whatever, who lived in the country and was rarely seen in town. But she was curious as well as flattered by his invitation. Theo had booked a table at a new place in Kings Cross. This was not a part of the city that Lillian frequented and she worried briefly about the safety of her car, left on the street under the belligerent gaze of a pair of strip club bouncers.

She was relieved that the restaurant looked reasonable: fashionably spare, its tables well spaced on the polished wooden floor. She was five minutes late and Theo was already seated, as she had planned. He stood and took her hand, not shaking it or kissing it, just holding it, then waited for her to sit before resuming his own seat. He waited that extra bit longer as though to emphasise that this was not a mere formality but a mark of respect, for himself as well as for her.

The food was good though Lillian would not have noticed if Theo had not made a point of savouring and commenting on each mouthful. She obediently murmured the appropriate phrases. Theo talked of this and that: his most recent trip overseas, to Lithuania, on the trail of icons; the state of the real estate market, which he could discuss eloquently while his mind was on something else entirely. Lillian became impatient. Why had he asked her to lunch? Was it possible that he was interested in her? She was just beginning to play with this idea when he finally said something to catch her attention.

'My house is coming along,' he said. 'I still need some furniture, if only I could find the right pieces.'

'What are you looking for?'

'A few things – dining table, chairs. Bookcases. That pair of your brother's would be perfect if he'd ever part with them.'

'They are very special pieces,' she said, noncommittedly.

'I've never been sure exactly how things stand between you...' Theo ventured.

'Oh, Raymond's collection is nothing to do with me.'

'I thought perhaps you were business partners.'

Lillian looked as though she had swallowed an ice cube. What had Theo heard about her business affairs?

'Not really,' she replied, trying to sound unperturbed. 'But I agree those bookcases could be better utilised, instead of lying about in bits gathering dust.'

'He hasn't pulled them apart, has he?'

'Raymond pulls everything apart. It's his hobby. But he'll never sell those bookcases. He wants them for Glastonbridge.'

Theo struggled to remain composed. 'He really is a character, your brother,' he said, trying to sound jovial. 'How's it going up at Glaston? Nearly finished?' He knew better, of course.

Lillian looked at him, suddenly soft, inviting sympathy. She put a hand on his arm. 'I don't think he'll ever finish, Theo. It would take someone like you, with discipline, to see through a project like Glastonbridge. I worry it might break him.'

'I haven't seen the house recently,' Theo said, 'but I admire it enormously. If there's ever anything I can do, you let me know.' He added: 'I'm very fond of Raymond.'

They both settled themselves back in their chairs and looked at each other.

'I've enjoyed this lunch, Lillian.'

'So have I. Very much.' She ventured a half-smile.

*

Raymond stood motionless in the centre of the great hall. Beyond the high mullioned windows, branches blew back and forth, casting dappled shadows across the floor and to and fro across his sagging shoulders. The tossing branches were the only indication of a high wind. No sound penetrated Glastonbridge except the occasional scraping of a branch against window or gutter. He had been standing like that for some minutes, unaware of time passing. Yet the passing of time preoccupied him. The time that was his time was rushing away from him, receding into an ever more distant past, while the present, in which he was trapped, clung to him like an impertinent petitioner. He found it more and more difficult to respond to the requirements of each day. Planning for a future had become impossible. He stood alone in the great hall, unable to move.

This house, which he had dreamt of for so long, had lain always in the future. But now it dominated his life, the burden of each day. At night he sometimes still dreamed about a dreamhouse and was filled with overwhelming joy that such a place awaited him. Then he'd wake, in the small butler's pantry at Glastonbridge, and the dream and the joy shrivelled within him.

There were times when he'd walk into a room or open a cupboard or climb the stairs from the cellars and fear would settle around him like a cold damp cloak. But he could not have said what it was that frightened him. True, the house was dim and full of dark corners, but that was just because so much light was blocked by the elaborate tracery on the windows. (Was there any other house in the country that had such extraordinary tracery?) The house was unnaturally cold. That was because of the thickness of the stone walls. Yet the coolness was welcome during a Glaston summer. Getting the heavy old drapes off the windows had helped to let more light in, yet it didn't change the feel of the place. In a small corner of his heart he had to admit that nothing made much difference. It was as if the effort they all put into the house was absorbed into the walls, soaked up.

He did not believe the house was haunted. But he could not deny that the place had an atmosphere all its own. Clover asserted that she could feel presences, but Clover would. Old Rose Harkness had lived in the house for fifty years. Whatever spirit it was could not have worried her too much.

Of course there were stories about the place: how the Harknesses inherited it from a bachelor relative who had lived in the place as a hermit for twenty years, died there and was not found for a week. How the Harkness children were sickly, generation after generation. How Reg Harkness had been sent away to school when he was five and never went home, not even for holidays, because his parents so feared he'd die, as his brothers and sisters had. Raymond didn't believe the stories. The only story he believed was that the building of Glastonbridge had sent William Berge bankrupt, then mad.

Raymond stirred himself, lifted his head suddenly and turned from where he was standing. He went into the hallway and climbed the stairs to the upstairs drawing room, where Clover was working. He stood and watched her a moment then asked, 'Do you think it's Berge's presence that you feel?'

'I don't know,' she replied, resting her slight arm on the stepladder, expecting Raymond to say more. But he didn't, just turned and walked back downstairs.

Raymond hadn't mentioned the letter from the National Trust to anyone apart from William. He decided to ignore it but it began to prey on him. Bloody busybodies! Watching and judging: he hated that. If only people would leave him alone so that he and Bob and Clover could get on with it. When Clover and Bob were with him he felt safe here, he felt he was getting somewhere.

Afternoon tea with Raymond was the favourite part of Clover's day. Work was over, Bob had gone home and it was just her and Raymond sitting quietly while Glastonbridge creaked and moved about them. Clover liked to think of these noises as the house settling itself for the night.

'It's so strange to think of someone building a place like this when this area was just grasslands and open forest and Glaston was only a scattering of houses,' she said. 'You can sort of see why they built Georgian in Tasmania – it was green and soft and Englishy – but why Gothic in the Glass Valley?'

'Gothic's never had much to do with reality,' said Raymond. 'More of an escape really.'

Clover waited for him to go on. These were the times she loved with Raymond.

'Gothic doesn't try to reconcile opposites. Contradictions – that's what it's all about. Imagine the contradictions that Berge was living with when he built this place! I sometimes wonder what he was trying to achieve, what he was doing here...' His voice trailed off.

'Perhaps there was something in his past,' Clover said. 'A scandal, a love affair.'

'I think he was just an un...unhappy man,' Raymond's voice was tremulous, and Clover sat very still, her knees tucked up underneath her on the day bed. 'Can't find out much about him but that's the feeling I get. When the crash came he just abandoned the house and left. No one knows where. His wife was dead by then and his surviving daughter had gone to New Zealand. They say he just walked away. Didn't take a thing.' He paused a moment then went on. 'In Tasmania you could take a piece of furniture and trace a whole family history through it – people going broke, breaking up, families dying out. Even as a kid I knew that furniture was somehow important, that if only it could talk it'd have stories to tell. Provenance should be more than making sure a piece of furniture is genuine. It should be about tracing its life, where and when it moved, family to family.'

'That's how I feel, too,' Clover said fervently.

'Maybe I take it too far,' Raymond said. Every day he learned something more about Glastonbridge. Sometimes he felt he was learning more than he wanted to know.

*

One afternoon at Hogarth's Clover moaned, 'I've just spent two hours re-oiling skirting boards and wrapping them in dust sheets. I wish Raymond would put them back on the walls but he can't make up his mind about the wall colour.'

Joan said, 'Really, someone should be keeping an eye on what Raymond is doing over there. I hear it's one step forward and two steps back.' She looked at Clover meaningfully. There was a way Joan had of looking – sort of large and soft and jolly on first glance, but when you looked closer, at the eyes, hard and penetrating.

It made Clover fidget. 'Oh I don't mean...I was only having a bit of a moan. Don't take any notice,' she said, and tried to change the subject.

But Joan would not budge. 'He really should be keeping the Trust informed.'

Clover frowned. 'If it weren't for Raymond, Glastonbridge would have fallen in a heap and none of you could have done anything to stop it. At least he's trying...' Her voice trailed away.

A late customer came in, wanting a book on quilting, and Joan fussed over her until it became clear that she didn't intend speaking to Clover again.

Joan Beaverstoke would not be a pleasant enemy. Even having to think such a thing shocked Clover. Driving to work the next day, she trembled at the thought. It was the sort of morning that would normally have made her spirits soar. There'd been a cool change. The breeze through the open window of her van was mild and a shower of rain the night before had settled the dust. She loved the drive along the Old West Road. It wasn't used much. On either side were simple nineteenth-century cottages spaced well apart, with market gardens and lucerne paddocks and the occasional horse or cow. But as she drove over to Raymond's this day even the beauty of the morning could not ease her mind. She approached the stone rampart of the Glaston bridge then on an impulse pulled over to the side and turned off the engine. She leaned back against the seat and ran her fingers through her hair.

'Wealthy eccentrics with more money than sense,' Joan had snorted, 'they're always taking on projects.'

That wasn't fair, Clover thought. Raymond wasn't just messing around out there, although it did sometimes look that way. When she'd tried to defend him, Joan had turned her back on her, literally.

Joan had been her friend and her mentor. Clover was swept by sudden grief for the innocence of that friendship, which seemed to have evaporated overnight. She hated to be caught between friends. Sitting in her van beside the Glaston bridge, Clover tried to decide what to do. She was thirty-one years old, living alone in a small town. She had no family here but it had never troubled her before because Joan and Norma had been like family. What would it be like here without Joan's friendship?

Then she thought of Raymond, and of Glastonbridge, and felt immediately protective. If Joan tried to make trouble for Raymond, there was no doubt in her mind whose side she was on. She straightened her back, started up the van and headed over the bridge. As she turned onto the track that led up to the house – Raymond still hadn't put a proper driveway in – she resolved what she would do. She wouldn't say anything to Raymond directly about Joan's potential trouble-making but in the afternoon she would go over and have a talk to Sally Austinmeer about it.

While Sally made tea, Clover looked around her. 'I always think,' she said, 'that you're not following style but sending it up.'

Sally glanced at her to see how she was meant to take this. Clover's pale blue eyes were fixed on her.

'It's a game,' she said, deciding that Clover was just being Clover. 'With houses, I play.'

'You know, it's not a game with Raymond,' Clover said. 'People think he's just messing around up there, playing about with Glastonbridge. But it's not a game. It's because he takes it so seriously. People don't...'

'Clover, what's happened?' Sally looked at her, concerned.

'It's probably nothing.' Clover picked up her delicate teacup and, delaying, turned the saucer over to examine the stamp underneath.

Sally took no notice; most of the people she knew did that sort of thing. She waited.

'It's just Joan, saying "the National Trust is concerned".'

Sally didn't respond. Part of her had been expecting something like this sooner or later.

'Can they do anything?' Clover asked, now clearly anxious.

'I don't know. I might talk it over with Philip Dexter.'

A car door slammed and a few moments later Titus's large frame blocked out the light at the front door.

'Is that you Clover?' he called up the hall. 'Bloody hell. Do you think you could move your car? I've got to get these barrels unloaded.'

Later, after Clover had left, Titus said in that brisk way he had of summing up a person or situation, 'She's a funny one, that Clover. So definite about anything to do with wood, so uncertain about everything else.'

*

I became closer to Sally than I did to any of the others. That's probably why I find it harder to describe her. I think she liked having me around because it was a relief to her to have someone she didn't have to worry about. She was surrounded by men who relied on her in some way or other. We did ordinary things together – went over to Brampton for the day, picked vegies, drank coffee, talked about movies and art.

I always thought there was a lot more to Sally than she let on most of the time. I suspect she had genuine talent but that she was afraid of her imagination. She kept it in reserve, like a box that she always intended to get out and unpack one day. Easier to worry about the colour of someone's wall, the fall of a curtain, than risk what might come from the end of her paintbrush.

We were over in Brampton on the day the article about Glastonbridge appeared in the Gazette. *We picked up the paper at the newsagents there. I saw the article on page three and read it to Sally while she drove. Then she stopped the car and read it for herself. 'I've always liked Brenda,' she said. 'Why would she write such a thing?'*

I told her I thought Joan and Duane had been in her ear.

Historic House Under Threat
By Brenda Watkins

The house that bears Glaston's name and which was 'rediscovered' only six years ago may be facing ruin.

Glastonbridge – owned by wealthy retired antique dealer Mr Raymond Tyler – formerly of Sydney and Tasmania – is believed by local heritage circles to be in danger of never being restored.

The house – which many locals believed was beyond repair when Mr Tyler bought it – is now thought by some experts to be in a worse state than when he began.

Glastonbridge was built in 1841 by Lt William Berge on land granted to him by Governor Gipps.

It was previously owned by Miss Rose Harkness. She died in 1986. She had not lived in the house since the early 1960s.

People concerned about the fate of the house believe it is time the Historic Houses Trust stepped in.

'Should I tell Raymond about this when he gets back from Melbourne?' Sally asked me as we sat in her car beside the Brampton Road. She was still holding the paper.

'You'll have to, won't you?'

She wasn't listening. *'No, I know what I'll do first. I'll talk to Philip.'*

*

'Not the Historic Houses Trust!' Joan exploded when she read the article. 'We don't need them nosing their way in. The National Trust! We can see to it.'

'Yes, I'm afraid Brenda made a bit of a mistake there,' Duane said. As a favour to Joan he'd put Brenda onto the story, but he didn't want to take responsibility for it.

*

If I had never met Raymond, if I had lived here and heard about Glastonbridge but never got to know its owner, I would probably have been like Joan – resentful of Raymond, disparaging, seeing him as a dilettante. But once I got to know him my critical instincts were blunted. You couldn't help but like him; the passion he had for the arcane; his disregard for the things that matter most to other people. Even his desire to own and restore and furnish a wonderful house was not like other people's. You couldn't call him materialistic and dismiss him. Look how he lived – the mess and discomfort he put up with quite happily, because in his eyes his vision was already half complete.

Sometimes he'd rant at Berge: 'Now why on earth did he do THAT!' he said once, pointing to a small stone staircase that appeared to branch off from the back stairs then ended in a stone wall. He shook his head as though exasperated, although I could tell he was actually delighted. He looked at me with a wicked grin: 'There's things like this all over the house. Upstairs there's a corridor that ends in a chimney.'

'Perhaps he made it up as he went along?'

Raymond shook his head. 'Mistakes? No, no, they're not mistakes. He knew what he was doing. They're there for a reason. It's like he was building blind alleys.'

I wondered about Berge's 'blind alleys'. Did he just have a childish sense of humour? Or were they metaphors for his own life? It was the same with Raymond. I was never sure whether he was a bright man trying to work something out through unorthodox means or a spoilt boy who'd become trapped in the maze of his own excess. Perhaps a bit of both.

There was a hillside just above the house that I grew to love. I sat there sometimes and tried to imagine how the Glass Valley looked before Europeans laid their hands on it, before Berge built Glaston-bridge or the bridge. Before Glaston existed. How many people lived here then? I'd close my eyes and, if I was lucky and there were no other noises – no distant screech of saw or Bob hammering timber in the house – the only sounds might be those that had always been here: the wind blowing through the eucalypts, the rustle of dry grass, a bird calling as it flew over, the whine of crickets. When I opened my eyes, it was like two images coalescing into one: a native landscape and a European one merging. Forming something that was both... and neither.

5.

There was nothing Philip enjoyed more than a long, complicated hunt for a unique piece of furniture. There was the subtle putting out of feelers, probing here and there with a quiet word and a promise or two. There was the thrill of following up possibilities, never knowing if one's approach would be welcomed or rebutted, whether he would meet with a knowing nod or a blank disavowal. There was the excitement as he first walked up to inspect a potential find, following in the footsteps of vendor or dealer, down long corridors or across stretches of dim warehouse. His nerve endings would be stretched taut, his nostrils alert, his eyes aching in concentration. Then, when he stood before it, stroking the smooth wood, noting the grain, assessing the patina, his heart began to pound. Running his hands down the legs, checking the joints, opening a drawer, examining the locks, his temples would ache. Sometimes he even felt weak in the legs.

This was the courtship – the seeking and wooing. Next came the marriage contract. He usually left it a day or two. Only once, in Paris, when he suspected someone else of having the same objective did he begin negotiations on the same day. Usually he would take his time, acting disinterested. He would suggest some adjustment in the price and not react when the seller shook their head in dismay and horror. He'd go away, the adrenalin coursing through him in waves so that he was alternately high, ravenous, on his power, and low, nauseous and hollow-stomached in apprehension. When, several days later, the deal was done, he was drained, euphoric, replete. 'Better than sex,' he'd once told Sally.

Sally had discovered that the best time to catch Philip was around ten in the morning, when he left his flat and went downstairs to the showroom and office. His assistant, John, a dedicated young man of nineteen, had just answered the phone when Philip appeared at the door, carrying a slim tan briefcase. John had often wondered why Philip bothered to take a briefcase home each night when home was only upstairs, but he never dared ask. He put his hand over the receiver and said to his employer, 'It's Mrs Austinmeer.'

Philip went through to his private office and picked up the phone. 'Sal!' He allowed his usual cultivated tones to drop away as he shoved the office door shut with his elbow.

Sally told him about the story in the *Gazette*.

'Raymond's been in Melbourne, thankfully,' she said. 'But he's due back tomorrow. Tell me, have you heard anything about the Historic Houses Trust getting interested or the National Trust? William tells me that Raymond had a letter from the Trust. But he didn't mention it to me.'

'No, nor to me. Who's behind the story in the local rag, do you think?'

'Probably Joan Beaverstoke, although I wouldn't have thought it of her. Do you know her?'

'Beaverstoke. Prompt me.'

'Runs a bookshop up here. With her partner. Lesbians.'

'Ah, the large woman with the imposing manner. I met her once at William's. Why do you think?'

'You know what small towns are like. The thing is, do I tell Raymond?'

'I think you're going to have to. He needs to say something to knock it on the head. When are you coming to town next? Haven't seen you since Christmas.'

'I'll be down next week to see clients. And I have to see Ro.'

Her sister, Rosemary, was a constant source of concern for Sally because she never seemed to be happy.

Rosemary was head of human resources for a large company in Sydney. She found the job mentally demanding but she didn't find it emotionally exhausting. She believed in leaving work at work. Rosemary's real passion was real estate.

She lived in Paddington in a two-storey terrace with a four-metre frontage, two bedrooms and an upstairs bathroom. It wasn't large but was very prettily restored, with the requisite amount of Sydney lace ironwork and tessellated tiling. Rosemary was inordinately proud of the tessellated tiling.

The house had been bought eight years before. It was almost time to upgrade and she was watching the *Wentworth Courier* for a suitable place in Woollahra. In the meantime, she had bought – for tax purposes – a studio unit in Elizabeth Bay, which was rented out and negative geared. Then there was the house in Petersham that she was restoring. Some philistine owner in the not-too-distant past had given it aluminium windows and a cement-rendered facade but she'd seen its potential. It was now beginning to resemble the sweet neo-Gothic cottage that it had once been.

After she left her office each day she went over to Petersham to see how the workmen were getting on. She consulted with the builder, scrambled up ladders and hopped from beam to beam across floorless floors. She had a knack with tradesmen. She always got what she wanted.

Except when it came to love.

Sally found Rosemary sitting at the dining table with a stack of decorating magazines in front of her. That's what has changed these past couple of years, Sally thought. She used to enjoy houses, now she's obsessed by them.

When she said something to this effect, Rosemary snapped: 'It's just a hobby. I do have a full-time career, you know. Unlike some.'

O-oh.

'You're looking tired again, Roey. Is everything all right?'

'Yes. And why wouldn't it be?'

'Well...you get yourself into a spiral, you know you do.'

'Yes, preach at me. You were always good at that.'

'I'm not preaching. I'm merely trying to...'

'What would you know? You don't know ANYTHING.'

Sally was stung. 'That's not fair.'

'You've been with Titus forever. You've never had to make it on your own.'

'I wish...'

'Oh, wish away dear sister. This is the real world.' Rosemary walked into the kitchen and put the kettle on, leaving Sally standing in the dining room.

What should she do now? Leave? Why was it that only her sister had the ability to rile her in this way? She followed Rosemary into the kitchen. 'You want to talk about the real world?' she asked. 'All right. It's about Philip, isn't it? Well, here's some reality for you. Philip's gay and always has been. He flirts with women because he flirts with everyone.'

'I know that. Of course I know that.' And Rosemary turned from the sink and looked at Sally so sadly that Sal felt like a total heel.

*

The money that Raymond had agreed to loan Lillian came through in February. She knew it was a loan. Well, in theory she knew it was a loan. But she hadn't realised that meant she would have to make regular repayments. She'd merely signed the papers that had been presented to her.

'I won't have any money!' she shrieked. 'He's done it on purpose.'

'Lillian,' said the accountant, who was the son of her father's accountant. 'You will. You'll just have to be careful. You really will have sufficient so long as you don't make any big purchases.'

When she left the office in Bent Street she was jumping out of her skin with fury. She stormed out of the lift, her arms and legs moving jerkily. How could he do such a thing, to his own sister! While he lived it up, spending, spending on that giant folly of his, she'd be watching every penny. She wouldn't be able to go out. She'd have to stay at home and eat TV dinners!

Throughout her life Lillian had been bitter with Raymond more often than not. When she was in New York her therapist helped her to see that it was all due to that two-year difference in their ages. She had always been just one step behind Raymond, not far enough behind to be the adored younger sister or long-awaited daughter. An accident, an afterthought, the one tagging along. When she was newborn, Raymond was walking. When she began to crawl, Raymond amused with his talk. He always had a way of swinging attention back on himself.

When Father died and Raymond took control of the Tyler estate, she'd been in America, happily married to Harry, with a full and interesting life. Australia, and the Tyler business interests, seemed a long way away. If only things could go back to the way they were when Harry was alive. She'd never had to worry about money then.

She was convinced that Raymond was trying to hide things from her, that there was more money salted away than he would admit. He was trying to cheat her. When she'd been at Glastonbridge, she'd seen furniture there that she'd never seen before.

'Where did that come from?' she asked him. 'How much did it cost?'

'I'm just minding it for Philip. He wants it out of circulation for a while.'

It sounded suspicious to her. She didn't believe him.

When, the year before, he gave her a fine walnut card table and said, 'I saw this piece and knew it was you and I got it for a really good price,' she was annoyed that he had given her something he had got on the cheap. She only considered an item satisfactory if it had cost a great deal of money. It made shopping an agony, because she battled with herself, and with the unfortunate salesperson, over every dollar. But in the end she always bought the most expensive item. Just like Raymond.

Lillian certainly had no doubts about Raymond's meanness. It dominated her thoughts as she lay beside the pool in the gardens of her

Darling Point apartment building. Sunning herself beside the pool was a large part of her daily routine. She hoisted herself up on one elbow and looked around. There was no one else in sight. At this time on a weekday morning she had the place to herself. She reached beneath the sun bed and felt for the chill-pack that held her beers. Beer, too, was a taste she'd newly discovered since returning to Australia. But she didn't like to be seen drinking it.

Perhaps she should go and visit Philip? Philip wasn't always nice to her but despite this she was drawn to him. When she'd discovered how close he was to Raymond, she was ready to hate him. But he wasn't easy to hate. He was always so gentlemanly, even when he disagreed with you. And he was so popular, too. It wouldn't do to go against the tide. But if anyone knew what Raymond was up to, he would. She'd go around to the shop after lunch. He had some new things in – she was on his mailing list – and she could pretend to be looking at them.

Philip disliked being caught between Raymond and Lillian. But he tried to get on with her. So when she came into the shop that after-noon he put down the papers he was working on, straightened his tie, and went out into the shop to greet her, smiling.

'Just dropped in to look at the new shipment,' she said.

'A few things have sold,' Philip said, 'the chest-on-chest, the fire-sur-round. But the best pieces are still available. This table, Lillian,' he said, walking over to a long elm refectory table, 'can't you just see this at Glastonbridge?'

Lillian smiled stiffly.

Now what? thought Philip. Then he said, 'I was sorry not to see you at the little do we had here last week.'

'Raymond did ask me but it was my night for the university.'

'It was good to see you together at Christmas. I hardly ever see you together.'

Lillian sniffed. 'We weren't seeing much of each other for a time.'

'Really?' he said, ingenuous.

'Tell me Philip, how do *you* think he's going with the house?'

'Wonderfully – except he needs to get the plumbing fixed!'

'Seriously Philip.'

'I don't know, Lil, you've been up there recently. You noticed some big improvements, didn't you?'

'Y-e-s,' she admitted. 'But he's obviously wasted a lot of time redoing things he'd done before. I worry how much it's all costing.' She paused. 'I wish I knew how things really stand.'

'He's quite astute, you know. I don't think you need worry that he's spending the Tyler fortunes.'

'Are there fortunes? I don't even know, you see.'

Philip almost felt sorry for her then. She looked so pathetic: her face, deep tanned but sagging around the mouth; her grey-brown hair, so light in contrast with her skin, curly and tight against her scalp like a bizarre swimming cap.

'He is your brother, Lillian. You should trust him.'

She looked at him as if she didn't know what he was talking about.

Philip occasionally wearied of living in a world where every decision was an act of pragmatism and each conversation was a tactical exercise. When that happened he needed to go somewhere he could drop his guard.

'I wish I'd never befriended her,' he said, sitting on the Austinmeers' verandah with Titus and Sally, glass of chardonnay in hand. 'She comes in and whines about Raymond cheating her. Then he comes in and whines about Lillian trying to screw him. They're as bad as each other. You know that money he lent her? You know why?'

'I thought it was because they got on so well at Christmas,' Sally said.

Philip laughed. 'That might have been the excuse. No, he was worried that she'd start finding out about the way he's invested some of the company funds. For God's sake, don't say a word!'

'Heehee!' Titus hooted.

'Of course not,' said Sal.

'It was basically to keep her quiet.'

'The weird thing is, I think they are actually fond of one another,' Sally said.

'Oh yes. Although I don't think "fond" is quite the word. They've got this weird fixation with each other. They can't leave one another alone. Have to keep gnawing away.'

'Dear me, why can't they just be civil?' Titus said.

'Quite. Well, at least we knocked this one on the head,' Philip said, picking up the copy of the *Glaston Gazette* that lay on his lap.

'Not that it was easy,' Sally said. 'Raymond got himself into such a flap I was sure he'd mess up the interview.'

GLASTONBRIDGE ON COURSE
By Brenda Watkins

The owner of the historic house "Glastonbridge" has told the *Gazette* that his restoration program is on schedule.

Mr Raymond Tyler said it was a massive project and he always knew it would take many years.

As evidence of the progress being made, Mr Tyler produced a photograph of the front of the house – showing recently completed windows and guttering (see photo at right) – together with one taken when Mr Tyler bought the house.

Mr Tyler said two local people were currently being employed full time – they are Mr Bob Pitts of Deweys Lane (carpenter/builder) and Miss Clover Cantrell of Brampton Rd (french polisher).

Mr Tyler also produced a letter from the Heritage Council of NSW, from Mr Peter O'Doherty – senior research officer with the council – who inspected the house two years ago.

In his letter Mr O'Doherty said "the work being done by you at Glastonbridge will ensure the house a place as a building of great significance in the heritage of this State."

Ms Joan Beaverstoke – president of the Glass Valley sub-branch of the National Trust – told the *Gazette* yesterday that the Trust looked forward to the day when Glastonbridge was ready to be opened for public viewing.

That weekend, with the last of the grapes harvested, Sally and Titus held a party, a 'harvest festival'. Their house suited a party: light and airy when one walked into it but, on closer inspection, rich and complicated. The paintings and fabrics and arrangement of furniture created quiet corners perfect for conversation. They'd bought the house for the cellar (Titus refused to keep his wine in a refrigerated shed) but then had to virtually rebuild it to make it habitable.

Jules had brought up a heap of food from Sydney and now he and Titus stood at the top of the external stairs that led down to the cellar, conferring about the wines. From the sitting room came the sound of William tuning the piano.

'When do you think we should have the grape treading?' Titus asked Sally through the kitchen window. 'Before or after we eat?'

'Definitely before.'

'Righto!' he said, with the enthusiasm of a boy.

'Now who is this?' Philip asked Sally, as a figure came up the path.

'That's Duane,' she said.

'Du-arne?'

'Duane Smith. He hasn't been in Glaston long. He's a bit of a dark horse and...well, what else can one say about Duane?' She raised a sceptical eyebrow.

'That he's gorgeous,' Philip said, and almost licked his lips.

'You're incorrigible.' Sally gave him a shove.

It was Robbie who went out and brought Duane in, and hardly left his side all evening.

During dinner there were people all over the house and out on the verandah, sitting on available surfaces, balancing plates on their knees. Raymond was sitting at the breakfast table with Titus and a woman who lived on an adjoining property. William joined them.

'I hate eating off my knees, don't you?' William said, putting his plate down and drawing up a chair.

'I do it all the time,' said Raymond. 'You know, in front of the tellie. I don't really have a table I can use.'

'Oh I think it's so wonderful what you're doing at Glastonbridge,' the woman said. 'What are your plans for it? Will you live there when it's finished?'

'I suppose so. What I'd like to do eventually is set up a trust. When the house is finished, and has my collection in it...that's how I'd like to leave it.'

'You'll have to set it up beforehand,' Titus said.

'Yes,' said Raymond, sounding vague.

A car pulled up by the barn and beeped its horn. The new arrival turned out to be Rosemary. She'd driven all that way and arrived so late it was almost not worth coming. As soon as she came into the room it was evident she was on something. There was a jarring over-brightness to her. All shiny and tinny like a metal surface. She got a plate of food and a glass of wine and sat next to Philip, who'd come over to talk to Raymond. She was very animated, too much so. While she ate, she talked, waving her fork about, the silver bangles on her thin arms jingling and flashing in the lamplight. Her wine glass emptied rapidly.

Philip went into the kitchen to help Sally. 'I've left Rosemary trying to persuade Raymond to become a hotelier. She wants him to turn the place into a country house hotel.'

Sally groaned and said: 'She's not STILL on about that, is she?'

Afterwards, while William was at the piano and Titus was singing, Rosemary walked uncertainly down the hallway to the guest bedroom. That's where Sally found her, fast asleep.

'But she didn't have that much to drink,' Sally said, perplexed.

'I think she might have mixed it with something,' Philip told her. 'Let her sleep it off. It's probably the safest place for her.'

Next morning Rosemary had an appalling headache but she was determined to get away early. She couldn't stand Sally when she went into elder-sister mode. Her worried frown made you feel responsible for having made her worry. Rosemary wished she hadn't come up. The only thing she didn't regret was telling Raymond what he should do with Glastonbridge. Such a place was wasted on him. If she had Glastonbridge, she'd turn it into something special *and* make money out of it. For the remainder of the drive, she diverted herself with an elaborate fantasy of how she would convert Glastonbridge into a guest house. The floorplan was laid neatly out in her mind, as if on graph paper.

She'd first had the idea when Sally and Titus took her over to see the house at Christmas. They'd been aghast when she suggested what could be done to it. They were so defensive of Raymond and treated him with such indulgence. When she'd said, 'That place is beyond Raymond. He'll give up sooner or later,' Sally had become quite frosty.

It was a mystery to Rosemary what people saw in Raymond.

'He's a character,' Titus had said, and chuckled. 'Who else do we know who keeps their groceries in a very good break-front bookcase? Row after row of tinned baked beans.'

*

Raymond had not heard anything more from the National Trust. But he didn't like the silence. He waited for another letter. Sometimes he was afraid when answering the phone that it might be the Trust ringing to check up on him. He worried about that article in the *Gazette*, too, even though his friends had told him it was nothing, and that his reply had set the record straight.

He worried about the money he had lent Lillian. He couldn't really afford it. And he worried about Theo Roth whenever he saw him, which seemed to be almost every time he was in Sydney. Sometimes he thought the man was stalking him. How else to explain that whenever Raymond went to a restaurant, Theo was there? These days it was usually Baillieu's. And whenever Raymond went to a pre-auction inspection, Theo was doing the same.

Raymond couldn't settle. After a few days in Glaston he'd go off to Sydney. A few days there, and it was on to Melbourne. It looked like jet-setting, but it wasn't that to Raymond. Worry made him restless.

6.

I arrived at William and Robbie's to find Duane standing at the bottom of a ladder while Robbie, perched at the top, dead-headed the climbing roses. Robbie's reddish hair glowed in the sun like burnished copper. I wondered, not for the first time, if he dyed it. I'd gone over to pick figs from their overflowing tree, to have a go at making fig jam from a recipe of Sally's. That's how I spent my days then.

Duane didn't stay long when he saw me. But long enough for me to catch the drift of their conversation.

'That story about Glastonbridge in the Gazette was stupid,' Robbie was saying. 'People around here don't have a clue, you know? It's another league from the Joan Beaverstoke school of heritage studies, that's for sure.'

'What d'ya mean?' Duane asked.

'Doesn't matter if a place is shit – as long as it's more than a hundred years old and you can open up twice a year and charge five dollars for tea and scones. It's true,' he said, seeing Duane scowl.

While I waited for Robbie to finish with the ladder, I wandered off to look at the garden. I never tired of Robbie's garden.

'Not much else to do in Glaston but garden,' he said gloomily, as he set up the ladder for me against the fig tree.

'William seems to keep busy.'

'Oh William. He's always trotting off here or there. He visits the old ducks in town. There's always one or other of them ill. Or he goes to the library. He's chair of the committee now, you know.' He rolled his eyes. 'Or sometimes he spends the whole morning playing the piano.'

'That's nice.'

'Yes, it is,' admitted Robbie. 'I can hear him while I'm here in the garden. Actually I think he does it when he knows I'm in a bad mood. Trying to get into my good books.' He tried to grimace but it turned into a pleased sort of smile.

'The thing about Glaston,' he said, 'it's okay as long as you can get out of it.'

'I hear you're going to Mardi Gras?'

'Yeah. Clover's never been. Can you believe that?'

Clover had asked me if I wanted to go, too, but I had no desire to go to Sydney even for a night. I said I'd seen it plenty of times.

'Just hope people in Deniliquin don't hear about me going.'

It was one of the few times I heard her mention the town where she grew up. It was as if she was afraid of the place and still shrank from the thought of it.

'Tell me about Deniliquin,' I asked her.

'There's nothing to tell.'

'So you agree with Duane – that one town is much the same as the next?'

'No,' she said quickly. 'The place where you grow up is never like anywhere else.'

*

Clover and Robbie went first for a drink upstairs at The Oxford. The place was already full at six o'clock and you couldn't get near the windows. Clover had had her hair cut very short for the occasion and kept pulling at it as if she wanted to make it longer.

'Leave it alone. It looks great,' Robbie said.

'I feel naked.'

'You've got more on than anyone else in the room.'

It was true. The place was awash with bronzed pecs and satiny stomachs, muscled thighs and velvety backs. Clover glanced at Robbie in his tight white shorts and black cutaway singlet that showed off his arms and shoulders, toned and tanned. His auburn hair seemed more brilliant, more burnished than ever. 'You look different tonight,' she said, half-shouting to be heard above the throbbing music. 'You don't look like you do in Glaston.'

'That's the point, Clover.'

Down the street, the white tablecloths were being spread at the Burdekin. There was a little less space than usual between the tables to cope with the demand from the socialites and voyeurs who booked the restaurant on parade night. It was nice to be able to wander out to the balcony to view the spectacle then retreat into the elegance of the dining room. Mardi Gras was an event one couldn't miss, but nor did one wish to be too close.

The Contessa had secured the best table. Hers would be a small but select party of only a dozen people. It was the first time that Raymond would be dining with her since that slightly embarrassing incident at the house. She was sure he had forgiven her; she had almost forgotten it. Raymond had declined to call at her place for pre-dinner drinks but it was probably because he had another engagement.

When he entered the dining room, her heart did a small flutter. Raymond could look so elegant when he tried. He was wearing her favourite light-grey Gieves and Hawkes suit. Personally, she would not have chosen a pink tie. After kissing her lightly on the cheek, he saw her looking at the tie. He said, 'My contribution to the theme of the evening,' and grinned his crooked grin.

The other guests arrived and they stood on the balcony drinking champagne and watching preparations for the parade. Traffic had already been diverted and yellow barricades lined two sides of Oxford Street. Marshalls moved about with walkie-talkies and loudspeakers. One directed a tow-truck towing away a parked car.

What a relief it was to get away from Glaston, Raymond thought. He wished he could be content there, as William was. 'It's a shame William couldn't join us,' he said to the Contessa. 'But he rarely comes to Sydney these days. He said he'd watch the parade on TV. Robbie's out there somewhere, though.'

'Really!' exclaimed the Contessa, stunned that someone she knew might actually be down there among all those people. 'Not in the parade, surely?'

'Oh no, as a spectator.'

That seemed to calm her. 'Look!' she suddenly exclaimed, 'There's Philip Dexter.' Everyone peered in the direction she was pointing. 'He always dresses so nicely. Is that Jules Baillieu with him? I read a very nice review of his restaurant in *Good Living*.'

'Mmm, you should give it a try. I think they're going to that new place, Lemons, this evening.'

Philip and Jules took their seats next to the plate-glass windows. The outfit that the Contessa had admired on Philip was an informal cream suit. But she would not have been impressed by the tie. At first glance it was inoffensive enough but the discreet pattern was of row upon row of naked men.

They were joined by two of Philip's friends: a lawyer and an architect. Jules offered the shorter of the two his seat near the window. 'Oh but I insist! We will be standing on our chairs when the parade goes by. You will not be able to see.'

By the time the main course came at eight-thirty, the pavement outside the window was jammed with people. There were cool dudes from the bars, decked out in skimpy white T-shirts and tight leather shorts, or leather jeans with nothing on top. There were the semi-scene guys in green or deep maroon jeans, one size too small, and the ubiquitous white T-shirt – so good for muscle definition and for flashing under the strobe lights at the party afterwards. There were more reticent onlookers in colourful shirts, shorts and loafers, or older gays in open-necked shirts, with one extra button left undone – just for the night. There were lots of young dykes in jeans and short hair and flamboyant ones in short skirts and lots of make-up. And there were lots and lots of straights. With a bottle in one hand and a milk crate in the other, they made their way up the street to their favourite spot for viewing the parade, as if going to the races.

Philip and his friends were just finishing their main course when the Dykes on Bikes roared up the road. Philip dropped his serviette, let out an uncharacteristic yodel and climbed up on his chair. Up and down the street, scores were doing likewise. From the balconies of apartment houses came the sound of innumerable cocktail parties in progress. Sydney's gay professionals were partying.

Robbie and Clover had positioned themselves at the corner of Flinders Street. Robbie nabbed a milk crate that someone had turned their back on, put it against a lamppost and stepped up on it, then hoisted Clover up on his shoulders. She perched there, hanging on to the lamppost to keep her balance. All along the street, people were climbing out of upstairs windows onto the shop awnings.

'This is amazing!' screeched Clover as the first of the marching boys swept by in a flurry of brown limbs, pink tights and twirling batons.

When a float rounded the corner with a huge banner, 'Wagga Wagga Gays and Lesbians', she dug her heels into Robbie's ribs and shouted 'Whoopee!' so energetically that they almost overbalanced. She clambered off his shoulders and Robbie gave her the crate to stand on. She leaned over and said in his ear: 'Let's have a Glaston float next year!'

'Heavens!' he shouted back. 'Glaston Gays and Lesbians, or what about Glass River Gays and Lesbians? I can see it now – in the shape of a glass boat with Joan Beaverstoke on the prow!'

Clover pushed her way through the throng to reach the bar of a hotel that was close by. She was dry and in need of a drink. She was already drunk with excitement. Euphoric. There was a crush of people at the door and windows of the pub but the counter was deserted, save for a plump blonde woman in a leopard-skin skirt, black boots and bare painted breasts. Clover's timidity had vanished for tonight: she offered to buy her a drink.

The noise and clamour from the street was as loud as ever, the patrons at the door cheered and hollered as the floats glided by, but all this receded and she was aware only of the proximity of the woman in the leopard-skin skirt. When the woman approached and ran her fingers down Clover's arm then caught her hand and led her towards the back passage, Clover followed in a trance. There, where the light was dim, she was aware only vaguely of other figures moving in the distance. After a time she was not even aware of that but only of the soft, pungent smell of the woman's skin and the taut heat of her own, and of the power of her beating heart as she traced with her tongue the rough dried paint on the woman's breasts and ran her hand into the damp recesses beneath the leopard-skin skirt.

'Heaven's, you were a while!' Robbie said when she came back.

When the last of the parade had passed, Philip and his friends resumed their seats. Their composure of an hour or two before had disappeared. The tablecloth was a mess of spilt wine. Jackets had fallen to the floor, shirts were unbuttoned, ties undone. Philip's face was damp, his eyes bright. My God, if my clients could see me now, he thought. This made him think of Theo Roth. He was reminded, momentarily, that he still hadn't heard from Theo whether he would take the bookcases he'd located for him in Chartres. But he wouldn't think about that tonight. Tomorrow, after the recovery party, it would be back to business as usual. They could put away for another year the Pride bracelet of multicoloured twine, the lapel button, the Valentino tie with its pattern of writhing bodies. He could hardly wear it in the shop! He could put on hold for another year the sentimental illusion of solidarity.

Not for the first time, he took a breath of deep relief that he and his had so far been spared. Another year and still the virus was kept at bay. All around, he knew, were thousands of men who had lost more friends and intimates than could be counted on two hands. Yet he and Jules knew only two who had succumbed, and they only acquaintances. At times such as this he felt equal measures of guilt and relief at his good fortune.

The Contessa's party were on to dessert, having risen between courses to view the parade from the balcony. Raymond was seated next to a rather obnoxious woman he hadn't met before. It appeared she had recently returned from living in New York. She said to him now, 'You're Lillian Tyler-Watson's brother, aren't you?'

It was not the way he was accustomed to hearing himself described, but nonetheless he agreed that he was. 'You know Lillian?' he asked politely.

'Not well. I met her a few times in New York. But I didn't realise she'd come home until I ran into her a couple of weeks ago. I was surprised to see her. She was having lunch with that fellow who sells houses... what's his name? Theo Roth.'

The meringue that Raymond had just bitten into almost exploded out of his mouth. He put the serviette to his lips as he struggled to swallow.

'Really?' he said eventually.

His heart was thumping painfully. *Why* would Lillian be with Theo? What could it mean? What was Lillian up to? He knew that Theo was up to no good. For the thousandth time he wished he'd never shown Theo Glastonbridge.

Raymond almost couldn't bring himself to return to Darling Point. The thought of walking into Lillian's flat and either speaking or not speaking of Theo Roth was too much for him. So he postponed it. The Contessa suggested a nightcap at her place but he declined. Instead he went down into the streaming crowds.

Those heading for the post-parade party surged up the hill towards Taylor Square, while the tourists and sightseers drifted away from the kerb towards their cars and the cafes of Darlinghurst. Raymond was jostled between these competing tides, sometimes picked up and carried forward, at other times confronted by a wall of people moving in the opposite direction. He weaved his way up Oxford Street until he reached Taylor Square. Here the partygoers veered off towards the showground, while bunches of skylarking straights headed in the direction of the Cross.

Raymond hesitated. Careless passers-by bumped him as they passed. He moved forward. He would walk. He would walk calmly, until his heart stopped racing. When his heart steadied so would his thoughts. It was foolish, he knew, to be thrown by a stranger's chance remark. It was probably an innocent lunch. He moved on, passed the courthouse, passed St Vincent's Clinic. Once, years before – an eternity, it seemed, but it was probably less than ten years – he'd gone there to collect Philip after the boy had been in to have a mole removed. He thought of him as 'the boy' in those days. Still did, sometimes.

'Dear boy,' he said aloud.

But things had changed. Ahead of him was The Albury, with multi-coloured balloons bouncing jauntily from its windows and a Mardi Gras flag draped from the balcony. The place was jammed, throbbing with music. Even the footpath outside the hotel doors was packed. The noise and animal heat of it scared Raymond and made him veer off down a narrow side street. Maybe Philip was in there now, partying, part of something that he never would be, never could be. He knew so little of such things and even what he knew he distrusted. He trod the steep and narrow footpath. The sounds of partying receded. He would walk and think calmly.

But when he tried to think of Lillian, he thought instead of Bamford. He imagined what it would have been like if he and Lil had stayed there; he as the gentleman farmer who dabbled in collecting, she as the country house hostess, running committees and organising balls, much as his mother had done. He imagined himself and Lillian as best of friends.

Then he remembered. Lillian standing in the stable doorway, tapping her riding crop against shiny black boots as he scrambled to his knees, pulling up his pants; the overseer's son diving over the partition into the passageway. There'd been silence as he struggled with his belt, silence except for Lil's crop going 'tap, tap, tap' against her boot. Then Lil said: 'You're a fairy. So that's what's wrong with you.'

But she hadn't told.

Raymond reached Bayswater Road and waited for the lights to change. The Saturday night traffic spewed carbon monoxide as it backed up on the approaches to the Cross. When the lights did change he had to dodge his way between the waiting cars. He wanted suddenly to be invisible, to be away from lights, from people. His steps took him towards the dark expanse of the park. He was drawn towards the shadows beneath the Moreton Bay figs, to the lapping water of Rush-cutters Bay. He was thirsty, so thirsty all of a sudden. There was not a bubbler or a tap in sight.

Maybe it meant nothing that Lillian saw Theo sometimes. Perhaps it was okay. Anyway, how could Theo Roth harm him? Theo might be jealous as hell but the fact remained that he, Raymond Tyler, owned Glastonbridge.

There was bound to be some water in the loos. He could see the squat shape of the small brick building beyond the oval. He made his way towards it. A doubt, a momentary hesitation drifted into his con-sciousness as he approached the toilets but he let it slip away from him. He was so hot; he just needed a drink of water. Inside, only one of three light bulbs remained intact, the other two were smashed, despite their mesh coverings. The walls, a dirty yellow, were covered in graffiti and glowed dully in the sparse light. Raymond splashed his face at the sink and cupped his hands to drink. He felt quite faint. He drank again, then leaned against the wall, its surface cool against his damp cheek. He stayed like that for several minutes until he gradually became aware of voices approaching. Before he had a chance to move, three youths appeared in the doorway.

'Look at the fuckin' poofter!' the tallest of the three said, moving towards him. He flicked Raymond's pink tie.

'Give us your wallet,' a second youth said, pushing himself forward.

'Shit, someone's coming,' said the boy by the door. 'Hurry up!'

Raymond fumbled in his jacket pocket and produced the wallet. Then they were gone. He wanted to sink to his knees but dared not. He followed them out but they'd already disappeared. A park ranger was driving slowly past in his van. He stared suspiciously at Raymond. Raymond merely nodded and turned away.

It was after two when he got back to Lillian's. He heard small snuffling snores coming from her room. He crept around the penthouse, trying not to wake her. He felt so ashamed.

*

That weekend Theo was at home with Julia. At first, Julia had been as keen on doing up Yarralong as he was. But now she was happy enough with the house and sick of spending money on it. She had other priorities, out on the farm. She couldn't believe he wanted to spend $200,000 on a pair of bookcases when the shearing shed was in such deplorable condition that the shearers might refuse to work in it this year.

'If occasionally you actually stepped out of the house and had a look around the property...' she said, when the subject came up for the third time in as many days.

But Theo waved her down. 'You know quite well that the farm is your hobby, and I leave it in your hands.'

'Then you need to give me enough money to run the place.'

'I thought it was supposed to *make* money.'

'It will. Next year. If all goes well.'

He stopped and looked at her. He thought he was marrying Miss Australia; how did he end up with Mrs Farmhand? She was still lovely but in a rather bleached sort of way. Her features and her hair had faded. Only her skin had colour: too much of it. He glanced at Julia's hands, the backs of which were brown and cracked. 'You should use more hand cream. And keep your gloves on when you're riding.'

She snorted. He should talk. Theo's white togs might look something in the eastern suburbs but out here they were a joke. 'If you're playing country squire, you could make some effort to look like one. When you're home why don't you at least put on those moleskins I got you? And the Akubra. Instead of that silly white thing.'

'I've dressed like this for thirty years and I'm not about to change now,' he said.

'Anyway,' Julia said, 'why are you so desperate to get those bookcases? It's not as though we have that many books. We'd be far better spending some of it on a decent dining table.'

'How much will it cost to fix the shearing shed?' Theo asked.

'Fifty thousand.'

'If I don't go overseas this year, we can do both.'

She smiled at him. 'Tell me, are these bookcases as good as Raymond Tyler's?'

Theo moistened his lips. 'Different...but better. I thought, if you don't mind, that we might sell the big George Third chest of drawers. Have to get it done up a bit first. We should get quite a bit for it once it's restored.'

'Yes, if you like,' said Julia vaguely. She'd already switched off from furniture and was studying a kennel magazine. 'I think I'll put Ralph's stud fees up – you should see the prices they're getting for Smithfield Heeler pups.'

*

Raymond slept late the next morning. When he woke his first thought was relief. Only his wallet was gone. He was almost light-hearted. Lillian was already up, dressed, breakfasted and sitting on the terrace reading the Sunday paper. He wouldn't tell her about the youths. She would want to know why he was in such a place. She wouldn't believe him.

There was a large picture of the parade on the front page of the late edition. 'Ridiculous! All this nonsense,' Lillian snorted. 'I'm surprised at the Contessa having anything to do with such vulgarity. I hope you behaved yourself.'

'Oh, Mardi Gras is just good fun,' replied Raymond.

'Huh.' She returned to the paper. She was resentful that she had not been invited to join the Contessa's party. Instead she'd spent a dreary evening playing bridge with friends in Mosman.

'Actually, I met someone who knew you last night,' Raymond said. 'Thin, sharp-faced, rather rude woman. One of the Contessa's New York mates. Can't remember her name. Said her husband – ex-husband now I gather – and Harold were on some board together.'

'I know who you mean,' Lillian said, watching Raymond guardedly. 'Junee Goldsbrough.'

Raymond nodded but did not look up. He concentrated on his Nutri-Grain, munching while Lillian watched him. Neither said anything for a while. Finally Raymond put down his spoon and said, 'Yes, she said she ran into you and Theo Roth at lunch.'

'That's right.'

'Didn't know you and Theo were in the habit of lunching.'

Lillian decided the best course was to brazen it out. 'We have done, once or twice. So?'

Raymond shrugged, apparently unconcerned. But when he put his teacup down, it rattled in the saucer. 'You really should be careful, Lillian,' he burst out. 'I don't trust him.'

'What are you talking about? I'll lunch with whoever I like. We have a lot in common, Theo and me.'

'No, no you don't – unless you're out to get me. Like him.' Raymond pushed his chair back. 'I know what's what, I know what people say. I know what that Theo is up to.'

'You're being irrational, Raymond. Sit down.'

After a moment's hesitation, he sank back down in his chair. 'It wouldn't be fair of you, Lil, to go confiding in Theo matters that are to do with you and me. I don't want you talking about Glastonbridge to him.'

'You're being ridiculous,' she said. But there was a quaver in her voice.

Lillian left Raymond at the breakfast table and went into her private sitting room. Half an hour later she heard the front door shut. When she went out into the hall, she found a note: 'Gone back to Glaston'.

All the way home unnameable fears assailed Raymond, anxiety shook him, so that every now and then Brutus swung from side to side on the road and sometimes hit the dirt. He collected himself then, forced himself to be calm and concentrate on the road.

He remembered suddenly that he was meant to be having lunch with Philip. At the next service station, he pulled in to make a phone call.

'Lillian's been seeing Theo,' he told Philip. '

'Seeing?'

'Lunching with, talking to. I don't understand why. I don't like it.'

'That's probably why she's doing it. Calm down. What harm can it do? Theo will be pumping her for information about you and Glaston-bridge, but as you don't tell her anything, she won't have anything to say, will she? You don't tell her things, do you?'

'I...I don't know. I don't think so. I might sometimes. I did mention to her about that article in the *Gazette*.'

The red light on the pay phone started flashing and he dug in his pocket for change. He slipped in a coin and heard Philip saying.

'Oh God, Raymond, you didn't!'

'We were getting on after I said I'd lend her that money. But she's back to normal now,' he added glumly. Raymond hesitated. 'There's something else, too, something happened. I...I...' How to tell it, even to Philip. 'I...' The red light was flashing again. Raymond fumbled for coins but he had none left.

'Yes, yes. What?' urged Philip.

'Something else happened, last night, after the parade, I...' The phone went dead. Raymond looked at it then put the receiver down. When he came out of the phone booth, a huge semi-trailer was bearing down on him, coming off the tarmac and into the rutted dirt parking area behind the phone booth, covering him and Brutus in a cloud of red dust.

He was surprised when he got home to Glastonbridge to find William there, standing on the porch, eating a peach. Raymond stared at him.

'Late lunch,' William said.

He'd forgotten William was to stay at Glastonbridge while the floors in his own house were being polished.

'They did the second coat yesterday,' William said, sucking on the peach. 'Final coat tomorrow. I didn't expect you back for a few days. How was Mardi Gras?'

Raymond was looking particularly distracted. William noticed that he seemed to be covered in dust. He said, 'I'm going to pop home for a while, to water the garden. I'll bring something back for dinner.'

Raymond nodded. He stood in the hallway a few minutes after William had gone, as though uncertain what to do, where to go. He noticed his hands, and the way dust was sticking to the hairs on his arms. 'I'll have a shower,' he said out loud, the sound of his voice startling him. Slowly he began to climb the stairs then remembered that the only shower was downstairs. He turned and descended the stairs.

At dinner that night, which they ate at a card table in front of the television, William thought he seemed better.

'Late night, long drive,' Raymond said in explanation of his earlier state. 'I had a nap. That put me right.' He chewed his food. How good it was to feel the jaws working smoothly, to feel no pain. What pain, if they had struck him! If they had bashed him up.

They went to bed early and had been asleep for several hours. The house was as quiet as a grave, the only sound the ticking of the clocks – the grandfather clock in the vestibule, the gold Louis XV on the drawing room mantelpiece and the Jacobean collection in the sitting room. At first, Raymond thought the banging on the door was part of his dream. He came up out of sleep to the sound of cast iron hitting wood and half-scrambled, half-tumbled off the bed. In the hallway he almost ran into William, who was heading towards the front door.

'Don't, don't,' whispered Raymond, his face as white as the nightshirt he was wearing. 'It's Lillian! It's Lillian! She's come to get the money.' His eyes were staring, enormous in their dark sockets.

William touched him lightly on the shoulder then he heard a voice. 'Oh, it's Robbie,' he said, going towards the front door.

Raymond stood still, transfixed, in the hallway.

'Sorry,' Robbie said as he came in, 'talk about sound sleepers! I've been banging for ages. I tried the back door first. The front door knocker was a last resort. Are you okay, Raymond? You look like shit.'

'Yeah, yeah, I'm okay,' Raymond said, touching his forehead. 'I might make a cup of tea.'

As William relocked the front door, Robbie said: 'I didn't think Raymond would be here.'

'He came back unexpectedly this afternoon. Do you know what he said just now? "It's Lillian. Come to get the money."'

They both began to laugh.

'Sshh. Sshh,' said William, holding his mouth.

7.

It started raining a few days after Mardi Gras. And kept on raining. Robbie and I sat in Hogarth's, lingering over a coffee and staring out the window. I wanted to ask him what had happened to Clover in Sydney. Since they got back she'd had an extra sheen about her. And her eyes often had a glazed look, as if she were thinking about something way beyond Glaston. But Robbie was preoccupied by the weather.

'If it keeps on going like this, it'll flood,' he said gloomily. 'In sixty-three it went right through our place, apparently.'

'They've built the levees since then,' I said. 'Did you and Clover stick together in Sydney?'

'Yeah. She was blown away by the parade. Clover's very...'

'Unworldly?' I offered.

'That's right – unworldly. She's a strange girl, you know?'

When I spoke to Clover, she gave me a quick look that clearly said 'don't ask me to explain'.

The kinks and curves in Glaston's main street roughly reflected the curves in the river, twisting and turning its way across the floodplain. Apart from this, the town took no notice of the river, turned its back on it. Out behind the shops, where people parked their cars and their garbage bins, that's where you could see the river. In the middle of a dry summer it shrank to a shallow stream a couple of metres wide. But after heavy rains it swelled and crept steadily up the banks. If the rain kept falling, it became a brown muddy torrent and people started eyeing it nervously. Floods.

Townspeople still talked about the big flood of 1963. In every street there were markers on the power poles to show how high it came. Up to ceiling height right through the old part of town. It was as if the markers were there as a constant reminder: 'Beware, or ye shall all be washed away!'

*

Whenever Raymond's thoughts turned to Lillian or to Theo, which they did sickeningly often, an image appeared before him of the two of them, heads close together, conspiratorial smiles on their faces. He told Sally about it, after about a week. He couldn't keep his misery to himself any longer.

He met Sally outside the newsagents. It had been raining for a week and the town was soggy and miserable. Muddy tracks from tractor tyres streaked the wet tarmac, and the grey power poles and shop fronts blurred into one another.

'Lillian and Theo having lunch together may be perfectly innocent,' said Sally. 'Logically, what could they be up to? What harm can it do?' Sally for once was only half interested. People in the town were beginning to talk about a flood and she was worried.

For a whole week after Mardi Gras, Lillian was furious with Raymond. It was so rude of him to leave just like that and not call later to apologise. He had no right to tell her who she could or couldn't be friends with. She had nothing to apologise for. He was just jealous because Theo Roth had chosen to make a personal friend of her, and not him. It was Raymond's own fault. The way he behaved around Theo, the things he said about him. Acting as if Theo was some sort of marauder. Raymond was so paranoid!

She decided it was time to invite Theo to lunch at her place. She chose her friends from Mosman to make up a third and fourth because they could make conversation without dominating it.

When Theo arrived he found the table in the dining room, which could seat twelve (although it never had), set at one end for four people with Lillian's Christofle dinner service. She'd brought the dinner service with her from New York, with visions of entertaining the best people in Sydney.

Lillian and Theo sat side by side, facing the view, while her friends Janet and Gordon were put opposite, with their backs to it. Lillian fussed about the food, jumping up constantly to check things in the kitchen, chastising Anna, her daily help, for forgetting finger bowls. Theo thought the food not worthy of so much attention. But he ate his way diligently through a few lukewarm slices of smoked salmon and the onion tart, conversing easily about the latest David Williamson play – which he hadn't seen – and about the revamp of the Opera House restaurant. Janet and Gordon were impressed by the menu. He told them bluntly there was nothing elegant about offal. On the rare occasion he felt like eating tripe he had no intention of paying thirty dollars for it.

The conversation turned from food to Theo's icon collection then to collecting in general.

Lillian said, 'The thing that worries me is how does one keep track of the current value of a collection?' She had Raymond's in mind.

'If one is a true collector, the value is irrelevant.'

'Oh, in theory, yes,' said Lillian impatiently. 'But surely in practice one likes to know the value of one's assets?'

'Not *this* one,' said Theo, drily. 'The icons have a value, certainly. But my icons are not an investment.'

'Oh come, come, Theo,' Lillian tittered, in what she thought was a coquettish fashion. 'I'm sure you are far too much a man of the world to let your emotions rule your wallet.'

'You have them insured though, surely,' Gordon threw in.

Theo, pointedly ignoring Lillian, said, 'Insured value and market value are not the same thing, as I'm sure you know.' His voice was as cool as the sorbet he was eating. 'In any case, my icons have no market value as they will never be for sale.'

Anna served the coffee then. Shortly afterwards, Theo left. 'Stupid woman!' he said to himself as he went down the front steps. That was the last time he'd waste time on her. Raymond, even with all his faults, was worth ten of her.

*

Rosemary was fed up with Sally and her coterie. The way she went into elder-sister mode: concerned and condescending. She was sick to death of the lot of them, with their houses and country lifestyles and their friendships. She couldn't stand the in-jokes, the way you had to see the world as they saw it or you didn't count. The way they made fun of Theo, for example. She'd heard Jules describing, in that absurd accent of his, the way Theo ate clam gazpacho – his chest and lap covered in four large napkins so as not to splash his white suit. Theo had more nous than the lot of them put together. And more money, taste and style.

Rosemary was thinking about Theo because there he was, across the room, standing to one side of the group of directors from Palisade Properties. He'd told her he'd be here tonight and suggested she might be interested in one of the new apartments Palisades was building. She wasn't, but she'd come anyway. Rosemary was always surprised when she saw Theo in the flesh because, unlike most men, he was actually taller than he looked in photographs. Both robust and refined. She hesitated only a moment. When she saw he was looking in her direction, she smiled and walked towards him. He probably wouldn't recognise her. He never did remember, even though they had met several times.

She held out her hand. 'Hello Theo, Rosemary Larsen.'

'Oh, Rosemary. Of course, you're Sally Austinmeer's sister, aren't you?'

She'd told him that this morning on the phone. Now she nodded assent.

'So, do you think you might buy into here?' he asked.

'Not really my sort of thing but it might suit Sally. Sally told me she and Robbie Grant were thinking of buying a pied-à-terre together. I thought a small place here might suit them, but it's probably more than they want to spend.'

'Oh it would be,' Theo said, surprising her. Then, lowering his voice: 'Tell them to get a little place over at Potts Point. Much better value.'

She laughed and he smiled a slow smile at her.

'How is everyone up at Glaston?' he asked.

'Oh, you know...' she said, waving her hand dismissively. 'Up there, they don't have a clue about the real world.'

'That's what country life does to one. I find the same thing with Julia these days.'

'Really?'

He shook his head resignedly then turned the subject back to Glaston. 'I'm going up that way myself soon. There's an auction at Armidale. Might call in at Glaston on my way back.'

'I suppose you'll be visiting Raymond?'

'Oh, Raymond's a bit spikey with me these days. I don't know that I'll get an invitation to Glastonbridge.'

'I spent a couple of hours crawling all over it at Christmas. That place would make the most fantastic hotel.'

'You think so?'

'God, yes. But...' she shrugged her shoulders.

'What do you mean by...that?' Theo asked, copying her shrug.

'Oh, you know. Raymond.'

'Ah, Raymond. He has very set ideas.'

'Theo,' Rosemary said, moving closer to him, 'this is probably terribly presumptuous of me. But do you think you might be able to have a look at a little place I've done up in Petersham? I'm just not sure if it's the right time to sell it.'

'Going into winter,' he said. He was suddenly very aware of her perfume: Giorgio, the same as Julia wore. 'But, yes, let me have a look at it.'

Rosemary, holding the champagne glass in front of her breasts, tilted her head to one side and watched Theo speculatively. It was so long since she'd felt any power in her femaleness that she chose to remain silent, revelling in the moment, aware that there was no need to rush.

Aware that she only need stand there, her breasts pointing towards Theo, her hip at a provocative angle beneath the soft fabric of her skirt.

*

It saddened Clover that the easy rapport she had once had with Joan was gone. She missed being able to call in at the bookshop at any hour for a chat or a coffee. Now each time she met Joan it was stiff and awkward, loaded with Joan's resentment and her own caution. She'd taken to driving past Hogarth's with her eyes averted, trying to avoid the pang she always felt when she spotted Joan's familiar bulk behind the glass window.

She would have liked to be able to tell Joan about the strange atmosphere she felt around herself ever since that encounter with the leopard-skin woman. But no chance of that, now. She couldn't identify exactly how or why things had gone wrong. Joan's attitude towards Raymond and Glastonbridge were only part of it. For a long time she'd been aware of subtle signs, or not so subtle if she'd had the wit to see what was happening. Ever since they'd met, Joan had been trying to influence her, to direct her. Who was it who had encouraged her to go into restoration? They'd even talked of setting up a business together. Until Norma said no. Norma was the only one who could say no to Joan.

'Don't waste time thinking about it!' Clover said aloud to herself, making the dog lift his head from the workshop floor and stare at her with sharp pale eyes.

Clover put down the piece of timber she'd been rubbing back and dropped to crouch in front of the kelpie, who immediately licked her chin. 'Let's go into town and see if Duane can lend us some wax.'

It was a Sunday afternoon and all the Glaston shops were shut. As she drove her van down the main street there was hardly a car in sight. The sun had come out and it was warm and muggy. She was hoping

Duane would be home and could lend her some beeswax so she could get Mrs Wyatt's skirting boards done before tomorrow. The front door of the shop was closed so she drove down the side lane to the flat at the back. Duane and Brenda were sitting on a pair of timber garden chairs on the strip of concrete outside the flyscreen door. Duane was stretched out with the sleeves of his T-shirt pushed up and a hat over his face, sunbaking, or maybe asleep. Brenda was reading. She didn't look up when Clover arrived. Neither of them did. Only when she was standing in front of them and said 'Hi!' did Brenda lift her head. Duane pushed the hat off his face and sat up blearily.

'That must be a good book,' Clover said to Brenda.

Brenda, flushed and distracted, nodded.

'What is it?'

Embarrassed, as if she and Duane had been caught in bed together, Brenda said: 'Keats.'

'Really?' said Clover, surprised.

Brenda closed the book and crossed her arms on top of it. 'I'm only just discovering poetry. Norma lent it to me.'

'Pull up a chair,' Duane said, indicating a broken bentwood that was propped beside the door. 'Just don't lean back too far in that one.'

'I won't stay long,' Clover said, straddling the chair. 'I've run out of beeswax. Can I get a bit off you, till tomorrow?'

'Sure. What sort do you need?' he asked, getting up.

'Oldbucks – clear, if you've got it.'

When he'd gone inside, Clover and Brenda sat in silence a while, until Brenda said, 'It was really good at Hogarth's on Friday night. Don't you go down there any more?'

'No, not as much as I did.'

'I feel really lucky to have met them. I'm learning so much.'

'Yeah?'

'Joan really likes Duane. I think she only tolerates me.'

Clover shook her head. 'She'd like to see you...blossoming.'

'Blossoming,' Brenda said, and thought about it. 'I suppose I am.'

'Just watch her...'

'Watch who?' asked Duane, coming out the door with a tin of beeswax.

'Joan,' said Brenda.

'Don't you trust her?' asked Duane, sharp as always.

'I think she likes to run people's lives,' Clover said in a rush. Then more quietly, 'To direct the action.' Like a ringmaster, she suddenly thought, in the centre of a circus tent, with a whip in one hand and a handful of treats in the other.

'Let her try,' Duane grinned.

Brenda and Duane were often at Hogarth's now. Brenda didn't mind that Duane was a favourite. It seemed to her right and inevitable. No one could compare with Duane. She liked to just watch him work. The slim brown arms, almost like a girl's. He could have passed for twenty-two. He seemed frail but wasn't. She'd seen him pick up a chest of drawers on his own. He was strong. Sinewy. A new word that. It suited him. Being with Duane, and listening to Joan and Norma talk. Nothing could compare with that. Norma lent her poetry books and Joan said she should try writing some poems. It was delicious. She wished she could fill the pages of the *Gazette* with poetry. Surely people would be different, surely Glaston would be different, if people read poetry?

*

Theo had not thought of going to Glaston until the moment he mentioned it to Rosemary. Then the idea took hold. He had no real excuse. It would make far more sense to fly to Armidale. Glaston was not really on the way. Glaston wasn't really on the way to anywhere. He wondered what he should do. Should he just front up to Glastonbridge, take Raymond by surprise? Raymond was far too well brought up to throw him out. Then he had an idea. He'd call Robbie Grant. Robbie had done the garden of his old house in Woollahra.

Robbie was surprised but pleased to hear from Theo. If he was passing through Glaston, he must certainly come and see them. Come for lunch, Robbie said.

'Will Raymond be there?' Theo asked.

'Most probably. Raymond's usually here if there's food going.'

Theo laughed, feeling suddenly light-hearted.

But Raymond, when he was invited, said no. 'No, no, really. Thank you, but no. I won't.'

Into William's puzzled silence he went on: 'Bob and I have a lot on at the moment. Got to keep at it. Sorry.'

And before William had time to press him, he hung up.

But Titus and Sally said they'd come. And at the last moment, Robbie invited Duane. In fact, Duane virtually invited himself.

'Oh I wish you hadn't,' William said.

'Well I couldn't NOT, you know?'

At that lunch, with them all sitting around the long table in the conservatory – actually a rather elegant enclosed verandah – a strange thing happened. Theo and Duane immediately took to one another. It was hardly surprising that Duane was fascinated by Theo – the Rolls, the white suit and hat, the general air about him. But Theo seemed almost equally intrigued by Duane. To start with they spent a good ten minutes discussing the etymology of his name, until William said, in a surprisingly catty fashion for William, 'I thought it was just a fancy way of spelling Dwayne.'

'Oh surely not,' said Theo smiling, 'I'm sure it owes more to Don Juan.'

While Sally was helping Robbie carry plates out to the kitchen, she asked, 'Theo is straight, isn't he?'

'Yes,' said Robbie equally intrigued. 'But then so is Duane.'

Duane had never met anyone like Theo. He wasn't even sure who he was.

'So you sell a lot of houses?' he asked.

'I've sold an AWFUL lot of houses in my time,' Theo beamed at him. 'And what about you? What do you do?'

'I sell antiques – and stuff – and restore furniture. I french polished this table,' he said, looking at William for confirmation.

'Yes, yes you did,' said William weakly.

'Theo,' said Titus, deciding it was time for someone else to take control of the conversation, 'I hear you're a regular at Baillieu's.'

'Yes I am. Of course, you must know Jules well. A wonderful chef.'

So for the rest of the meal they talked about food.

Afterwards, when they were walking in the garden, Theo said to Sally, 'I hear Raymond's doing marvellous things with the house. I'd love to see it again.' He looked over in the direction of Glastonbridge, even though it was miles out of sight. 'Do you think he'd mind if I called in?'

Back inside, Sally disappeared to the kitchen to make a phone call. She rang Raymond.

'No, no, I don't want to talk to him.' Raymond was highly agitated. 'Why should I! Oh…pretend I'm out.'

Sally talked on soothingly, 'He only wants to have a look.'

Finally, he said, 'Oh, all right, tell him I've had to go out but he can look at the outside.'

Driving to Glastonbridge, Theo recalled what Rosemary had said about the Glaston crowd: out of touch with the real world. There were benefits in that. It was odd being in the same room with Rosemary's sister. Not that they were at all alike, but still. What had developed between him and Rosemary was sudden and unexpected. Rosemary said she'd never discussed her love life with her sister and she wasn't about to start now. 'Presumably you are not going to tell Julia,' she said, 'and I shan't tell anyone either. I'm used to keeping these things to myself.'

There was a dynamism about Rosemary that he appreciated because he was familiar with it in himself. But what about her mad idea for Glastonbridge? He'd gone along with it because he enjoyed hearing her talk about the house. She knew its layout even better than he did. He didn't tell her that he would never allow the house to be turned into a hotel. Small bedrooms turned into bathrooms! Never.

Although he'd only been to Glaston once before, he found the Old West Road without difficulty. He stopped when he reached the original Glastonbridge gateway. It no longer led to the house but to a neighbouring farm with a 1960s red-brick farmhouse stuck in the middle of a bare paddock. Now, if he owned Glastonbridge, he'd buy the gateway and relocate it to the new entrance. Further along the road, at the new entrance, he turned onto the rutted track. The weld-mesh gate was shut and he got out to open it. The air was still and brisk. Streaks of white cloud dashed across the slipstream of the sky. He stood a moment and looked back towards the town, the pepper trees and lines of poplars, the church steeples, the stone parapet of the bridge peeping above the willows. Was it his imagination or did he really feel more at home here than at Yarralong?

He left the car in what had once been the stable yard. There was no sign of Brutus and he assumed that Raymond had gone out. How was it, Theo wondered, that this place – which in reality he barely knew – worked on him in such a powerful way? Why should he, at heart Russian and Jewish, feel an affinity with a strange neo-Gothic house from the early Victorian era, built on an Australian hillside, above a town as Anglo-Saxon and ordinary as Glaston?

Without looking too closely at the rear of the house, he walked past the remains of the stable yard gates onto the path that had once been the main drive. He followed it until it reached the front gate into the garden. The wooden gate had long since ceased to open and was tied up with rusting bits of wire. On either side a barbed wire fence, erected long ago to keep cattle away from the house, sagged to the ground. Theo stepped over it and, pushing past an overgrown plumbago hedge, emerged onto a shabby gravel apron before the main porch, its slate roof steeply pitched and supported by timber arches on a sandstone base.

Instead of walking up to the porch, Theo moved to one side, so as to better view both the porch and the stone tower behind. Glastonbridge was distinctly ecclesiastical from this angle. The steeply roofed porch reminded him of any number of nineteenth-century village churches, and the stone tower was a version of a Norman church tower. Of course, Gothic had begun with churches. It was when one moved further around the side that the true extent of the house revealed itself. The actual front of the house, with its row of long windows and pair of high gables, looked across the grassed terrace to Theo's right. He moved that way now.

Perhaps it was the very incongruity of the place that drew him: a Jacobean reproduction stranded on *terra australis*. He knew the purist in him should be prepared to laugh at this place, at the folly of the man who built it, or at his presumption. Yet he couldn't. Wouldn't he, in the same time and place, have done something similar?

The terrace was littered with blocks of sandstone and the detritus of a building site. A couple of wooden sawhorses, as if only recently abandoned, stood surrounded by off-cuts of timber. With his eyes averted from the house, Theo walked to the edge of the terrace, then turned to survey the front in one sweep. His eyes were immediately drawn to the windows and he gazed at them in admiration. When he'd last been here, most of the front windows were boarded up, the delicate wooden tracery in the arches lost or broken. Now all was as it should be, on the ground floor at least. Raymond had not yet got to the first-floor windows, but in any case they weren't too bad.

Theo stood for some minutes, unable to move.

Raymond was hiding in the back passageway when Theo arrived. Now he peered out from behind one of the windows of the long gallery. What's he doing? Raymond asked himself. Why is he staring so? What's he spotted? Raymond grasped the fabric of his tracksuit pants between his fingers, as if to stop himself jumping about. He withdrew slightly from the window so as not to be seen and walked in a small circle. When he looked out again, Theo was walking towards the house, dodging the blocks of stone that were in his path.

Raymond ducked out of the gallery and ran down the main stairs, nearly tripping on the drop sheets that covered the treads. At the door to the morning room he stopped and peered around the corner. Theo, outside the French door on the other side of the room, stood peering up at the timber architrave. Like a termite inspector, Raymond thought. What's wrong with the thing? Still Theo stood there, peering up, his white fedora pushed back from his forehead, his little pointy black beard jutting forward.

Theo was looking not at the top of the door but at the tracery above it, at the way the original had been saved and repaired so carefully that it was hard to see where the new bits had been added. He shook his head in astonishment. Where did Raymond find such a craftsman?

Raymond saw Theo shaking his head and cringed. He felt sick. What right did he have to come here and start criticising? Did Theo realise how long Bob and he had spent on those windows, learning the skills as they went along? He went back to the staircase and sat on the bottom step, chewing his fingernail. You can't just go to a shop and order windows like those, you know! Had he made a mistake trying to save them? Perhaps he should have just put simple fretwork panels in. But fretwork was so geometric and symmetrical. And there was nothing symmetrical about Glastonbridge. What was Theo up to now? He went back and peered across the breakfast room but there was no longer any sign of him. Raymond retreated back to the central passage and hurried along past the drawing room and the dining room to the sitting room at the far end. He always called the rooms by their correct names, even though their present appearance gave no indication of their true function. He had left the old drapes on the sitting room windows to protect his clock collection from the sun. He wrapped himself in one of these and peered out the bay window. Theo was only a couple of metres from him, with his back half-turned, inspecting the base of the dining room chimney.

Well, you can't blame me for anything there, Raymond thought. I haven't touched it.

Theo rested his hand on the stone, which was warm from the sun. Cicadas droned in the tufts of grass nearby. Only a light breeze disturbed the air, rustling through the oak trees behind him. He turned and strolled towards them. The leaves were changing colour and falling. A few drifted to the ground as he watched. He left the terrace and went down the rough slope and the fallen leaves crackled under his feet. There could be nothing more peaceful than this place on such a day as this. So why did he still feel a vague uneasiness? He was not the sort to be influenced by the tales about Glastonbridge, yet even he felt presences here, felt the house imposing its personality. Felt it watching him. He stood in the hollow beside the house, looking down across the river towards Glaston. He had his back to the house but still he couldn't rid himself of the feeling that he was being watched.

That's right, Raymond thought, admire the view. Don't bother turning around to see the work I've done on the parapet of the western wing. Remember last time you were here, you tripped on some of the rubble that had fallen from the parapet? Well, that's all gone now. The battlements are back in place. But don't bother looking at something that I've done well. No one ever notices the work I've done.

Theo turned around and climbed back up the slope and as he did so he looked up at the western wing. My God, Raymond has fixed the parapet! He paused. His suit suddenly felt hot and out of place. Why were people always saying that Raymond wasn't getting anything done? Just look at it!

The western wing was the tallest part of the house. At ground level there were small half windows that gave light to the cellars, above that the secondary reception rooms, including the library and sitting room, and above them the guest bedrooms. And in the attic hidden behind the stone parapet were the female servants quarters.

The pine trees that ran parallel to this wing had been planted when the house was built and were now as tall as the roof. Theo remembered the wind that had roared through them the first time he was here. How the trees had howled and he had howled inside, because Raymond had beaten him to this incomparable house.

Briskly, Theo walked along beneath the trees to the rear corner then went around towards the kitchens.

'Where's he going now?' Raymond said out loud as Theo disappeared from view. He wasn't going to let him inside. Never. He wasn't going to have him sneering. How could someone like Theo Roth, a real estate agent, understand a place like this?

Theo liked the back of the house; the way bits jutted out at odd angles, the flagstones on the court, the low roofs of the outhouses. It reminded him of an Elizabethan inn.

Raymond, scurrying along the upstairs passages, had trouble seeing where he had gone. Then he spotted him in the courtyard, inspecting the well. I suppose if you had this place, you'd want to pull down those back bits because they're later additions, because they're the wrong style. You don't understand that houses grow, that they've always grown. Eclectic was itself a style, you know! Raymond glared from an upstairs window, not caring any longer if he were seen. But Theo had turned away.

He reached the car and sat in it, staring at the house. He felt suddenly tired, heavy. What had he been expecting? To find the place tumbling down, worse than when Raymond had bought it? He knew what he'd wanted. He'd wanted to be able to walk away shaking his head, saying 'poor, misguided Raymond'. He'd wanted to believe that, as Lillian said, the house was too much for Raymond. He wanted to believe the Glaston rumour mill: that the house was being mismanaged, that the restoration was a ruination. But he saw no signs of any of this. Should that stop him? Should he give up now? Reconcile himself to Raymond's ownership?

But he could not. Few people saw the house. Fewer people, on seeing it, understood it. Some people would no doubt carp about the use of new timbers. Some would be scandalised by Raymond's use of colour. (Theo had glimpsed some of the painted plasterwork through the windows.) But Raymond's loyalties were not to fashions – either the heritage fashions of now or the sometimes tasteless decorative fashions of then – Raymond's loyalty was to the spirit, the eccentricity, of the house. Theo understood this. He thought, maybe that's why Raymond allowed me to come – he's showing off.

If most people didn't realise what Raymond was doing, there was a benefit to be gained from that. Who was to know that he, Theo, was impressed by Raymond's work? He could pretend to be just the opposite. He'd heard it said that Raymond was mad. He probably was. It was what made him so daring, and so stubborn. The question remained: how was he to be dislodged?

8.

Two boys drowned in the river that week. And the town went into sudden shock. They were swinging on the willows above the swollen water and a branch broke. Just being kids. Daring one another. Taking risks.

At the church, people spilled out onto the porch and steps. Gruff, silent farmers and women wailing. A man standing at the side of the church, his forearms resting on the rough stone, the same stone as Glastonbridge, and by the hunch of his shoulders you could tell he was sobbing.

Even Raymond showed up. 'Those kids, huh. I remember what it was like, the risks you took.' It turned out he knew one of the families. I was often surprised by the people he knew.

Norma stood at the elbow of one of the mothers, holding her arm in a tight grip. 'Auntie Norma' they called her.

Autumn came. Long, warm days with chilly nights. The leaves on the plane trees changed colour slowly, yellowed, and fell to the ground. Sometimes I'd go out to Glastonbridge and talk to Raymond, or not talk to him. Or I'd sit with Clover while she worked, or climb my favourite hill and look out across the valley. Or I'd take a book and lie *on the pine needles on the slope below the house and read and dream and sometimes even sleep. Bob found me there one evening, just as it was getting dark.*

'Thought you were still here,' he said. 'You lot are mad.' With that he seemed to summon up some collective of weird interlopers who had landed on his planet solely for his amusement.

*

Theo's flat on the sixth floor of the Astor in Macquarie Street was normally just a place to lay his head while in town. But for several days after his return from Glaston he barely left it. He spent a lot of time staring out the window, watching the bag ladies and lovers, and the pedestrians in too much of a hurry to notice either. He didn't call Rosemary; he spoke to Julia only briefly on the phone. He had a few business calls that could not be avoided. But the rest of the time he sat in his darkened study, so tired he thought he must be getting the flu. His mind kept returning to Glastonbridge. He relived his stroll around the house, examined each small detail again and again. Several times he saw Raymond's face before him – the Raymond of the auction room, smartly suited, cunning. Or another Raymond, the one who had first shown him Glastonbridge: enthusiastic, boyish, jigging from foot to foot in gleeful excitement. Finally, a third Raymond appeared, one he had not himself seen. This Raymond was of untidy appearance and distracted eye. His movements were nervous and his expression suspicious. This Raymond had been described to him; a man driven half mad by a project and a place that were too much for him.

Theo didn't doubt that Glastonbridge had a peculiar atmosphere. He imagined that one could wrap oneself in it until, eventually, the outside world receded to a hazy distance. There was enough power in Glastonbridge to drive a wedge between present and past, and to make the past the more inviting. It could happen if one let it. Theo wondered if that was what was happening with Raymond? He thought Raymond's connections to the real world had always been pretty tenuous.

On the third day, a cold and squally day when the autumn leaves in Macquarie Street rose and fell in whirling eddies, Theo forced himself to again take up the familiar reins of his life. Sighing, he turned away from the window. There was a business meeting that he would attend, instead of cancelling; there was a fine arts auction that he should view. He would even ring Rosemary. He wasn't sure what he wanted from Rosemary. A diversion? Uncomplicated sex? Suddenly the word 'companionship' leapt into his brain. That had never really been a motive before.

'So?' Rosemary asked, tilting her head. 'How was Glaston?'

She had resisted ringing Theo for several days. Finally, when her patience was almost up, he had rung her and suggested dinner.

'Did you see the house?' she asked.

'The outside,' Theo said, not looking at her, his eyes on the wine list. The trouble with having a clandestine affair was that you could never go anywhere decent in case you were seen. This wine list was pathetic.

'Was it still looking a mess?'

He put the wine list down and rested his fingertips lightly on the edge of the table. Now, he said to himself, watching himself, this is how it must begin: 'Raymond does seem to have got himself into a bit of a muddle.' He paused. Rosemary was watching him closely. There was something almost canine about her when she was on the scent of good real estate. She had the look of a pointer dog: lean and intent.

Theo looked down and ran his finger along the edge of the pale wooden table. 'Poor Raymond,' he said. 'I think he's heading for trouble with the Trust.'

'*Poor Raymond*,' Rosemary snorted. 'Why? What's he done?'

'His methods are rather unorthodox.' Which is true, Theo thought. And which is just as it should be. 'It's still a wonderful house, of course, but one does worry about its future.'

'You didn't get inside?'

Theo shook his head.

'Damn!' Rosemary said. 'I wanted you to see the inside, to see the potential.'

Theo looked non-committal.

'I should have gone with you,' Rosemary said.

'You could hardly have done that. I saw your sister. It was only because of her that I managed to see even the outside. God knows what the inside is like. I did see some rather garish plasterwork.'

'Oh, the ceilings! Yuck! I suppose Sally defended Raymond.'

Theo nodded. 'She's a good friend.'

'Her and Philip. They nanny him.'

Theo regarded her. She had lit a cigarette, even though she knew he didn't like it. 'Watch out, I won't kiss you.'

She smiled at him flirtatiously, took two quick puffs, then put the cigarette out. 'When are you going down to the farm?'

'Tomorrow,' he said, unblinking, holding her eyes. 'Julia is expecting me.'

'Pity,' said Rosemary, 'the new flat in Elizabeth Bay settles tomorrow. I'm picking up the key at lunchtime. We could have christened it. Don't you love making love in an empty house?' she asked.

'Only if it's carpeted.'

'It is,' she said.

Standing at the open window of her office next morning, wearing a little brown woollen suit and smoking a cigarette, Rosemary mentally ran through her plans for the new apartment. It would be a symphony in muted tones: pale cream and several shades of taupe. To emphasise the stateliness of the living room she might even add a couple of columns. The deep beige carpet was in good condition so she wouldn't need to replace it. The kitchen would be the main expense. She thought she'd have classic panelled cupboards, painted the same cream as the woodwork, and a taupe benchtop, and a wooden venetian on the window. She liked a kitchen to have clean, elegant lines. Sally's kitchen always looked so cluttered. So many different colours and textures that it assaulted you as you walked in the door, what with the painted frieze and tiled benchtop and open shelves everywhere. All right for a country house kitchen, she supposed.

She thought about Theo and smiled. She could see him in the apartment. She could see him on the carpet, the smooth alabaster of his skin – almost the same colour as the woodwork – against the beige. The strong black hairs on his arms and legs and chest. She liked the way the hairs on his chest formed a perfect Y down to his navel. He didn't have hairs on his back, thank God. That was such a turn-off.

What a team she and Theo would make! She wondered how long it would take him to tire of Country Julia, of the driving back and forth, of the routine of weekends at the farm. Theo wasn't handsome, but there was something magnificent about him. The way his thinning black hair glistened against the dome of his skull; the neat, almost pretty beard; his dark eyes, so mysterious and meaningful. She couldn't wait for people to hear about their alliance.

131

Within a few weeks of his previous visit, Theo was again on his way to Glaston, this time with a chest of drawers in the back of Julia's Range Rover.

'Why on earth are you taking it all the way to Glaston?' she had asked.

'There's a fellow there does very good restoration. And much cheaper than getting it done in Sydney.'

Theo was taking the furniture up to Duane so as to somehow prolong the Glaston connection. Duane intrigued him. He recognised something in him, a kind of hunger. The boy was bright, street-smart. Wouldn't trust him though, Theo thought to himself, amused. Still, it might be handy to have someone in Glaston who could keep him informed about Raymond's activities. Lillian had been no use.

Theo arrived in Glaston the same day that Brenda's first poem appeared in the *Gazette*, on page three, set in Gothic Bold.

A Token of Love
In the brackish waters of a small town
A spirit that for years had been kept down
At last shook off its unbecoming gloom
Drawn and drawn again to a delightful room
Wherein were magic potions freely found
Enough to make a head spin round and round
Here books abound and in them lives revealed
So touching that a lovesick heart reeled
Shaken but comforted by words both read and spoken
For in this special place joy is yours with just a token
Take this small verse and follow whichever paths
And you'll get 15 percent off any book at our Hogarths.

Skimming the pages of the local rag while waiting for his coffee, Theo saw the poem and chuckled. Then he looked up and saw the name of the shop hanging from the awning outside the window. A slim, almost wizened woman with curly greying hair brought him his cappuccino.

'I see I'm in the famous Hogarth's,' he said, tapping the newspaper with his finger.

'Indeed,' Norma replied drily. 'But don't hold me responsible. We have a reporter with literary aspirations.'

'Do you know who that is?' Joan hissed at her as she went past the front counter. 'It's Theo Roth.' Then she added, 'I wish you'd go home. You're not looking at all well.'

'Don't fuss!' Norma snapped.

When Theo came up to the cash register to pay, he asked, 'Would you happen to know where I could find Duane Smith, the furniture restorer?'

'He's a friend of ours,' Joan said. 'You're Theo Roth, aren't you? I thought it was you. I'm Joan Beaverstoke. I'm president of the National Trust up here.'

Theo inclined his head. 'You certainly have some wonderful buildings, as well as one quite unique one.'

'Oh you know Glastonbridge?'

On hearing the name, Theo felt a frisson. He swallowed. 'I've been there. I saw it when Mr Tyler first bought it.'

'Well, it's not that much changed,' Joan said. 'Duane will be able to tell you more. He gets out there from time to time.'

Theo parked in the side lane. He found Duane in the workroom behind the shop, running his hands and his eyes over a delightful burr walnut dressing table that had just been waxed. When he saw Theo, he walked towards him, wiping his hands on his jeans.

'I do love the smell of wax,' Theo said, and smiled benignly.

He held out his left hand and Duane wondered what he was meant to do with it. Kiss it? Theo squeezed Duane's hand briefly, then dropped it.

When the pieces were standing side by side in the workroom – the George III chest of drawers and the pair of early Hepplewhite chairs – Theo said, 'I heard you were very good with chairs, so I thought I'd bring them as well. This one is quite rickety,' he said, putting his hand on the one nearest him and rocking it.

Duane bent forward and picked the chair up with one easy movement. He turned it upside down and rested it on his knee. 'You see the joint? Someone has tried to fix it by glueing. Doesn't work with these mortice and tenon joints. It needs a new wooden dowel, if you want to be authentic.'

'Can one get those?'

'I make them.' Duane stood back. 'They're nice pieces,' he said. 'Well worth spending money on.'

'Yes, I've decided to keep the chairs. They go well with a new bookcase I've bought.'

'What sort?'

'Chippendale, with Gothic glazed doors. Quite unusual.'

'Raymond Tyler's got a pair of bookcases with doors like that.'

Duane had replaced Clover in Joan's affections. Here was another waif waiting to be moulded. And despite his slight appearance and diffident manners there was a strength in Duane which appealed to Joan. He was a mystery, a challenge. No matter how much she teased him, he refused to reveal his antecedents.

'My family is an accident that's best forgotten,' he said.

And another time: 'I've lived all over – Bathurst, Albury, Geelong, Wagga.'

He had so many different anecdotes that it was hard to believe that all these things had happened in one short life. She didn't care about the inconsistencies. She liked the idea of a life lived on many fronts. If she had one ambition for her own life, that was it.

'What's a boy like that doing with all you old history freaks?' Norma asked when Joan came home and told her that Duane was now a member of the Trust committee.

'He's not a boy. He's twenty-eight. Anyway, I think it's very heartening to see someone like Duane so involved,' Joan said. 'Just because you don't care about our heritage.'

'Heritage! It's an excuse for nosing into other people's business. No, don't turn away Joan. You know I don't agree with some of the things you do.'

'Then it's best if we agree to disagree.' Joan didn't like to upset Norma. Her face took on an unpleasant colour when she was upset. She hadn't been well lately but she refused to see the doctor. Sometimes, when Joan looked at herself in the mirror then looked at Norma, she was shocked to be reminded that they were well on their way to being old women. Why hadn't they met earlier?

'I wouldn't have been ready for you,' Norma said, lying in bed on a Sunday morning, weak autumn sunshine streaming through the twelve-pane window. 'I would have been too afraid. I set a cut-off point for myself of fifty. After that, I told myself, you do what you like. Take no heed of nobody. Before that, at forty or thirty, I still spent half my time looking over my shoulder. Looking at all those Sells who went before me, at family respectability, family history. See? That's what you won't concede, with all your love of history. That it's a trap, a bind. The one good thing I got from the family is money. The rest of it I don't want to know about.'

'What about this house?' Joan asked. She loved Norma's house. It had belonged to the Sells since 1862.

'The house is just a house.'

Joan frowned. 'How can you say that?'

'Easy. Don't try and turn me into one of your renovators and restorers, Joan. Look at William and Robbie,' Norma continued. 'Now I like them, especially William, but really! All that time and money on a house that's in one of the worst parts of town.'

'But when you get inside the garden you could be anywhere...'

'They're still over-capitalising.'

Joan tut-tutted. 'They've rescued a once-valuable house. It wasn't always the worst part of town.'

'It's just excessive,' Norma said. 'All that effort, all that expense. For what? What does it *mean*?'

Joan wasn't sure how she really felt about Glastonbridge. She admired it because everyone else did. But she also recoiled from it. It was overwhelming. It didn't fit with her image of a colonial house. To her mind, the house that bore Glaston's name should have been a truer example of colonial architecture. Like Norma's, except bigger. Norma's house had the low, wide verandah, the square-paned windows, the simple, geometric layout of a true Georgian house. Balance and harmony combined with age and history. That's what Joan liked. The truth was she found Glastonbridge grotesque.

Thankfully, Glastonbridge was a one-off. All the other buildings that the Glass Valley sub-branch of the National Trust concerned themselves with were more manageable examples of the colonial period. But Glastonbridge could not be ignored. It was a renegade that must be tamed, brought within the fold. Joan decided to write to head office about it. She would send them the clippings from the *Gazette*. It wasn't right that everyone else stuck to the guidelines while Raymond went and did what he liked!

*

When Raymond was a boy, Bamford's ten thousand green acres were the limit of his experience. Bamford, with its order and conformity, the neat symmetry of its Georgian buildings and serried rows of crops, was for him unexceptional. Its mellow stone and small-paned windows represented the comforting architecture of his childhood. A Georgian house, devoid of verandahs, bare-faced, glinting in the Australian sun. When it was built, it was surrounded by raw paddocks and fallen timber. But this rough patch of earth was to become, if its pasty-faced new owner could make it, a place that would be forever England. In Tasmania they almost managed it. There, where the land was greener, the sky greyer, the light softer, they imposed their solid homes and neat hedges, grew crops and reared sheep, wore their tailored clothes and played their English games, ate off Worcester china and Sheffield plate. All the time trying to master and structure, order and contain, to mould the new world to their ancestral pattern. And the houses: square, box-like, stately; doors centred, windows paired, roofs even. The houses, transplanted from Hertfordshire to Hobart, clamped on untrustworthy soil, demanding compliance.

There was one day in his youth when it all crystallised before him. He was standing in the front hall with his father. In front of them was the grand double front door with its arching skylight and pair of handsome side-panes. Behind them, his mother and Lillian stood on the landing of the wide central staircase, where it paused before dividing into twin return flights up to the first floor. On either side of the hall were double doors, and on either side of the doors, a pair of family portraits. Everything in pairs! Everywhere he looked was a desire for order, balance, symmetry. Everything, every one, was one half of something else. His family, caught there in tableau, was no different: mother, father; daughter, son. And so it was meant to continue. The next generation and the one after that. He would not, could not, do it. He stood there, hearing his father out.

'All the sons in this family have gone to Geelong and you will, too. I won't argue about it. You'll do what's expected of you.' His father picked up his hat and opened the front door. 'What makes you think you've the right to be different?'

Sir Anthony left the house and went off to Hobart for the week. By the time he returned, Raymond had left home. He fled to an aunt in Sydney. He was sixteen.

*

'It's only a dinner party,' said Sally on the phone to Philip. 'I just thought it might help if Joan could be helped to understand Raymond's—'

'Obsession?' offered Philip.

'Vision,' countered Sally. 'You're being very sharp today.'

Philip, on the other end of the phone, paused a moment then said: 'Do you understand it?'

'What?'

'His vision.'

'I try to,' Sally said. 'I do admire him, his depth of knowledge.'

'Yes, yes we all admire that,' said Philip impatiently. 'I'm just not sure if I know, any more, what it all amounts to. What "Raymond's vision" has got to do with the real world.'

'Heavens Philip, what has any of it to do with the real world? If you come down to it. What you do, what I do.'

'At least we're running businesses. I just get annoyed with covering for him. Can hardly get him to talk business these days, and sometimes there are things I need to discuss with him.'

'Oh, he's just going through one of his off phases,' Sally said. 'He'll come good. He always does.'

It was not like Norma to be ill. Joan was concerned, of course. But she also couldn't quite believe that she *was* ill. Each morning she woke expecting to find Norma restored to health, smiling and getting out of bed to make the tea, putting out clothes to wear to the bookshop. Instead, when Joan woke, Norma remained groggy, drifting in and out of sleep – the effects of the drugs the doctor had given her, when she finally consented to see him. Norma's sandy grey curls were squashed and lacklustre, her sharp, intelligent face uncharacteristically slack. When she did finally wake properly, she'd say, 'I'll be fine by tomorrow'. But she wasn't.

Joan got a young woman in to help at the shop. 'Just for a couple of weeks, till you're back on your feet.' Sitting at her dressing table on the Thursday before the Austinmeers' dinner party, Joan twisted her auburn hair up onto the back of her large head and turned from side to side to check there were no loose strands. She'd have to ring Sally Austinmeer tonight, if Norma was no better. She didn't really want to go without her.

Norma sat up in bed, watching her. As if reading Joan's thoughts, she said, 'You'll enjoy yourself far more on Saturday night if I'm not there.

You know it's not really my sort of thing. They'll be talking of nothing but houses and furniture.'

Joan turned towards her, 'I thought I might ask Sally if we can postpone it.'

'No, don't do that.'

Joan picked up her lipstick, the same scarlet that she wore day in, day out. After she'd applied it and squeezed her lips together, she said, 'If you're sure.'

'Don't go getting into any fights,' Norma said. 'If you want to keep on living here after I'm gone, you'll need to get on with people. People who make waves often get caught in the backwash.'

'Don't talk nonsense.' Joan busily began rearranging the things on her dressing table.

'It's true. Stop fiddling and come over here. What's the matter?'

Joan moved slowly towards the bed and sat on the end of it. 'You do talk some nonsense. I might die first, and if I don't…well, I haven't even thought about it.'

'Well, you should. You like Glaston, don't you?'

'I really don't want to talk about it,' Joan said, heaving herself up off the bed. It took two attempts. 'I mean, look at me! I'm the one who's unfit.' They began to laugh, and Joan leaned down and wrapped her arms around Norma's thin shoulders.

Raymond agreed to the dinner party because he didn't want to disappoint Sally and her good intentions, but he had no desire to sit at the same table as Joan Beaverstoke.

'What am I going to say to her?' he grumbled. 'I don't think we've got a single thing in common.'

Sally reassured him it would be easy. 'I'm sure Joan is well meaning. Just talk about Bamford if you like. That will keep her fascinated all evening. Tell you what, why don't you bring over that painting of Bamford? I could hang it on the dining room wall. Pretend you've lent it to me.'

'What painting?' Raymond said nervously, feeling trapped, like a thief caught in the act.

'The one you showed me years ago, the big oil of Bamford in the eighteen hundreds.'

Raymond had forgotten that, once, in a moment of rare ease and confidence, he'd shown the painting to Sally. 'I never hang it. But all right, just this once. It might distract the Beaverstoke woman from Glastonbridge.'

'Exactly. It will also show her that you've far more experience of old houses than she has.'

Joan saw the picture as soon as they entered the room. Carrying her champagne glass, she walked around the table and stood in front of it. 'Where's this place?'

'That's Bamford, Raymond's family home,' Sally said from the door-way to the kitchen.

After that, it was as easy as Sally had predicted. Raymond at first had to be coaxed to talk. He was still convinced that Joan had it in for him. But once he got going his usual stock of stories flowed forth – stories about Tasmanian colonial life, the families, their marriages and their homes. Stories that even William and Sally had not heard before. The talk was of nothing else until near the end of the venison. From time to time William contributed a titbit from his own stock of tales about the upper classes. Occasionally Robbie yawned. He quickly stifled it. They were all doing their bit for Raymond. Not that he noticed.

'Bloody hell,' said Titus in the kitchen as he brought in the empty plates, 'do you think we're going to talk about anything *else* tonight?'

'It's good, it's good,' Sally said, inspecting her pudding. 'It's just as I hoped.'

When they re-entered the dining room, Joan was saying, '...but Raymond, being so familiar with a house like that, and I imagine furniture to go with it, how was it you became interested in this other sort of thing? What do you call it, Jacobean, Gothic? It's so different from Georgian.' She looked at Raymond expectantly. Raymond looked blank, then he looked at William.

William said, 'You knew all about the Georgian period because you were living in it. Maybe you were looking for something different.'

'Not that you didn't love the Georgian,' Sally said hurriedly, for Joan's benefit.

'I loved it and I hated it,' Raymond said. He looked at Joan. 'I became fascinated by the Elizabethans. James the First, Cromwell, because they were exotic to me. And later, all that Gothic revival. Hugh Walpole, Sir Walter Scott. And Pugin, of course, the great architect.'

'So you think he designed Glastonbridge?'

Raymond shook his head. 'There's a house like it in Lancashire that Pugin did. I think it was the inspiration. Berge was from Lancashire.'

The phone rang in the hall and Titus went to answer it.

'This is really very interesting,' Joan said.

'Joan,' said Titus, coming in from the hall, 'it's for you.'

Joan pushed back her chair and hurried out with a whoosh of fabric.

'You see,' said Sally quietly to Raymond, 'it was a good idea.'

'I suppose so. She's not so bad – just doesn't know much.'

There was a small noise from the hallway, like a strangled sob. All their heads spun simultaneously. Joan appeared in the doorway.

'I have to go! It's Norma.'

9.

From the time of Norma's death, people's lives started unravelling. Not in any spectacular way – just that we'd all had a jolt and the comfortable pattern of our lives shifted gear. People were suddenly reminded that this was all we had, that there were no second chances.

Norma realised the same thing towards the end, I think. Of course no one knew the end was approaching. But one time she rang the shop while I was helping out and when she heard my voice said: 'Oh, it's you. Good, I'm glad it's you. I've been meaning to say something to you.'

'What?'

'Don't you think it's time you got on with your life instead of just watching everyone else's?'

I didn't know how to respond.

'If there's one thing I've learnt, if life means anything it's what you make of it yourself. I learnt that – too late, or nearly. Is Joan there?' she asked briskly. 'Tell her to call me.'

I was shaken, like she'd given me a slap.

When she died so suddenly I kept remembering that conversation – the last words I heard her speak.

Vale, Norma Sells

The sudden death last Saturday of Miss Norma Sells has left many Glaston residents in shock. Miss Sells was the last member of the Sells family – who first settled in the Glass Valley in the early 1850s.

Miss Sells was known for her quiet good humour and her generosity – a large number of people attended her funeral at All Saints Presbyterian Church on Tuesday.

Mourners have since been surprised to learn that Miss Sells was the mystery owner of more than two dozen buildings in Glaston – including the Pitt Street terrace-houses and the Rundle Street warehouses.

There was a creek behind the house I was renting, its banks lined with thorny bushes and thistles. If I followed it, as I sometimes did, after about ten minutes it joined the river at floodgates set into the levee bank. I'd sit on the bank and look across the river to the hills. I had come to Glaston because what I thought of as my future had evaporated. The past looked more inviting. But that wasn't strictly true. The past was messy, complicated. The only thing about it that was inviting was that it was unchangeable. It was there to be uncovered, whereas my future had become a terrifying void.

I did a lot of walking that winter, a lot of walking and sitting and trying to think. I wondered if I should just go. In a sense, Norma's life showed me the futility of trying to reshape the past. Her past had never left her, was known to everyone. Yet she died an enigma even to those who knew and loved her best.

Sitting on the levee, I could just see the top of the bridge around the corner, it's four stone 'towers', two at either end, miniature versions of the tower at Glastonbridge. When Berge built the bridge he did the puntman out of his livelihood. I don't imagine that such a thing even occurred to Berge.

If I hadn't found the little house where I was living – the house where my great-great-grandmother lived till she married – I would not have stayed. Just as I would not have stayed had I not met Raymond and heard the story of Glastonbridge.

It was after Norma's death that I said to Raymond, 'Have you ever heard of Tom Harkness?'

'Yes.' He looked at me. 'Old Rose's great-uncle. He got the house after Berge disappeared. Why?'

'He was born in my place.'

'Really? I didn't know there were Harknesses on that side of the river.'

*

Trying to break through Joan's frozen state ten days after Norma's funeral, Raymond told her the story about his mother's death.

'She was with me less than two years,' he said, as they sat having tea in front of the fire in the house that was now Joan's. Joan made no response. Raymond continued, 'I went up one evening to see why she hadn't come down for her usual nightcap and she was lying on her bed, fully dressed, as if she was just having a nap. She was still warm. I didn't believe she was dead. Do you know what I did?'

Joan stared into the fire, her large face impassive, and shook her head.

'We'd been talking a few days before about driving to Scone to see her family's old property. She wasn't from Tasmania, you know, only went there when she married my father. She wanted to see Scone again but we hadn't got around to it. So I picked her up and carried her downstairs and put her in Brutus. And that's what we did – we drove to Scone.'

Joan looked at him in surprise, the first expression of interest she'd shown in anything for a fortnight. Raymond was encouraged. He continued, 'I can't remember much about the drive. It was dark, of course. The sun was rising just as we reached Scone. I drove up the driveway to the house. There were poplars on either side, and at the end was the house, a nice, two-storey brick place. It was sort of silhouetted against the dawn sky. The sky was gold streaked with red. I remember that. There was a light on in the house so I didn't go any closer. I said to Mum, "Look Mum, we're here, here's the house". She didn't respond, of course. She was dead. But I still couldn't believe it.

'I turned around and drove back here. I went in to Doctor Con. I went in and said to Con, "Mum's outside in the car. Can you come and have a look at her?" He came out and took one look at her sitting up in the car and said, "You know she's dead?" She was stone cold by then. I didn't really believe she was dead until Con said it.'

'I didn't believe it even then,' Joan said. 'I yelled at him: "You stupid Greek!"' She giggled, then looked at Raymond with such sad eyes that he had to look away.

Raymond had taken to calling in to see Joan most days. Ever since Norma's funeral. She had behaved so oddly at the funeral. Not like herself at all. There was a vacancy about her, as though whoever she was was being buried under the sods of earth with Norma. It wasn't pity exactly that drew him, but something like.

'I had no idea about all those properties, you know,' Joan said now. 'Can you believe that? I wonder sometimes if I knew her at all. Sometimes I just feel this incredible *rage*.'

'Ooohh,' Raymond crowed, 'you don't need to tell me about rage. I felt cheated by Mum dying.'

'Yes, cheated.' Joan passed him a quick look. 'And now a mess to clean up. But it's more than just cheated. It's like she was making fun of me. Keeping all these old buildings a secret. And me working for the Trust. She heard me criticising landlords who let old buildings fall apart. Now I find out I've been living with one of them!'

'Huuh,' Raymond sighed. Then after a short silence, 'I'd better be going. Got to get some meat for Miffy.'

Left alone, Joan was again swept by one of those tidal waves of anger that left her breathless and powerless. Too late now to argue with Norma, too late to have it out. Part of her wanted to flee, to flee her humiliation and the bleak knowledge of Norma's impenetrability. She'd had an image of the two of them: two gnarled brown figures joined at the hip, living out their days in cosy comfort like two walnuts in a shell. What a joke! Who was this person with whom she'd shared a bed?

*

A Facelift for Glaston?
By Brenda Watkins

It has emerged in recent weeks that a local philanthropist – the late Norma Sells – had been allowing dozens of local families in need to live in her properties for nominal rent.

The tenants – who have been living in the properties for between ten and 25 years – are grateful for the subsidised accommodation, but many are now complaining about the dilapidated state of the buildings.

Help may be at hand. The new owner of the buildings – benefactor of Miss Sells' estate, Miss Joan Beaverstoke – has for a number of years been president of the Glass Valley National Trust. It is expected that now that she has control of the properties substantial improvements will be made.

National Trust sources say that Miss Beaverstoke has been keen to improve the architectural face of Glaston and now is her chance. Some of the buildings date from the early to mid 1800s.

One – which is said to be in most serious disrepair and has been unlived in for several years – is believed to have been built by the father of Glaston, Lt Berge.

A friend of Miss Beaverstoke – Mr Raymond Tyler – said yesterday, 'Joan had no idea that Norma owned the properties until she
was shown the will. This has shaken her badly.'

*

'There's too much death around lately,' William said to Sally. He'd
called in with a big bunch of early jonquils, knowing they were Sally's favourites, the ones with the deep yellow petals and gold centres.
Sally was arranging them in a green vase that matched the stems.

'Norma. Who else?'

'Oh,' said William, waving his hand. 'You know...'

Sally didn't. She waited but when he didn't continue, she said, 'Do you
remember Betty Tyler's funeral? God, wasn't that a weird day. All
those bored-looking women in pearls. A bit different from Norma's. I
wish now I'd known Norma better.'

'I imagine Joan is thinking much the same thing,' said William with
one of his flashes of droll humour. 'I was very fond of Norma. She
wasn't someone you could easily get to know. But I didn't mind that.
She had a wicked sense of humour sometimes.'

Sally smiled and concentrated on her flowers. After a few moments,
she asked, 'Does it worry you, dying?'

'Only when I think about it,' William said quickly.

'Raymond says he's rather looking forward to it. Expects all sorts of
revelations.'

'I wish I could be confident that it'll be that interesting.' He bobbed his
head up and down and moved to the other side of the room. 'But let's
not talk about it.'

Sally remembered that William still refused to go into the room where Raymond kept Lady Tyler's ashes in a box on the mantelpiece.

'All right,' she said, taking William's arm. 'Come and have a look at this piece I bought last week. It's like Staffordshire but it's German.' William perked up immediately and padded after her into the dining room. There was nothing like porcelain to ease his mind.

*

It wasn't yet five o'clock when Theo arrived back at the Astor but already the high-ceilinged rooms were deep in shadow. He resisted turning the main lights on and instead went through to his bedroom and switched on the picture lights. The heavy brocade drapes were still drawn and he had left his bed unmade. He pulled the cover roughly over the crumpled sheets and lay down on it, kicking his shoes off. Before closing his eyes, he looked around him. Beneath each wall light was an icon. Half a dozen of his favourites. There wasn't room for more in the flat. Most of his collection was down at Yarralong, in three big interconnecting rooms that Julia refused to go into because she said the icons gave her the creeps. That was another thing in Rosemary's favour: she did admire the icons. She loved sleeping in this room. Theo closed his eyes. But it was more peaceful here without her. It was after all a bachelor pad and he intended to keep it that way.

Half an hour later he was woken by the door buzzer. By the time he reached the intercom he realised who it must be. Duane. He'd forgotten he was delivering the chairs today. Five minutes later, Duane was standing at the apartment door with a chair under each arm. His hair had fallen into his eyes and he swished it back with a toss of his head as Theo opened the door.

'No, no,' Duane said as Theo reached for a chair. 'I can manage.' He came in through the door sideways, looked around then walked over to the bay window and put a chair down on either side of it. He stood back. Theo switched on the main light and walked over to the chairs to inspect them.

'Very nice. Very nice indeed.' He rocked them both to see how steady they were. There were no loose joints. Duane hurried over and picked the nearest chair up and turned it over to show Theo.

'You see this here?' Duane said, pointing to what looked like an old nail. 'That's new, and so is that one there. But I bashed the tops to make them look like original nails.'

'Well done! I'd never have known.'

'Of course it wouldn't fool everyone.' Duane stopped, realising that probably wasn't a diplomatic thing to say.

'For example?' Theo asked. 'Who wouldn't it fool?'

'Well, you know. Experienced dealers, restorers. But they'd have to look close,' he added, just a little proud.

'Raymond Tyler?'

'Nah, Raymond would know that trick.'

'So how is Glaston? Much happening?'

'Aw, the usual. Oné thing, though. This woman, Norma Sells, died and it turns out she owned half the town. And no one knew. She left it all to Joan Beaverstoke. Joan's a mate of mine.'

'I think I've met her. At the cafe, bookshop, whatever. A large, red-headed woman?'

'That's her.'

Theo sat down in one of the chairs and leaned back to try it out. Satisfied, he smiled up at Duane. 'Do you want a drink?'

'Yeah, sure.'

'Tell me more about this Glaston business,' Theo called as he went through to the kitchen to get glasses. 'Are we talking about a lot of property?'

'About twenty houses and a dozen commercial buildings. Most of the houses are dumps – a couple of long terraces near the station. The others are mainly shops in the main street. Oh, and one big warehouse near the river. You know, there used to be boats on the river, paddle steamers! These days it's not much more than a trickle.' He took the drink Theo handed him and perched on the edge of a sofa.

'What's she going to do with them?'

'Dunno. Everyone expects her to do them up. But I don't know if Norma left her much cash.'

Theo said nothing. He was lounging on a dark red brocade sofa, wearing a white collarless shirt and cream waistcoat. Duane thought he looked like some sort of priest.

Duane went on: 'Raymond has become real friendly with Joan now.' Seeing Theo look interested, he said, 'Yeah, it's surprised a lot of people. Particularly as Joan was behind those stories about Glastonbridge falling apart.'

'Ah, Glastonbridge,' said Theo.

'You like it?'

Theo moved his face about, as if uncertain what to say. 'It's special,' he said at last.

'I might be doing a big job out there for Raymond soon,' Duane said.

'Oh?'

'Yeah, the kitchen. He wants it to look like it used to, except with modern appliances.'

Theo looked at Duane speculatively then leaned forward, his elbows on his knees, and looked intently into his face. 'If you ever hear there's a chance Glastonbridge might be coming on the market, I'd really appreciate knowing about it early.'

'Uh-huh.' Duane looked around him at the sombre tones, at the dim wall lights and chandeliers that looked like banks of candles. More like a church than a home.

He looked down at his empty glass. 'I suppose I'd better be going.' He wondered suddenly why he had been asked here. To bring the chairs back, of course. But was that all? 'Thanks for the opportunity to do some work for you,' he said formally, standing up. He looked around for a place to put his glass.

Theo stood, too, and took it from him. 'You'll send your bill?'

'Oh,' said Duane, reaching for his back pocket. He'd almost forgotten the bill. He took out a folded invoice and handed it to Theo. It was substantial, but Theo's expression never altered. Duane had heard it said once that it never paid to undercharge.

'No doubt we'll talk again,' Theo said and held out his hand for Duane to grasp in a parting gesture.

When he'd gone, Theo poured himself another brandy. He believed in fate. It did not pay to ignore opportunities that fate put in your way. Taking his drink, he went through to the study. He looked at the phone then took up pen and paper instead. At the top of the page was his letterhead, which consisted simply of his name and below it, on one side, his post office address. He addressed the letter to 'Joan Beaverstoke, c/- "Hogarth's", High Street, Glaston'.

'Dear Joan,' he began. 'You may recall we met...'

*

That winter was a bitter one for Lillian. So many things were not as she expected in Sydney. Her position in society, her relationship with her brother, the weather. People always assumed Sydney was warm; people from New York – or Tasmania. But it wasn't. In winter it was cold and people never heated their houses, so on the rare occasion she was invited out she usually spent most of the evening freezing her tits off. The evening gowns she'd stocked up on over the years were meant for central heating and mink stoles. But you were likely to be shot if you wore mink in Sydney. Some greenie would probably throw paint over you. Suits were the safest bet, dull but safe. That is, until some tired and emotional fellow at a dinner party, with a red nose and tufts of hair above his ears, told her that her favourite little Hermès number reminded him of David Jones wrapping paper. 'And what a nice little package you are,' he'd said, trailing his tie through the raspberry coulis as he leaned towards her. That was the last time the Hermès had an outing.

It wasn't just that her social life was a failure, that the only men she met were gout sufferers or heart attack candidates. It was that she'd had this picture of comfortable familiarity. Coming home! Before her marriage, she'd been the prize of Tasmanian society. And she fancied that she had aged well. Her hair might be greying but she'd kept her figure. She had expected that now, in her maturity, she would slide easily into a place among the upper echelons in Sydney, appreciated for her New York sophistication. But she discovered that Sydney didn't work like that. The Contessa, when she was in New York, did not mind being treated like a small-time colonial eccentric, because she knew that in Sydney she was queen of it all. Lillian, however, did object to being seen in Sydney as a Tasmanian hick, as if her New York years had never existed. Now she knew how Clive James felt.

She had hoped and expected that Raymond would ease her way. He'd lived in Sydney for four decades. He was well known. He could have introduced her to people, escorted her. But it never occurred to him. Typical! He introduced her to Philip Dexter, that's all. Philip had once or twice taken her to functions, which was sweet of him. But that was in the beginning. It was a long time since Philip had invited her to anything other than his own exhibition openings.

Lillian put a hand across her heart and tapped her shoulder lightly, nervously. It was a habit that had developed lately which she was totally unaware of and which, living in solitude as she did, no one had pointed out to her. What she needed was something to occupy her time. She had offered her services to the Black and White Committee and the overture had been received with polite smiles and no more. She considered joining Friends of the Opera but feared being made to feel uncomfortable and dull-witted. She would have to sound knowledgeable, which she wasn't. In fact, she found opera rather tiring.

Perhaps Friends of the Art Gallery? She'd heard they held very good cocktail parties and art was something that she could have an opinion on. She could honestly say that in New York she had regularly gone to the Guggenheim. Its coffee shop was one of her favourite places in town. So convenient for meeting people, particularly out-of-town guests. When her father was alive there'd been a lot of those. Seemingly every Tasmanian who visited North America had been given her phone number. She complained about it but secretly enjoyed it. She liked the role of worldly escort, showing the colonials the finest city in the world. Oh dear, Lillian thought, tapping her shoulder, they were good days. She should have savoured them more.

What was left to her now? For the umpteenth time she wondered whether it had been a mistake to return to Australia, to come and live in Sydney. Perhaps she should have gone back to Tasmania? They wouldn't have ignored her there. She would still have been Sir

Anthony Tyler's daughter. She could have gone back to Bamford and picked up where she'd left off. A few of the old beaux might even have come calling. She'd heard that Wally Barton's wife had died. Her mind was about to dance off into a reverie about the kind of life she might live in Tasmania when one inescapable fact loomed before her: Raymond had sold Bamford.

She had a recurring dream about Bamford. She dreamt that Raymond had sold it. Then she'd wake in the morning thinking, 'Oh dear, I dreamt that Raymond had sold Bamford. Thank heavens it was only a dream.' Then, fully awake, she'd realise it wasn't a dream. What right had Raymond to sell their ancestral home? She forgot that at the time she had raised no objection, that with their mother newly dead, their father gone, secure in her own life with Harold in New York, she had given her assent with barely a thought. How quickly things had changed. It was as though her life had disappeared from under her feet. Now here she was in Sydney with no husband and no position in society, with nothing but a difficult and unreliable brother. It was all Raymond's fault! He could have helped her more. Instead he'd turned her into a virtual pauper. How could she entertain on what was left her each month? Oh little dinner parties, maybe. But it would take more than that to prove her colours with Lady Regan's crowd. And that Junee Goldsbrough – she'd been back in Sydney barely three months and already on the Contessa's invitation list! Lillian had seen a picture in the *Wentworth Courier*. She never did like Junee. Trust her to be the one to tell Raymond about Lillian's little lunches with Theo Roth. Not that Lillian had heard from Theo lately. Even he had stopped calling. Oh, what was she to do?

That very evening Philip was invited to the Contessa's. The crystal chandelier in the drawing room blazed and beneath it the Contessa's guests hovered as a bevy of black-suited waiters ferried champagne bottles and trays of canapés from guest to guest. Crumbs were ground into the fine pile of the enormous silk carpet and champagne spilled onto the parquetry floor that surrounded it. This was a grand room of a very particular kind. The Contessa had lived on this side of the world for fifty-nine of her sixty-four years – her accent was more firmly Australian than that of most of her guests – yet her style, her tastes, were still grandly, unabashedly, European.

It was to her that the director of the Art Gallery turned when he was wondering how to entertain a visiting art curator, a chauvinistic Belgian on his first journey south of the equator. The Contessa was always ready to do her bit for The Arts. The visiting Belgian looked quite at home. A portly man with a balding pate and long wispy beard, he was sitting on the edge of one of the Contessa's brocaded sofas with his mouth full of canapé and nodding vigorously at a talkative Jules.

What a blessing that Philip had brought Jules, the Contessa thought. What a nice, refined young man. She didn't even mind the long hair because it looked so good tied back like that. So chic. So French.

'I do like your...I do like Jules,' the Contessa said to Philip, hesitating only slightly.

Philip inclined his head but said nothing. He had only recently begun taking Jules with him to these sorts of events. Now that they were living together it was, he supposed, time to be more up-front.

'I do miss Raoul and Patrick,' the Contessa said. This might have appeared a non sequitur, but Philip was aware that it was not, that it was, from the Contessa, an acknowledgement and an acceptance. Patrick and Raoul were good friends of the Contessa's who had recently retired to France. Philip was about to enquire after them when the Contessa's conversation took a sudden change in direction.

'Such a pity Raymond couldn't be here,' she said.

'He's rather preoccupied at the moment.'

'Has he had another row with that dreadful sister of his?'

'Now, now Tessa. You're very hard on Lillian.'

'Oh, she's an annoying woman. Poor Raymond.'

'That's very loyal of you.'

The Contessa looked at Philip closely, her tiny frame leaning backwards as she gazed up at him, holding his gaze.

'Some people need loyal friends more than others,' she said.

'Quite,' said Philip, then surveyed the room. He looked down at her. 'What have you heard?'

'Nothing, nothing. Just that the last couple of times I talked to Raymond it was clear he wasn't himself. He was ranting about Lillian.'

Poor Lillian, Philip thought suddenly. No one ever took her side. What was she doing with herself these days? Hard to imagine a life so empty. 'You shouldn't take too much notice of Raymond when he's like that,' he said.

The Contessa sniffed then patted his arm. 'I should go and talk to the guest of honour. Can't leave poor Jules to talk French to him all night.' She was about to move away then suddenly turned towards Philip, her face stricken. 'Quickly, quickly,' she said, 'remind me. What is this exhibition about?'

Philip leaned down and said in her ear: 'Flemish masters. Seventeenth century.'

'Of course, of course. How silly of me.' Then she sailed away towards the curator, calling gaily to people she passed on the way. Just as she was about to reach her destination, a figure in white blocked her path.

'I'm so sorry I'm late,' Theo said, taking the Contessa's hand and kissing it.

'Oh Theo, you're always welcome, whenever you arrive.' She smiled up at him. Such a figure of a man! 'Come and meet our visitor.' She took him by the hand. Despite what she said, Theo did not always get invited to the Contessa's evenings. There were some people, she knew, who did not entirely approve of him. But tonight there could be no objection. Who better to meet the curator?

'Theo is a collector,' she beamed as she introduced him. 'He collects icons.' Theo and the Belgian shook hands politely, but both were at a loss as to what to do next. Theo made a few polite remarks about looking forward to seeing the exhibition. Privately, he didn't like the Flemish painters much – he found them too overtly personal. What he really wanted was to get away and have a quiet word with Philip, who must be here somewhere although he couldn't see him yet.

Philip, meanwhile, had taken the opportunity to chat up the wife of a leading QC, a woman with a great appetite for antiques but uncertain taste.

'I'm never sure that I've made the right choice,' she was saying. 'And Rodney is no help at all. He thinks furnishings just happen!'

'It's too big a responsibility to do it all yourself,' Philip said soothingly.

'That's right!' After a pause, during which Philip was studiously silent, she asked: 'Do you do that sort of thing? Give advice, choose appropriate pieces?'

'Of course.'

'Oh well, we must talk more. Perhaps I could call in and see you?'

'Do that. You know where we are.' Philip never did anything so crude as hand out a business card. Now he steered the conversation away from business, lest it occur to her later that he had deliberately wooed her. He set himself the task of entertaining her. Within minutes, her cultivated laugh came in waves from their corner of the room.

Throwing his head back to laugh with her, Philip spied Theo advancing towards them.

'Now here is someone I don't know if you know,' he said. 'Theo Roth, a delightful man.'

'I know *of* him, of course.'

'Theo,' Philip said and extended his hand.

A moment later the tall-panelled doors to the dining room opened and the Contessa urged her guests towards the buffet table.

Raymond was in Sydney that evening but not with his sister. There was a place in Woolloomooloo that he liked to go to, a discreet establishment. He didn't go often – it was a pleasure to be rationed. He was always rather nervous when he arrived but that soon passed. He enjoyed the preliminaries nearly as much as the main event. To have a drink and watch the slim figures of the youths as they moved through the rooms. Such gorgeous creatures, golden or quicksilver. Which would it be tonight? He thought perhaps quicksilver. His eye was drawn again and again to a lad with fine black hair and extraordinary eyelashes. He liked the sardonic curl to his lip.

It was such a relief to let the chatter wash over him, to allow himself to be handled in a most pleasurable way. One of the greatest pleasures was the knowledge that no matter what he did tonight, there would be no one ringing him tomorrow demanding that he explain himself. There was nothing so erotic as the combination of biting leather straps and cold steel – binding him, restraining him – together with the total freedom from responsibility. He groaned as his pale-skinned, dark-lashed paramour tightened a strap.

Later, when he was spent and the youth was giving him a light rub-down, he thought of Joan and Norma. As so often in the past, he wondered about love. What it felt like, how it changed people, how the loss of it left them bereft. Was the comfort of her years with Norma worth the pain Joan was going through now? He had sometimes wondered what he might be missing out on. But he could not regret, at this moment, that love had passed him by. There were peaks and troughs aplenty in life without that.

In the weeks after Norma's death, Raymond was curiously drawn to Joan's misery. He approached her out of sympathy at first. Then in fear and fascination, as if she were some kind of precipice. Joan's grief was deep and genuine but there was another side to it, a towering, raging anger that not only consumed her but seemed to threaten everything around her. Her bulk – which had been comfortable, homely, respectable – swelled noticeably. Even Titus, large enough himself to overlook others' size, remarked upon it. Her face had a hot and clammy sheen; her eyes, always bright and piercing, became crazed blackcurrants in her swollen face. It was as if half of Glaston waited in trepidation to see where Joan's fury would vent itself, in which direction she would erupt and who might be engulfed. The town seemed suddenly very small.

'I don't know how you can spend so much time with her,' Sally said to Raymond when he called in on his way home one afternoon. 'I ran into her in town yesterday and she made me feel so nervous I had to get away from her.'

Raymond shrugged. He couldn't have explained why he was curious about Joan, why he felt compelled to watch her. That's what he did most times he visited: he watched her. They didn't talk much. Sometimes Joan took no notice of him at all. Other days she raved at him and Raymond just sat there silently, taking it in.

'I don't know which of them is the craziest,' Sally said one evening to Titus. She was a little annoyed with Raymond's defection.

Titus grunted and Sally looked at him in exasperation. They were normally so in tune with each other but lately they'd been bickering a lot. She sighed.

For Joan, the hardest thing to bear was the humiliation. President of the Glass Valley National Trust one moment, slum-lord the next. She was furious that she hadn't been re-elected as president of the branch. The committee made excuses, said she wasn't well. But she knew what it was about. She was an embarrassment. She knew what people were saying: that she'd lived with Norma, that she must have known about the properties, that she was complicit in allowing heritage buildings to fall into disrepair. That she was a hypocrite.

At this point in her recurring inner monologue Joan usually thumped something – a windowpane, a table, the mantelpiece. Every time Raymond visited he had to step over shards of glass and broken bits of crockery. He was becoming quite accustomed to it.

But towards the end of June, Joan changed. The humiliation fell away, the fruitless railings against Norma ceased. She went on a diet. She had her hair cut. All this happened after she'd been to see the solicitor. Afterwards she wondered why she had postponed the visit so long. Because, whatever else Norma had done, she had transformed Joan into a woman of means. For the first time Joan grasped the extent of those means and the opportunity that was now before her. She stepped out with a renewed sense of confidence.

At home that evening she tackled the mail that had accumulated. After making a mental note of who had and had not sent a condolence card, she pushed the pile of cards to one side. Then she opened the bills, including the funeral bills, and pushed them to the other side. That left one letter in the centre. She opened it carelessly, expecting another condolence letter. Her attention was caught by the name at the top.

'You may recall,' Theo had written, 'that we met a few months ago in Glaston...I realise that you may not wish to think about such things at this time...if and when you feel like it...I am very interested to be involved in the preservation of historic properties and believe Glaston has great potential...perhaps next time you are in Sydney we could have lunch together.'

10.

The cottage I was renting was on the edge of town. Four small rooms and a bathroom out the back, off the verandah. When I looked out my window, the floodplain stretched into the distance. A vivid expanse of green after summer rains; in winter, yellow and tussocky. But even in the midst of drought there were always patches of green on the floodplain, kept that way with water pumped from the dwindling river. The large arms of the irrigators circled remorselessly through summer heat and winter drought.

I spent a lot of time looking out that window. There wasn't much in the garden: the remains of a giant willow that a high wind had brought down, wisteria climbing its rotting trunk; a few ancient roses in the garden bed; a chaotic jasmine smothering everything else and winding its way up the verandah posts.

What I liked best about the place was its endless untidy vista. Five miles of flat country broken by dips and troughs, straggly fences and lines of willows, then the steep blue hills, more purple than blue. But there was nothing idyllic about it. The main road was a stone's throw away, there was a fruit market down the way a bit, and a nursery where I bought a few plants, despite myself. Not knowing if I'd see them grow.

Across the creek I'd often see a cloud of dust rising where a truck was being driven along a dirt track, on its way to the turf farm. Not only was water being taken from the river, soil was being taken from the plain in rolls of turf. Robbie tried to reassure me once, said they kept adding new topsoil, but I was not convinced.

And then there was the railway line. There's no passenger service to Glaston any more, hasn't been since the early eighties, but the freight trains still rolled through and the long grain trains, hauling in the wheat from further out west. Just behind the house was a railway bridge across the creek and at night I'd lie there and hear them coming, then the whole house would shake as the train crossed the bridge, the glass rattling in the old wooden frames.

But in the daytime, in between the trains, I'd look out that window and it was easy to imagine how Glaston was a hundred or more years ago when those unknown forebears of mine had lived here. I'd tried to find out a little more – that's how I knew Tom Harkness had been born in my cottage. But the trail was thin and petered out. Only Tom's name carried on, part of the family that made their fortune with paddle steamers, trading up and down the river. The fortune that allowed him to buy Glastonbridge.

*

Robbie, in his usual long shorts but with a sweater on top against the winter chill, lounged in a low armchair that was in Duane's workshop to be recovered. He said to Duane, 'Norma must've just been one of those people who like collecting real estate, you know. I wonder what Joan will do now?' When Duane didn't respond, he asked, 'Is that Theo's chest-on-chest you're working on?'

'Yep. He wants me to take it down this week.'

'Oh, so you and Theo are seeing quite a bit of each other. Buddies now, are you?'

Duane straightened up and grinned. 'He's a man worth knowing.'

*

When their affair began, Rosemary could not honestly have said she even found Theo particularly handsome. His looks were not the main attraction. But now she could not get enough of them. She'd never known passion like it and wondered where it had come from. Not even the most gorgeous house had ever had this effect on her. Why should Theo, of all the lovers she'd had, inspire this? But she wasn't about to analyse it too closely. Sexual delight was a mysterious, unknowable gift that had blessed her unexpectedly.

She let her fingers stroke his balding pate as he snuggled into the hollow between her hip and thigh.

'What are you thinking?' Theo asked, rearranging himself so he could look into her eyes.

'Just that this is most unexpected. I never thought it'd be this good.'

'Me neither,' Theo admitted. He couldn't precisely pinpoint when things had changed between them, when it had gone from being a pleasant part-time affair to something far more compelling and time-consuming.

'Usually it's either hot right from the beginning or not at all.'

'That's true.'

'At least in my experience,' Rosemary added.

'Not that it wasn't good in the beginning...'

'But it's better now.'

'Yes,' said Theo, and pulled her earlobe fondly.

He had found lately that even when he wasn't with her, he thought about her. This was almost a new experience. It was also a new experience for him to have a lover busier than he, one he had to wait for. He would have liked to spend time during the day with her, but she had her work and, after work, her builders. Time lay on his hands in the daylight hours. He needed a new project.

He rolled onto his back, stretched and took her hand. 'Pity we can't go and see your sister.'

'Well, we could. Sally wouldn't say anything.'

'But what about the rest of them in Glaston? Julia would be bound to hear, one way or another.'

'We could go in camouflage,' Rosemary smiled. 'In my car, and you could wear black instead of white.'

'And it would have to be a weekend, I suppose?'

'Of course.'

'When I'm supposed to be down at the farm. It's getting complicated.' He rolled off the bed.

Rosemary looked at him in silence for a while then propped herself up on an elbow and said, 'If we keep going like this, Julia's going to have to be told.'

'Yes. But not yet.'

His tone told her that was the end of the matter. Rosemary was surprised that she wasn't more distressed. But she was simply confident, confident that it would all be resolved in the end and that nothing would stop them, not Julia, not her sister, not unwelcome gossip. All this was unimportant. They had a great future. Of that she was certain. There was so much they could do.

'Do you know what I'm looking forward to most of all? Working with you. Undertaking some big project with you, something magnificent.'

He leaned down and kissed her throat. 'Something like Glastonbridge perhaps?'

'Now wouldn't that be fun!'

'You weren't serious about wanting to see it turned into a hotel, were you?'

Rosemary shrugged. 'Why not? Almost every building I go into, I hatch plans as to what I could do with it. It's a game, a habit. Maybe I'm a frustrated architect.'

'You're far more inventive than I am,' he said.

'What would you do with Glastonbridge?' she cocked her head.

'Live in it.' He'd said it now, for the first time out loud.

'That'd be all right, too. We'd be near Sally and Titus.'

Joan had a fantasy, too. About the sort of town Glaston could be. From the moment she first saw the rows of old wooden-framed shop windows, the fancy brickwork on the two banks and the town hall, the once-grand department store with its crenellations, she had played with its possibilities in her mind. Joan dreamed of a colonial town with enough of its English parentage showing through but with modifications appropriate to the climate of New South Wales. Like verandahs. She loved the verandahs that jutted over the footpath, supported by shapely wooden or iron posts. She hated it when the verandahs were ripped away and replaced with self-supporting awnings.

When Coles knocked down a row of shops and put in a supermarket at one end of High Street, she refused to go into the ugly pebblecrete and steel monstrosity. She continued to shop at the privately run mini-market at the other end of town. The first hint of a falling out between her and Raymond was because of Coles.

Late one afternoon Raymond sat in her living room hunched in front of the fire, while Joan sat at the table doing paperwork for the shop. From time to time when something Raymond said required an answer, she'd look at him over the top of her reading glasses. But for the most part she displayed no great interest in his being there.

Finally, Raymond looked at his watch and said, 'I'd better get down to Coles before it shuts.'

'You don't shop there, do you,' Joan stated rather than asked.

'Well – well, yes. There's nowhere else, really.'

Joan sniffed. 'There's Denhams.'

Raymond didn't know what to say to this. He rather liked Coles. Everything spread out there before you. No need for a shopping list, which he found impossible to compose. You just walked along the aisles and picked up whatever took your fancy. He spent at least an hour in Coles every week.

'It's very convenient.'

'But it's so ugly. I would have thought, Raymond, that you had more taste.' She slapped an invoice face down on the table and took up the next one.

'It's only a supermarket, Joan.'

Joan ignored this comment. 'They've ruined that end of High Street,' she said. 'I hope you don't buy meat there?'

Raymond dared not admit that he did.

'One should support independent shopkeepers,' Joan declaimed. 'Especially butchers. My father was a butcher.' She glared at Raymond accusingly over her glasses.

'Really? I thought you were related to the Adelaide Beaverstokes. You have lived in Adelaide, haven't you?'

Joan tucked her chin in. 'I was born there. And we are related, distantly.'

'Oh.' Raymond was on the point of asking her which Beaverstokes she was related to: the Basil Beaverstokes or the Beaverstoke-Trents. But he thought better of it.

Joan continued to look stonily at her papers.

'It doesn't matter, I was just interested,' said Raymond.

After a few more moments of silence, he said, 'I'll be off.'

'Goodbye then.' Joan did not get up from the table.

Bloody hide! she thought when he had gone. Bloody snob, preoccupied with family pedigrees.

*

The heat was on in Jules Baillieu's kitchen. Jules gave the heavy saucepan he was holding in one hand a quick shake that sent the melting butter swirling around the pan in a smooth and sizzling curve. He reached out his other hand and adjusted the burner under a second pan. Behind him his staff of three ducked and darted, passing plates and arranging garnishes and wiping spills from the edge of dishes. It was near the end of the lunchtime rush hour and Jules was in his element. Amid the steam and clatter he presided with nonchalance. Turning to the bench behind him he deposited three crisp golden quail on to waiting plates with a calm flourish. Then he stood back to allow Trudi, his assistant chef, to spoon the sauce over the birds. There was a derisive glint in Jules's eyes as he watched Trudi. The glint was directed at himself and his new concoction, the grapefruit sauce that Trudi was ladling. This latest addition to his menu was not as outlandish as some but was still very successful: 'Marinated quail on a bed of radiccio with a piquant grapefruit sauce and toasted almonds'. It had proved almost as popular as last week's special dish, 'Chargrilled black capsicum marinated in Umbrian olive oil with sea urchin infused with iodine and a dash of Pernod, pureed and served in a cornet of sourdough brioche on a bed of Homebush Bay seaweed studded with barnacle meat'. This had been described as 'daring and innovative' in Tuesday's *Herald*. As a result there'd been such a run on it that it was now almost impossible to get a sea urchin in all of Sydney.

It was becoming a game with him to see just how far he could go. It almost seemed there was no limit. Each day as he was doing his preparations he thought of his *grandmaman*, of her kitchen in the old family home in Lisieux where he'd first fallen in love with cooking. It was she who had taught him the first rules of great cooking: sift the flour three times; always stir a roux in the same direction; empty the blood from the neck of the chicken into the pan to thicken the coq au vin. And always throw salt over the left shoulder after salting a cooking pot. He did that now; he wanted his luck to hold.

'I always follow your rules, *ma cherie*,' he told her silently. 'The sauces and garnishes and silly names are just a joke, to see what these foolish *nouveaux gastronomes* will swallow.' And he'd hear her full-bellied laugh, and smile.

When the last of the main courses was served Jules went out the back, sat on a garbage bin and lit a cigarette. He smoked it slowly, listening through the open door to the banter and wisecracking of his young staff. He was preparing for the second act of his performance. Back inside, he removed his soiled apron and cap and took fresh ones from the cupboard. He washed his hands and face, combed back his long dark hair and redid his ponytail, then put on the clean apron and cap. Thus attired he went through to the dining room to greet his customers.

The first person he saw was Theo Roth. 'Hello Theo,' he said and bowed his head. 'You enjoy your meal? What did you 'ave?'

'Ah, I went for one of the simpler dishes,' Theo said, after a slight hesitation. 'I had the filet steak. Very nice it was, too. The *pommes frites* were excellent.'

'A very good choice,' said Jules.

'Perhaps I am not adventurous enough...'

'No, no,' Jules held up his hands, 'you are quite right. There will *ol*ways be one classique dish on the menu, just for you.'

He beamed at Theo in what Theo thought was a rather mischievous way. Surely he wasn't flirting?

'My friend here – perhaps you've met Joan before? Joan Beaverstoke, from Glaston. Joan this is Jules Baillieu. Jules, apart from being Sydney's most innovative chef,' Theo paused for effect, 'is a good friend of Sally and Titus Austinmeer.'

Jules held out his hand. '*Enchanté*.'

'Joan had the osso bucco of salmon with vanilla puree,' said Theo and raised his eyebrows.

'Wonderful,' said Joan, 'very light. What do you recommend for dessert?'

As Jules ran through the desserts, Theo surveyed the room. He was disappointed in the direction Jules's cooking had taken, but others obviously were not. The restaurant was packed.

'What are you having?' he asked Joan.

Jules said, 'I can recommend the iced cappuccino parfait wrapped in chocolate with Kahlua Anglaise.'

'I'll pass on the sweet and just take a short black,' Theo said.

Jules motioned to a waiter to come and take their order, then said goodbye and moved on to chat to other diners.

'Thank you so much for bringing me here,' Joan said. 'I'd heard of Baillieu's, of course, but I never made the connection. Doesn't Jules live with that antique dealer, Philip Dexter?'

'Yes,' said Theo, 'You know Philip?'

'Only by sight.'

'Of course, you've probably seen him in Glaston. He and Raymond are very close. I suppose you see a bit of Raymond?'

'Oh Raymond. He can be so irritating. But he was sweet to me after... after Norma died so suddenly.'

'Yes, it must have been a shock. How long has it been now?'

'Nearly three months,' said Joan, picking at a few crumbs on the tablecloth. 'I'm not from Glaston originally, you know. My first reaction was to pack up and run away. I just felt...well, I won't go into it. Now that I'm over the shock I realise I've been given a great opportunity.'

'That's what I wanted to talk to you about,' Theo said, leaning forward and resting his elbows on the table. 'I like Glaston very much. I think it has a lot of potential.'

'In what direction, do you think?'

'Tourism,' said Theo. 'It's the only way.'

'I didn't know you were interested in tourism?'

'I'm not. I'm interested in buildings, same as you. But there's no way buildings can be restored unless a use can be found for them.'

'I haven't got them yet.'

'But you soon will. Doesn't hurt to plan.'

'Funny,' Joan said, diffidently, 'for years I've dreamt of being able to do this sort of thing. Now I can, I almost don't know where to start.'

'Probably the first thing to do is for us to look at the properties together and start throwing some ideas around.'

'That would be wonderful!' said Joan, her eyes alight. 'Yes, let's.'

*

Raymond stood at the window of the upstairs study, gazing out across the low rolling hills and river flats of the Glass Valley. There was little green to be seen. It had been a cold, dry winter and the grass in the paddocks was short and brown. Raymond was cold. He seemed never to be warm this winter. He'd made a little nest for himself in this room because it was small and faced north-west and had a fireplace that worked. An oak settle stood near the fireplace, loaded with cushions and rugs to soften its hard edges. Beside it was a footstool that was piled with newspapers and magazines. A reading lamp balanced precariously on top of the pile. Around the edges of the room were assorted pieces of furniture in various stages of repair and reassembly. A drawer full of handles, locks and catches sat in the middle of the floor. A marble fire-surround leaned against one wall and a pile of rugs against another. He had unfurled two thick Turkamans to cover the floor and to stop draughts coming up between the floorboards.

As he stood at the window he saw a cloud of dust moving along below the lip of the hill. Bob, going into town to get some pies for lunch. Raymond hunched his shoulders against the cold. He should light a fire. He had a sudden vision of Joan's house and a fire burning cosily in the grate. Yes, a fire would cheer him up. He set about it, taking newspaper from the pile and kindling from the broken-down cardboard box beside the fireplace.

When the fire was blazing he stood up to observe it. It was warming but there was also something utterly depressing about a fire in the middle of the day in an empty room. He turned his back on it, just as Clover knocked on the door.

'Oh, wonderful,' said Clover, 'a fire. It's cold down in that hall.'

'Quickly then,' he said, 'come and warm yourself.'

They stood side by side with their backs to the fire.

'That's better,' said Clover and sat down on the settle, smiling.

Raymond dropped to his haunches and smiled back. What a delight Clover was. The room was suddenly cheerful.

'What were you and Bob arguing about this morning?' she asked, not looking at him, picking at the piping on the sofa.

'Oh, he's annoyed because I've asked Duane to do the kitchen cupboards. Bob wants to do them. He's in a bit of a huff.'

'He'll get over it.'

'Yeah.'

'So Duane's going to be working here?'

'Probably. Joan speaks very highly of him.'

Clover looked away. For weeks she'd been wanting to warn Raymond about Joan, but didn't know how to. There were so many things she couldn't mention to him any more. What she used to love about Raymond was that you could say anything to him; nothing shocked him, no subject was out of bounds. Now almost everything was. She couldn't keep up with the sudden changes in his humour. His moods swung like an erratic pendulum.

'When are you going to Sydney?'

'Tomorrow. A few things I need to do. Better go and see Lil, I suppose.'

*

Raymond was again using Lillian's apartment as his Sydney base. He had worn out his welcome with Philip and Jules. 'It's not that I don't enjoy seeing him,' Philip told Sally, 'but I prefer it to be when we are both washed, shaved and fully clothed. Raymond before breakfast is not an appetising sight.'

Lillian actually preferred Raymond unarmoured. She liked to catch him off guard by going into his room first thing in the morning, on the pretext of bringing him a cup of tea, and haranguing him before he'd even rubbed the sleep from his eyes.

A few times he tried to ward her off, saying, 'I don't want the blasted tea. I just want to be allowed to wake up in my own time.' She'd go away grumbling loudly about how ungrateful he was. He could hear her taking out her rancour on poor Anna in the kitchen.

Then she would sit at the breakfast table grumpily eating. When she had finished, she'd clear the entire table, including the place that had been set for Raymond. Half an hour later, Anna would quietly set out the breakfast things again for Raymond. If Lillian noticed her daily help's small betrayal, she pretended not to.

On this particular morning there was no sign of Lillian when Raymond reached the breakfast table. Anna was relaying his cutlery. He smiled gratefully and she smiled back shyly.

Lillian was in her sitting room, pretending to read a magazine while counting the minutes and thinking, 'Let's see how he enjoys eating breakfast on his own.'

Raymond was enjoying it immensely, particularly with Anna popping in every now and then to see if he needed more toast or extra hot water. He propped the *Financial Review* against the teapot and slathered his toast with honey. At Bamford they had clotted cream with the toast and honey. Clotted cream straight from their own dairy. He hadn't eaten it in years. The next time Anna was passing through the room, he asked, 'I don't suppose there's any clotted cream?'

Anna looked as if she didn't understand him. 'Cream?'

'Yes, clotted cream.'

'I will look,' Anna said. A minute later she came back with a tub of double cream. 'This?'

'Not exactly but it will do,' Raymond said. This Anna really was a gem. He wondered how Lillian managed to keep her.

Unable to restrain herself any longer, Lillian arrived in the breakfast room as Raymond was draining the last of the tea from the pot. 'Good breakfast?' she asked sardonically.

'Oh yes, very nice. Anna's been looking after me. She's a gem.'

Lillian looked away slightly and said in an injured voice, 'I'll probably have to let her go soon.'

'Why's that?'

'Well, I can't afford her, can I?'

Here we go, thought Raymond. 'Now, now, Lillian. I'm sure it's not as bad as that. I don't imagine you pay her much.'

'Thirteen dollars an hour.'

'As much as that?'

'She wants fifteen.'

'Still,' said Raymond dubiously, 'I'm sure she's worth it.'

'I don't know where I'd be without her. Sometimes she's the only human being I speak to all day.'

'It would be a shame to lose her,' Raymond agreed. 'I suppose I could contribute. How many hours does she work?'

'You could pay half. She works three hours five days a week.'

'As much as that!'

Lillian looked offended.

'Oh all right,' said Raymond.

'Well, really,' Lillian said, annoyed at his grudging tone. 'It's the least you can do seeing you've turned me into a pauper!'

'Rot.'

'It's true. I can't even hold my head up in society. What would Daddy think?'

'I haven't worried about what *he* thought in years.'

'That's right,' Lillian snapped, 'mock his memory.' She passed her hand across her breast and started fluttering her fingers against her shoulder. She was close to tears.

Raymond got up from the table and folded up the newspaper. 'I have to go out,' he said, and left the room without another word.

It wasn't true that Lillian never went out. That very night she had been invited to view an art collection that Sotheby's were to auction. She'd ordered the catalogue the week before. Not that she could afford to buy anything but she wanted to give the impression that she could.

In the middle of the afternoon, she had a phone call from Philip. 'I thought you might be going this evening, and wondered if we might go together and perhaps have a bite to eat afterwards?' She had been on Philip's conscience. It was a small thing to pay her a little more attention.

Lillian was almost pathetically grateful. 'I…I thought maybe Raymond and I would go together. But I haven't seen him all day. I wasn't looking forward to going on my own.'

'Oh no, that wouldn't be much fun,' Philip said lightly. 'You must come with me and Jules.'

*

William and Robbie were arranging their dinner service on the shelves of the newly painted kitchen. William was counting the tureens.

'The tureens should go on the top shelf,' Robbie said, looking down from where he stood on the highest rung of the stepladder.

'Oh dear, I'm sure there was ten,' William said, and began to count again.

'There's only nine. The other one got broken when we moved. Remember? Hurry up, I can't stand here forever.'

Robbie tossed his head, making his extraordinary crop of thick red hair glint in the afternoon light. He held out a hand for the next piece of china. He was already surrounded by it, rows and rows of Copeland blue and crimson porcelain: plates and bowls, cups and saucers, sauce boats, platters and vegetable dishes, stretching from bench to ceiling around three sides of the long high-ceilinged kitchen.

'Do you think there?' William asked, passing up the last tureen. 'Isn't it too close?'

'William,' said Robbie testily, 'it'll be fine.' God, William could be irritating.

After arranging the last piece on the top shelf, Robbie stepped down off the ladder to survey the arrangement from the floor.

'You don't think it's too much?' William asked now, uncertainly.

'No, it's good,' Robbie decided. Arms folded, he looked around the kitchen. 'I wish we had enough for the end wall, you know.'

Robbie never shrank from the grandiose. While other garden designers bought sixteen of a particular plant, Robbie bought sixty. While they created white gardens and blue gardens and yellow gardens, each discretely separated from the others by greenery, Robbie planted purples and oranges and pinks all in together then split the garden up into sections using voluptuous swathes of white.

'I'll have to get Raymond over to look at this,' William said. 'He was with me when I bought this set.'

Robbie was up on the ladder again, moving a pair of jugs. He said, 'Oh, I forgot to tell you. Sally rang earlier. Dinner at their place tomorrow night.'

11.

Duane was the only one who knew that Theo had been in town to look at Joan's properties. Theo had made a point of calling in to see him. Duane was immediately intrigued – and a little jealous. He would have liked to have been the one to go into business with Theo, to profit from his experience, to get into something big where he could make real money.

'Could be a great thing for Glaston,' he said to Brenda.

'What's the point of a lot of tarted-up buildings?' Brenda retorted. 'Won't be much help to the families she's going to toss out.'

Duane looked at her scathingly. 'Theo's an important person. Joan's lucky he's interested. Anyway, you oughta be pleased that at last something's going to happen in this town.'

She knew he was right, but Brenda rather liked Glaston just the way it was.

That afternoon at the *Gazette*, she took out a single-column item on the forthcoming Anglican Church sesquicentenary, which she had intended for the front page, and wrote instead:

Entrepreneur for Glaston?

A well-known Sydney property dealer is believed to have visited Glaston to discuss plans for a major redevelopment.

Mr Theo Roth is best known for his chain of real estate agencies. It is believed he came to Glaston at the invitation of Ms Joan Beaverstoke – beneficiary of the estate of the late Norma Sells.

Ms Beaverstoke has inherited about two dozen commercial and residential properties – most of heritage significance but in poor condition. Mr Roth could not be contacted yesterday. Ms Beaverstoke declined to comment.

Joan did more than decline to comment. She told Brenda to mind her own bloody business.

'Glaston is my business,' Brenda replied, more hurt than angry. 'It's my job.'

When Joan rang Duane to chastise him, he said simply, 'Sorry. I didn't realise it was a secret.'

Of course she forgave him.

'So that's what it was all about,' Sally said when Titus brought the newspaper back from town. Sally had heard about Theo and Joan's lunch at Baillieu's. Jules had told Philip, who had passed it on to Sally. But no one had told Raymond.

Then the telephone rang. It was Raymond.

'Yes, I've seen the paper,' she said to him. 'I've just been reading it... Calm down Raymond, we don't know the details...Well, why don't you go and ask Joan? You're friends with her...Oh, that's silly...she's going to need help...Yes, I know. You still could offer to help her. You've said yourself, she is really rather ignorant...I'm disappointed myself. On the other hand it could be a good thing for Glaston...Look why don't you come over tonight? And calm down...All right. About seven.'

'Raymond a bit upset at having Theo on his patch, is he?' Titus asked.

'Out of all proportion.'

'Dear me, he does let things get to him.'

Raymond stood at the door of Joan's house, his arms clamped against his sides, his hands clenched. A cold August westerly blew leaves and twigs across the stone flags and from somewhere nearby came the sound of a loose piece of iron flapping noisily on a shed roof. Raymond knocked on the door and waited. He was not sure what he was going to say to Joan. But he couldn't bear it any longer – he must say something.

'Oh, it's you,' said Joan, and held the door firmly so the wind wouldn't catch it. 'Come in then. Quickly! Before the leaves blow in.'

She shut the door and walked through to the living room and Raymond followed.

'Haven't seen you for a while,' she said.

'Well, you've been pretty busy with someone else, I gather.' There. He'd said it now. He felt sick with apprehension.

Joan just raised her eyebrows at him.

'You're letting yourself be...be influenced. This scheme – it's harder than you think, you know,' Raymond said, his agitation mounting. 'Restoring old buildings. It'll send you broke. He'll have you spending a fortune, and for what?'

Joan turned away from him. Going broke was exactly what she feared. For the first time in her life she had money; she didn't want to lose it.

Raymond went on, sneering now, 'Who in Glaston gives a damn about those buildings except you? Most of them aren't even worth it. You'll have no end of trouble. People won't like it.' He went on and on. Now that he had started, he couldn't seem to stop. She'd have trouble with the council, he said. She'd have trouble with all sorts of people. 'You wait,' he said. 'See what it feels like to be on the other side for a change, to have the heritage people after *you*.'

Joan had very few Trust friends left but she wasn't about to tell him that. Stiffly, she said, 'If you do things properly and keep good relationships with people then you don't get into trouble.'

Raymond was jigging nervously around the periphery of the living room, his body angled away from her. 'What has that Theo said?' he shouted suddenly, facing her. 'What have you two been up to?'

Joan looked at him with disgust. 'If you can't control yourself, you had better go.'

Raymond did one more nervous circuit of the room, his footsteps loud in the silence. Then he headed for the front door. Somehow he got himself outside. The wind was so strong now that he had to lean into it and force his way across the fifty metres to where Brutus was parked under a tree. The car was covered in dust and grit and bits of leaf. He crawled into the driver's seat and sat panting a moment before he had the strength to turn the key.

Sometime in the middle of the night the wind dropped and by next morning an icy calm had settled over the valley. The frost on the low slopes and river flats shimmered like glass in the first rays of sun. No sounds disturbed Glastonbridge, out on its lonely hillside. As the sun rose higher the quiet was broken only by the cawing of a flock of black cockatoos flying over.

The isolation of Glastonbridge had never worried Raymond. Indeed, it was one of its attractions. He didn't want to be reminded of the world. All that interested him now was having the time and freedom to bring to life the image he carried in his head of Glastonbridge as it could be.

Yet he felt forces conspiring against him. Who could he trust? He trusted Clover and Bob. Yes, he did trust them. When they asked for instructions each morning as to what they should work on next he went into a spin of indecision. But at least he could trust them.

Sally had said to him, trying to calm him, 'Why does Theo worry you, upset you so much? To get those buildings restored would be good and if Theo wants to be involved, well…it's not necessarily a bad thing.'

But it was a dreadful thing. Couldn't she see that Theo was stalking him! Couldn't she see it? Now Raymond did feel truly alone. After that evening with Sally and Titus, he went back to Glastonbridge and closed the door on the world. In the library, he pulled from the shelves the books he'd pored over as a youth, the long lists of families and genealogies, the spidery notations he'd made in the margins, adding links and stories of his own. It was soothing to retrace familiar steps, to look for unexplored connections, to immerse himself in lives that were not *this* life. Houses and the people who'd inhabited them spoke to the part of him that yearned for connection, but also to that stronger strand in him: the lure of mystery and the unknown. He opened a clean page and in the middle of it wrote 'Tom Harkness'. A little below it he wrote 'Rose Harkness'. That was all he had so far on the Harknesses. Just two names. But it was a start.

*

The new kitchen at Glastonbridge was not so much a renovation or a restoration as a re-creation. Duane had got hold of a stack of secondhand cedar and drawn up some designs, which Raymond liked. Duane thought this job could really set him up. There were plenty of tradesmen installing 'ye-olde-style' kitchens, but very few who could create something that might almost pass for the original.

Clover was working in the upstairs hallway when the argument started. She went to the top of the stairs, not so much to hear better, more out of concern. She could hear raised voices, Raymond's querulous and demanding. She couldn't quite make out the words. Then she heard a sharp retort from Duane: 'Aw, come on, that's not fair!'

The tempo of the argument was quickening. She wondered what it was about. She felt guilty suddenly, eavesdropping. She went back to her work. Picking up the steel wool, she rubbed it around the tin of wax until it was evenly smeared, then began applying it to the timber panelling, leaning her weight into it as she worked. This was the best part of the process and normally she found it soothing, almost mesmerising, and she would drift off into a reverie from which it was hard to rouse her. But today she could not ignore the raised voices downstairs.

Suddenly, clearly, she heard Raymond screech, 'Are you threatening me?' Then a low murmur from Duane. After a few seconds, during which she remained motionless, her hand poised above her work, she heard a door open and Duane saying: 'Have it your own way then!'

Raymond cursed. The next moment Duane was crossing the downstairs hall. She heard Raymond spit after him, 'Go on, get out. Just get out!' before retreating down the back passage.

Clover stood looking down at Duane. He glanced up at her. 'Silly old coot.'

As he was opening the front door he stopped, as if about to say more. Then he thought better of it and left, leaving the door wide open.

Clover walked slowly down the stairs and across the hall to shut it. Duane was climbing into his utility. She heard the gearbox crunch as he put it into gear. He accelerated away fast, his wheels spinning as he went around the corner of the bumpy track, sending up a cloud of angry dust.

*

When Clover told me about the argument between Duane and Raymond, neither of us thought much about it.

'I'm not surprised really,' she said, 'now that Raymond and Joan aren't getting on...' and left the sentence unfinished.

I still loved to watch Clover work. The concentration, the wood-stained fingers, her lithe grace. But if she caught me watching her, she didn't like it. Or at least pretended not to.

'Don't stare!' she'd say, half severe, half laughing, and try to hide herself behind a nonexistent post. If Raymond happened to be passing, he'd look from one to the other of us, puzzled.

One day about this time he stopped me as I was leaving and asked, 'Have you found out any more about the Harknesses?'

'Only that they operated the boats on the river.'

He nodded. 'But there's a bit of a mystery about Tom. I heard a story once that he went mad. And when he died he wasn't found for a week.'

He gave me a piercing look. Then grinned and turned away.

When Sally hadn't seen or heard from Raymond for a week she called by Glastonbridge. Raymond was on the terrace, transferring several cumquat trees into stone tubs.

'I'm going to put these along the parapet,' he said. 'It had to be something that could take the heat. What do you think?'

'Good,' she said. 'I heard you'd been making progress.'

'Who from?' he asked quickly, suspiciously.

'Clover.' Sally held her hand up against the sun, bright for August. It glinted against the blonde streaks in her hair. 'She said the front hall's finished.'

'Yeah. Want a look?'

When they were inside he said, 'I haven't put any furniture back in yet. I'm hoping to get that monk's settle that Philip found. I thought it would look good in this corner.'

'Mmm. Very ecclesiastical.'

Raymond grinned, lopsidedly. Almost his old grin.

Sally looked around her. 'Raymond, it looks just fabulous. Didn't the floor come up well! You're really getting somewhere. I think it deserves a celebration. Why don't we have a dinner party here? Robbie and I could do the cooking. What do you think?'

'Well, if you like.' He seemed doubtful at first but then the idea seemed to grow on him. 'Which table would we use?'

'Let's have a look.'

He led her from the hall into the morning room. Sally's heart sank. It was even more disorganised than usual. Cupboards, chairs and small tables were piled up, half obscuring the windows.

'Nothing in here,' he said, roving his eye over the stacks of furniture.

The next room, the drawing room, had at one point been quite presentable. Now it was a shambles. More a workshop than a drawing room. But Sally did notice that the walls and ceiling had been repainted.

'Yes,' Raymond said vaguely. 'This room's ready now. I really should clean it up. That table's a possibility.' He pointed to an object covered in a paint-splattered dust sheet. An elegant pair of pedestal legs were just visible. On top were an assortment of paint tins and brushes. 'Oh, but we'd have to move everything,' he said and dismissed it.

'It would be an opportunity to straighten out the room,' Sally said, but Raymond was already going through to the dining room. Here was another pile of furniture.

'I think the best bet is in the library,' he said. 'A nice oak refectory table. Would suit the hall very well.'

He passed through the sitting room with Sally trailing behind. She always thought of it as the clock room because of the collection. Last time they'd been there, Titus had quipped, 'More clocks than Keating,' alluding to the PM.

'Oh yes,' Raymond had said. 'But he only collects French empire. My tastes are a little more...eclectic,' he'd said with his impish grin.

Finally, they reached the library. The Sly bookcases stood on either side of the fireplace, their doors open, books spilling out. In the centre of the room was the refectory table where Raymond had been spending his nights hunched over his books and papers.

'Well, the table is lovely but it would be an awful hassle to try and move it to the other end of the house.'

'I suppose so,' said Raymond, suddenly sounding weary of the whole project, as if ready to abandon the idea.

'I think the one in the drawing room,' she said decisively. 'Where is that table meant to be?'

'The morning room...eventually. That's where the chairs are.'

'That settles it. It will be quite easy to set it up in the hall and move it into the morning room later.'

'The place is a bit of a mess at the moment.'

Sally thought that an understatement but said, 'You *are* getting there! The mess is easily fixed.' She sounded more confident than she felt. 'Just look at the drawing room and the hall – they look terrific. Aren't you pleased?'

'I suppose so.'

*

Theo was waiting for someone to ask him what he intended to do in Glaston and why. But so far no one had. Rosemary would have asked him if she had known about it. But for some reason he resisted telling her. How could he rationalise such an unlikely endeavour? But instinct told him that moving in on Raymond's territory was the only way to keep ownership of Glastonbridge within his sight.

He felt drawn to the place, tied to it almost, by something so profound he found it impossible to analyse. Glastonbridge had a solitary arrogance. He felt that in himself. It was right and proper that he have the house. He refused to contemplate disappointment. Yet how was it to be achieved? Could he wait until Raymond died? But Raymond, he calculated, couldn't be more than sixty or so. He could live another twenty or thirty years! Theo was fifty. He might well die before Raymond. Even if he didn't, he could be into his seventies before he got hold of the place. Too late. He wanted Glastonbridge not in twenty years but soon. Next year.

He suddenly realised that he wanted to live there with Rosemary. He pictured Rosemary as she was the night before: pixie-faced, her hair dishevelled, her soft limbs wrapped around him. He smiled to himself and felt an immediate sexual stirring. She had become essential to him.

Then he was brought up short by the thought of Julia. Julia must be told. It could not be put off much longer. Already, she and Yarralong were receding, retreating into the past even though still part of the present. He would have no regrets about leaving the farm. He imagined that Julia would want it.

Rosemary came into the kitchen and he smiled at her, at her trim loveliness. She was wearing a tight-fitting soft blue woollen suit that showed off her slight shoulders and shapely legs. He loved the way she dressed.

'You know what I was thinking,' she said, taking the bread from the fridge and switching on the toaster. 'Maybe we should think about buying something together. For later.'

'You mean for when we go public?' he teased.

'Yes.'

'I thought you liked my flat.'

'I do, but it's not really big enough for both of us full time.'

'But if we had another place, in the country?'

'Mmm, maybe.' She looked at him curiously. 'I hope you're not think-ing to install me at Yarralong?'

'No, not Yarralong.' He wouldn't tell her yet, not until he was sure.

*

I don't know if Theo knew why he was doing what he was doing. He thought it was to do with a house and perhaps it was. But I don't think it is ever that simple. Glastonbridge was a receptacle for his imagin-ings. A house like Glastonbridge is a window to another world. Isn't that what these places are to any casual tourist who wanders through the vast and glorious rooms of former palaces and tries to imagine what it must have been like to live there?

Glastonbridge wasn't a palace. But that only added to its mystery. There was no logic in such a house in such a setting. It was aping elsewhere. Yet I can't criticise Berge for that. If you are to live in a place, to make a home of it, how can you do that but by transplanting what you have known before on to what you have here, now? The past matters because it never leaves us. The present disappears each and every instant but the past lingers on, growing in our imagination as it fades in our memory.

12.

Lillian sat up in bed reading her bank statements. A lemon headscarf of sheer silk protected her hair and across her shoulders was a mohair shawl. She was adding up how much money she had handed to Raymond in the past six months. The figures horrified her. She could have bought a new car for that. And she needed a new car. Perhaps one of those nice new E series Mercedes that were advertised in the colour supplements of the weekend papers. She had a vision of herself motoring up the coast: the soft-top down, her scarf blowing in the breeze, the brilliant blue of the sea reflecting in her Ray Bans, on her way to holiday with friends at Port Douglas. She did not dwell on who the friends might be. Only on Port Douglas, which must be a nice place if the President had stayed there. She had never been to Queensland. It was time she went.

She picked up the phone beside her bed and rang the Glastonbridge number. Raymond was just turning down the covers, ready to get into bed.

'Raymond,' she said peremptorily, 'I want to go on a holiday.'

'That's a good idea, Lil. Where to?'

'Port Douglas.'

'Oh yes, nice and warm at this time of year.'

'I'll need a new car.'

'Why's that? Surely you'll fly.'

Lillian paused. That hadn't occurred to her. 'I'd rather drive.'

'Well, if you like, but it's a very long way.'

'Doesn't matter, doesn't matter. But I need a new car.'

'Your Audi's only about three years old...'

'Four.'

'Four, then. That's not old. Look at Brutus. You're being silly, Lillian.'

'Don't you patronise me!'

Raymond held the phone but said nothing.

'Raymond!'

'Yes, I'm here but I'm going to bed now. We can talk tomorrow.'

He put the phone down. As he was about to walk away from it he stopped, bent down and pulled the plug from the wall.

Next morning, within half an hour of his plugging the phone back in, she was on the line again.

'I will have a new car if I want and I will go on holiday if I want!'

'All right then, do as you like. The bank'll probably lend you the money.'

'The bank!'

'Yes, I certainly can't...'

'I've given you a hundred and twenty thousand so far this year. I want some of it back!'

'You haven't *given* me anything – you're repaying a loan. You owe *me*, not the other way. Maybe it's time you sold something. You're not using your place in New York. You could sell it and repay me and have money left over.'

'Never!' She slammed the phone down.

She phoned the next day, calmer and determined to be conciliatory. She remembered how easy it had been to get her own way with Harold. She schooled herself to handle Raymond the same way. But Raymond said: 'Lillian, I can't talk now. I've got people coming to dinner...no, of course I haven't got caterers in. Sally and Robbie are doing the cooking...Look, I'll ring you tomorrow...Yes, yes, I'm sorry, too. We'll talk about it tomorrow.'

Titus was about to hang one of Raymond's favourite paintings above the drawing room fireplace when they discovered there was no power. He pushed the trigger on the drill and nothing happened.

Clover and William had gone upstairs to look for the large Chinese carpet that Raymond intended for the drawing room floor. He was sure he'd put it in the nursery.

'Raymond,' said Clover, coming back into the room, 'the lights aren't working. There doesn't seem to be any power.'

Raymond put his hand to his lips. 'Oh dear, I'm sure I paid the bill. I did. I paid it myself about ten days ago.'

'Great,' said Titus. 'How are we going to manage tonight?'

'Oh dear yes, it'll be dark soon,' Raymond moaned. 'Maybe we should call dinner off?'

'Oh no, it will be lovely,' Clover said, eyes shining. 'It will. There's plenty of candles. And some kerosene lamps out in the coach house.'

As dusk fell they fetched candelabra and candles, lamps and matches.

'I put a kerosene lamp at the top of the stairs,' Titus said as he, William and Clover were leaving to get changed, 'and candles in the guest bedroom for Philip and Jules when they arrive. Aren't they in for an interesting night!'

Only the hall, the drawing room and the makeshift kitchen were lit, a soft glow that didn't reach the corners. How strange, thought Raymond, I've never been in the house like this. This is how it must have been when it was first built. It suits.

Clover had laid the table in the great hall with his best silver. He walked around it, fingering the cutlery glowing gently in the candle-light. On the mantelpiece the flickering lights from the candelabra were reflected in the gigantic Jacobean mirror.

A sudden sweep of light across the morning room windows told him Philip and Jules had arrived. He took his torch and went out to the porch.

'My God, Raymond, what *are* you doing? It's black as pitch.' Philip's figure emerged out of the dark.

'No power, but it's rather nice,' said Raymond. He led the way inside. 'It suits the old place, don't you think?'

'Yes, it's nice,' Philip agreed.

'*C'est magnifique!*' exclaimed Jules.

By eight o'clock they had all reassembled in the hall. The men were in evening jackets and bow ties, the women in long skirts. The first toast was, of course, to Raymond, to what he had achieved at Glastonbridge, and the great things still to come.

'Well, I do have hopes,' he said tentatively, 'that by this time next year all the main rooms will be finished, both upstairs and down. The hardest bits are done now. This hall here...well, Clover can tell you how much work's gone into it. Pity you can't see it better.'

'We can see enough to know it's a credit to you both,' Philip said, raising his glass.

'I was thinking,' said Raymond, 'that because candlelight seems to suit so well – the way it reflects in the mirror – that I might replace the electrical sockets in the chandelier with candles. Back to how it used to be. Put the chandelier on a pulley, so it can be lowered to allow the candles to be lit.'

There were a few murmurs of agreement.

'I always thought it was foolish to get too carried away with authenticity. But this house seems to demand to have things done its own way.'

'That's for sure,' said Clover.

'Jules, you must tell me how you did this trout,' Robbie said. 'It's delicious.'

'It is an easy recipe. I give it to you.'

'The thing is,' said Philip, 'what *is* authentic, when you're talking about Gothic? Are we talking about pointed arches, about Norman churches, about eighteenth-century romanticism, Victorian Gothic?'

'I didn't mean stylistically authentic,' Raymond murmured.

'Then what did you mean?'

'I meant, in keeping with the spirit of a place, whatever that spirit might be. Fashion is irrelevant. Arches and curlicues and ornate capitals with birds and beasts and reptiles – that's just decoration, flights of fancy. I-I'm not against flights of fancy,' he said when the others laughed, 'but the essential character of Gothic is...is the materials, the way they're used. Stone and wood, used with skill and...and *passion*. Ruskin said the essence of Gothic was its savageness and naturalism, its rigidity and redundance. Contradictions. All contradictions. Not like the classical, all straight lines and symmetry. That's what I mean about the spirit of the place,' he said with a rush that ended in silence.

'You're quite right, of course,' said Philip quietly. How he enjoyed Raymond when he was like this. He saw it so rarely these days.

Clover got up to replace some of the candles. She loved the candlelight, the way it moved and flickered across the walls, casting sudden shafts of light when reflected in mirror, glass or flashing knife. Tonight, for the first time ever, the hall felt warm and welcoming. It was usually such a cold room. But tonight the logs in the enormous fireplace had succeeded in dispersing the persistent chill. The dozens of candles cast a yellowish glow across the stone walls so that they seemed almost cheerful. She replaced two candles in a wall bracket, then stopped and looked back towards the group gathered around the table. How she would love to freeze this image: the heavy silverware glinting dully on the rich brocade cloth, the murmuring voices, the glasses filling with wine. It was a scene that could be from any time if one didn't look too closely; if one didn't see Philip's short-back-and-sides or the Rolex on William's wrist. She wondered sometimes if Glastonbridge did something to people as soon as they walked in the door. Took them over somehow, so that everything that belonged to the world outside became odd and out of place within its walls.

Tonight, for example. She felt that tonight the house was flaunting itself, wooing them all. Just at the point when some of them, at least, had been beginning to despair. It seemed to say, 'You see? This is how I am meant to be.'

And this is how it would be, Clover told herself. Eventually. When Raymond finished.

Later, while Titus went through to the kitchen to dish up dessert, the rest of them sat around the table, sipping their wine, their chairs pushed back and top buttons undone.

'Thank you Sally for suggesting this,' Raymond said fervently. 'It really, really is wonderful to have you all here. It's made me feel much better about the place. I suppose I was starting to get a bit down.'

'You need to enjoy the house Raymond,' Philip said. 'What's the point otherwise? Life's too short to bury yourself alive up here.'

'You're right,' Raymond sighed.

'Tomorrow, said Jules, coming in from the kitchen, 'we are going to arrange the furniture.'

'Yes Raymond, it really is time,' Philip said.

Raymond grimaced guiltily. 'Except that – there's not much point really because I've decided to change the ceiling colour in the three main rooms down here.'

'Oh Raymond!' several of them chorused.

Philip just looked at him.

When Philip and Jules had gone to bed and the others had departed, Raymond sat for a while at the empty table. He had forgotten what it was like to sit around a table in his own home, with friends, relaxed. It made him think of Bamford. Was it the last place where he'd had this same sense of contented belonging? Everywhere in between had been a staging post. At the flat, he'd hardly even tried to make a home. And at the Hunters Hill house he'd never been really comfortable. It was his mother's house, chosen by her to fit the kind of life she'd wanted to lead at that stage in her life. He hadn't minded; she'd enjoyed it. Not like Lillian. It didn't seem to matter what Lillian had, she never enjoyed it. He must ring her tomorrow. He clicked his tongue nervously.

One by one the candles gutted until there were only two. The house was silent save for the ticking of the clock. He'd brought his favourite James II clock in for the occasion and put it on the mantelpiece. While he was contemplating it, it struck the quarter hour. He could just make out the clock face. After one – time he was in bed. Still he didn't move.

This was how he would like it always. The room ordered and magnificent around him, a full meal in his stomach, good friends asleep in a room upstairs. It wasn't so much to ask, so why had it taken this long to achieve it? And would it look and feel the same tomorrow, when there was no sympathetic candlelight? When the harsh sun came in the windows and showed up all the faults, all that was still to be done. He knew he'd look up at the ceiling tomorrow and be unhappy with it. Should he just let it be, as the others urged?

But it had to be right.

And tomorrow morning he must ring the electricity company. Find out why the power went off. He was sure he had paid the bill. What could it mean? Using his elbows he pushed himself out of the high-backed chair. He turned on the torch and blew out the remaining candles. Then he crossed the hall and shuffled down the narrow, back corridor towards his bed in the butler's pantry.

13.

Theo had taken to ringing Duane every week or two.

'I suppose Joan has told you what we're thinking of doing in Glaston?' he said.

'Yeah, yeah, she did. It'll be a good thing for the town.'

'You like the idea?'

'Sure.'

'I gather Raymond isn't so keen.'

'Oh Raymond – I wouldn't take too much notice of him. He's a mad old coot. I had a big barney with him.'

Barney. Theo hadn't heard that word in years. He wondered sometimes which crack in time Duane had crawled out of. He was both older and younger than his years; innocent and cynical, streetwise and old-fashioned. 'A fight? Why?'

'Aw. He wanted me to do his kitchen. I bought a whole lot of timber. Would have been perfect. Cedar – beautiful. Hard to get. Then he accuses me of trying to cheat him. So now I'm stuck with the stuff.' Duane had a sudden urge to confide in Theo, to tell him about cutting

Raymond's power off. It was a good joke, particularly doing it the night they were all going to be there. Serve the old bastard right.

'Well, you never know,' Theo laughed, 'Joan and I might be able to use that wood.' Then seriously, 'Could be quite a lot of work for you if our project comes off. If we get development approval.'

'You serious then?' Duane asked. There was something in his tone that caught Theo off guard.

'Well...yes.'

'I thought it was Glastonbridge you were after?'

Theo laughed. 'Glastonbridge isn't available, is it.'

'Beats me why anyone would want it. Place gives me the creeps. You know they say it's haunted?'

'I have heard that.'

'Just thought I'd better warn you,' Duane joked. 'I bet they reckoned it was haunted the other night!'

'Why, what happened?'

'Power went off, didn't it. My little joke. Don't you tell a soul!' he added quickly.

'I won't. You mean you cut his power off?'

'Yeah, it was easy. Just rang up the power company. But, listen, I shouldn't have told you...'

'Don't worry,' Theo said, 'I won't say a word. And speaking of that,' he lowered his voice. 'People know I'm keen on Glastonbridge but I don't want to fuel the gossip.'

Duane assured him he wouldn't.

'Right then,' said Theo before he hung up, 'keep up the good work!'

There was a time, not long after Theo married Julia, when he thought he had reached the peak of his desires. She was such a beauty. They made such a team. It was as though he had, finally, arrived. And now? Now all of that was nothing. It wasn't that his wife was a stranger. He knew each small tremor of her being, each tiny reflex. Yet he viewed them from a distance. He had the knowledge but had lost the reverence.

What then did he revere? Glastonbridge? How he longed for it. For the test of it. He waited for it to push him that one step further. It was for this that he most resented Raymond. That he could live in that sublime space so carelessly.

But it was just a house. Theo told himself this, many times. To think as he was thinking was wrong, he knew it. To plot against another person, even if you didn't act on it – he didn't believe he would act on it. It was one thing to fantasise about Raymond suddenly disappearing off the planet. It was another thing to actually do it. How would he do it? He knew people who knew people who could arrange such things. One did not work in the property industry in Sydney for thirty years without making such acquaintances. But he had always been careful that they were no more than that.

Usually Theo reached this point in his reverie and stopped, shocked at himself. He and Raymond had once been friends. Or, at least, theirs had been a friendly rivalry. He was becoming obsessed. Theo always tried to balance his conscience by making a point of being generous if he knew he had been tough; by allowing himself to be occasionally ruthless as long as he was thoughtful. But there was no counterweight for obsession on the moral balance sheet.

And then there was the problem of Julia. Theo knew it was time to tell her.

She heard him out in silence. He waited for tears, remonstrations, anger. But they didn't come. Instead, she continued to sit on the lounge with Ralph, her favourite dog, lying across her knees. After about a minute's silence, she pushed Ralph off her legs and stood up.

For the first time, Theo dared to look at her. He couldn't believe it. She was smiling!

'This is, well, this is quite a relief,' she said. 'I didn't know how I was going to tell you.'

'Tell me what?'

Julia ran her long brown fingers through her sun-bleached hair. 'Um, well, I'm involved with someone, too.'

'Who?' he asked, astounded. He hadn't expected this. It had seemed to him that the only thing Julia expended any passion on was her dogs.

'Ted Grover.'

'Who the hell is Ted Grover?'

Julia looked at him with disgust. 'The vet's locum. The guy who came out in the middle of the night to pull that dead calf.'

'Oh, him.'

'You would have met him if you'd bothered to get out of bed,' Julia said.

'So it hasn't been going on long?'

'Three weeks. Long enough to know that this is it, the real thing.'

What had he been? he wondered.

'And you?' she asked. 'Is she anyone I know?'

'You don't know her. Her name is Rosemary Larsen.'

'How long's it been going on?'

'Five months.'

'You bastard.'

*

When it rained, my cottage was dark inside, mysterious. On wet days, I'd sit by the window and listen to the drip-drip of rain in the downpipes, the drip-drip from the drooping shrubs. Or, if the rain was heavy, watch it cascading out of the overflowing gutters onto the garden bed. On such days it was a forlorn place and truly looked its age.

I finally started going through the boxes I'd been schlepping around for years: boxes from my mother, and from her mother. In one I came across folders from my great-aunt Sarah, the one I stayed with here in Glaston years ago. She was obviously interested in family history, like a lot of old people. I had no such interest. But because I was in Glaston, and some of these people had lived here, I found myself running a finger up and down family trees. Mostly the names meant nothing to me. But occasionally the name Glaston would leap out at me: a place of birth or the site of a wedding.

It was a wet spring after the winter drought, day after day of drizzle, so I had plenty of time. Raymond went off to Melbourne to stay with one of the old ladies he was always mentioning.

'The rain depresses him,' Clover said. 'I don't think he really likes Glastonbridge when it rains.'

But a few days later he was back. The rain cleared and he and Bob started getting out the paint tins again.

After the dinner party, I began to think about Glastonbridge in a new way. Since I'd been in Glaston the house had really been two separate houses to me. There was the one I took an interest in because it was Raymond's home, and there was the other Glastonbridge, the one buried deep in a child's memory; the one my great-aunt had taken me to.

There are mysteries in life that one can live with, filaments of the shadowed past that add intrigue to one's life but do not dominate it. And there are half-told stories that get passed on in bits and pieces from one generation to the next and seem to grow in the telling and retelling. Family myths. And perhaps it is only when an event occurs again that the kernel of an old myth explodes into the present. Then you know there are ghosts and that their purpose is to make sure one never forgets.

I knew I was pushing away my own story – how a woman my age washes up in a place like Glaston – and dwelling instead on those names from a past I never knew. There was a name my great-aunt Sarah had kept writing, over and over again, in her notebooks, with question marks, as if she didn't know where she fitted, what became of her. Kathleen. She was linked somehow to my family story. And I tried to imagine what her life might have been. Did she grow up here beside the river? How different it must have been then, flowing full and fast. Great forests of cedar running down the slopes onto the floodplain. The Worimi people newly dispossessed of their country. Chased away, killed, as the forests fell.

A forest of cedar must have gone into Glastonbridge alone.

*

It was when the power went off for the second time that Raymond became uneasy. Could it really be a mistake, as the electricity company said the first time? He rang them again. He got a different person this time, not the nice young woman he had spoken to ten days before, but a rather surly man.

'What, you changed your mind, have you?'

Raymond tried to explain that he had never asked for his power to be disconnected. 'I-I don't mind about the lights so much but I really need it for the refrigerator and the telly. And for the power tools.'

'So you want it back on?'

'Yes, please.'

Raymond tried to pretend to himself that the whole thing was a silly mistake. But in the pit of his stomach he felt threat hanging over him.

By the second week in September, winter had departed Glaston. The daffodils were out in Sally's garden and she brought a large bunch of King Alfreds over for Raymond. Brutus was parked outside but there was no sign of Raymond. In the kitchen was one of the ornate black and gold vases that they'd used at the dinner party. Sally arranged the daffodils in it and put it on the mantelpiece in the hall. There was no point in trying to decorate any of the other rooms. She stood back to admire the effect, then went looking for Raymond.

She found him in a makeshift workshop behind the coach house, cleaning an elaborately carved oak fire-surround. He looked up and saw her standing in the doorway.

'Oh hello Sal. Didn't see you there.'

'I brought you some daffodils. They're in the hall,' she said.

'Oh that's nice,' he said. 'Lillian likes daffodils.'

'Is she coming up?'

'She says she is. Tomorrow. But I don't know if she will. She keeps changing her mind. Ring, ring, ring, ring, ring. And every time, she's doing something different. Frankly, I hope she doesn't come. She wears me out.' He sighed.

Just then Clover shouted from the house: 'Raymond, Lillian's on the phone.'

'Oh dear.'

'I've got to go,' said Sally. 'I have to get to the bank.' She paused to admire the fire-surround while Raymond went inside. A few minutes later, when she was about to leave, he reappeared, looking paler than before and agitated.

'She really is horrible,' he said. 'Horrible. Horrible things she says.'

'What sort of things?' asked Sally.

Raymond just shook his head.

*

Within a week of telling Julia, Theo had moved out of Yarralong and Ted Grover had moved in. Theo and Julia agreed they would split the furniture. Julia of course would keep the children. It was too soon, and they were too young, to talk about them spending weekends with Theo in Sydney. He was going to miss the kids, he realised, as he loaded the remaining icons into the boot of the Rolls. He'd never been a very involved parent but he had enjoyed the limited time he spent with them. The little one, Alexander, sat on the hall floor and watched with wide expressionless eyes as Theo carried the icons out to the car. Sasha was hiding in the garden somewhere. She emerged reluctantly when he yelled out to her that he was going. She let him hug her goodbye but turned her head away to avoid his kiss.

Back in Sydney, Theo stacked the icons, each wrapped in bubble wrap, on the floor of his study. Rosemary, seeing them there, gave a sad sigh.

'If only Raymond could be persuaded to sell Glastonbridge,' she said out of the blue. Then she slipped an arm around Theo's substantial waist. 'That's the setting they need.'

'Who knows, anything is possible.'

'I'm seeing Sally tomorrow night,' Rosemary said. 'I'm going to tell her about us.'

'That'll cause a bit of a stir in Glaston,' Theo said.

'Not to mention Queen Street,' said Rosemary.

In Queen Street, they already knew. At the opening night of the new Barrie Kosky opera, Lady Regan told Philip that Julia Roth had gone off with a jackaroo.

'I don't think he's a jackaroo,' Philip said, adjusting the collar of his shirt. 'I heard he was a vet.' Lady Regan waved her hand as if the difference was insignificant.

'And from what I understand,' Philip went on, 'it's Theo who has moved out. And left Julia the property *and* half the furniture.'

This is what surprised people the most.

Jules said, 'He must 'ave spent a great deal of money on that 'ouse. To just walk away from it...' he twisted his shoulders theatrically. 'And,' he lowered his voice, 'for that 'ysterical Rosemary Larsen.'

'Jules,' warned Philip, then said, 'they are both very interested in property. They have that in common.'

'Who is this Larsen woman?' asked Lady Regan, wiping the remains of a chicken and lettuce sandwich from her lips.

'Rosemary is Sally Austinmeer's sister.'

'Oh really? I imagine she has some taste then.'

'Very tasteful.'

'Do you realise,' said Sally to Titus a few days later, 'that we may end up with Theo as a brother-in-law? Isn't it strange?'

'Little doubt about it, I'd say. Ro seems to think she's found her man,' Titus said from behind the pages of *Cellar Talk*.

'Yes,' said Sally slowly. 'Well, I quite like Theo. I wonder how Raymond will take it.'

'Oh God,' said Titus. He put down his magazine. 'I hadn't thought of that.'

'Hadn't you? I've been thinking of little else. I suppose it's up to me to tell him – before anyone else does.'

*

Raymond sat on a pebblecrete bench in the shopping plaza with his trolley load of plastic bags in front of him. He'd bought his groceries an hour before but he continued to sit in the shopping centre, watching weary working mums and dads with trollies loaded high. It was Thursday evening – late night shopping. He should go home now, before it got dark, but he didn't want to. Lillian had been telephoning. She kept abusing him, snarling at him. Sometimes six times a day. It was worse than ever before.

Then there was this other business with the electricity. What could it mean? Every time he went into the house he dreaded flicking a switch in case the power was off again. It made him nervous, even though he tried to talk sensibly to himself. Accidents did happen, coincidences did happen. An awful sense of foreboding settled on him whenever he went inside the house. He couldn't bear it.

Life was so simple for some people. You went to work each day and came home each night. You went out into the garden and picked a bunch of flowers. You flicked a switch and there was power. You answered the phone and someone spoke to you pleasantly, coherently. Not like the horrible screeches, and worse silences, that he was getting. Sometimes the phone rang and there was no one there.

He hauled himself to his feet and pushed his trolley towards the car park.

Sally dropped by Glastonbridge on her way into town that Thursday evening. On the drive over she steeled herself to tell Raymond about Rosemary and Theo. 'I know he's going to take it badly,' she told Titus. 'He's going to blame me. I just know it.'

She found the house wide open but there was no sign of anyone. The daffodils, dead by now, were still in the vase where she'd put them. Sally wandered through the house looking for Clover. The mess, if anything, was worse. The drop sheets and ladders and tins of paint were back.

She couldn't find Clover. When she got back to the hall, Raymond was there, sitting half-slumped at the table, surrounded by shopping bags. 'Oh hello,' he said, straightening up.

'The door was open so I thought someone would be here somewhere.'

'Ah, I just ducked into town. Thought Clover was here, though,' he said, looking around as if he expected her to pop up from behind a cupboard. 'We tend to lose track of each other around here. Thank you for the flowers,' he said, looking up at the dead bunch. 'I should get them some more water.' He stood up and moved towards the kitchen, carrying some groceries. Sally was struck by how frail he seemed.

'No sign of Bob either,' she said. Sally didn't have much confidence in Bob. She thought it was typical of him to skip off home and leave the place wide open.

'Ah,' said Raymond again. 'I sent him home this morning. Couldn't get anything done today. No power.'

'Again?'

'Third time.'

'Raymond, you're not serious. What's going on? What did the power company say?'

He shook his head and sat down again.

Sally flicked a switch and the lights came on. 'Well, it's on again now. Should I put the kettle on?'

'Oh, oh, I've got to go out again. Sorry.' He moved towards the door.

She followed him. 'Raymond! Raymond, there's something I have to tell you...'

But he was already out on the steps. 'Just realised I forgot something in town. Sorry.' He got into Brutus and gave her an ineffectual little wave as he turned the ignition.

He had nowhere to go, really. But being in the house was intolerable, and trying to explain to Sally even more so. He drove off down the rutted track, Brutus bumping and swaying. At the gate, he turned towards town, but only in case Sally was watching him. He would just drive around for a while.

It was getting dark and it was still chilly in the evenings. He didn't have a jumper with him. Still he went on. He drove for a long time down a straight, narrow road that ran between lucerne paddocks, right across to the far side of the floodplain. As he reached the hills the road began to rise. Steep curves took him between tall ghost gums. The massive trunks loomed towards him as the headlights illuminated them. A black canopy of branches met overhead. It spooked him. He took the first turnoff he came to and double-backed towards the town. When he saw the first lights he began to breathe more normally. He drove over a rise, past a line of solid brick homes set in wide gardens and overlooking the floodplain. Through the lighted windows he could see families settling down for the evening. The flickering glow from television sets behind sheer curtains. He felt like a visitor from Mars.

He knew that if he wanted to, he could go to one of his friends and be welcomed. Yet he hesitated. Not because he didn't wish to intrude. He'd often timed his visits to William and Robbie's so as to arrive just as Robbie was putting the spuds on. But tonight he hesitated because he was afraid. Too afraid to talk about it, too afraid even to admit to the fear.

It was after nine when he finally returned to Glastonbridge. Clover had left the porch light on for Raymond. It glinted cheerfully at him through the bushes as he drove up the driveway. Raymond smiled in relief when he saw it.

Next morning, however, when he opened the fridge to get some milk for breakfast, the interior of the fridge was dark. The power was off again.

Sally telephoned later in the morning. Raymond hadn't even rung the power company yet. He didn't know what to say to them. He sat in the kitchen, shivering. When he answered Sally's call, his voice was little more than a murmur.

'Raymond, what's the matter? Speak up.'

'The power's off again,' he said, louder.

'You're joking! Oh this is ridiculous. Have you rung them? Look, let me do it. I'll call you back.'

Later she rang to tell him that she had arranged with the power company that his power was not to be disconnected unless he went into the office in person and requested it. 'Someone's been playing a practical joke on you,' she told him, trying to make light of it.

'Not a joke,' he said.

'Well no, it's not funny.' She did think it very odd. Who in Glaston would do such a thing? And why?

'I-I-I won't give in.'

'Give in? What are you talking about?'

'I won't, I won't.' And he hung up.

When she told Titus, he said: 'Poor old chap's had a fright. I mean, that house, without any lights, it's bloody creepy. It was okay the night we were all there. But when he's there on his own…Maybe we should invite him over here to stay? I'll call him.'

But Titus's conversation with Raymond was even odder than Sally's. Titus related it to William and Robbie.

'When I asked him to come and stay, he said, "It's very nice of you, but I can't. I can't leave the furniture." That's all he kept on saying: "I can't leave the furniture".'

Robbie said, 'You could hardly suggest he bring it with him. I think Raymond's going a little odd, you know?'

'Oh Robbie,' said William nervously.

'He's afraid of something,' said Sally. 'He's terribly afraid.'

'It could be that Lillian has shaken him up in some way,' said William. 'Did I tell you about that time I was staying at Glastonbridge? When Robbie arrived in the middle of the night?'

Titus and Sally shook their heads.

'Well, it was like Raymond had woken in the middle of a bad dream. He stood in the hall in his nightshirt hissing, "It's Lillian, it's Lillian. She's come to get the money".'

'Oh dear,' said Sally, half laughing, sadly. 'And you know I *still* haven't had a chance to tell him about Rosemary and Theo. He's not going to like it.'

'He can hardly blame you for what your sister does,' Robbie said.

William and Sally looked at each other.

*

Glastonbridge recast its spell on all of us the night of the dinner party. I had a sense of what it might have been. What, perhaps, it could be.

'This old house has some stories,' Raymond said to me one day when I was visiting. He put his hand against the stone wall. 'People look at a place like this, at the house or some of the furniture, and the first thing they ask is "How old is it?" It's never the right question.'

He said no more, just stood there, with his back half-turned to me. Finally, out of curiosity, I asked: 'So what is the right question?'

'Why,' he said quickly, turning to face me. 'That's the only question – why?'

Most of us find meaning in the most ordinary of places. But some go looking for it down bizarre byways. Was he burrowing into the past to find a meaning for his own life? Was that what he was trying to do? Perhaps that's what we were all doing: Titus with his antiquated methods of wine-making; William with his encyclopaedic knowledge of early porcelain – the social conditions under which it was made, the reasons behind the methods. Finding meaning in very personal and individual ways. Robbie said to me once, 'I never feel so alive as I do when I'm in the garden, with my hands buried in soil – the plants, the soil, the wind all seem to be speaking to me, you know?'

*

Theo sat in his study surrounded by his icons. They looked at him and he looked at them. It was as if he were waiting for them to tell him something. He had sometimes wondered why it was that the icons mattered so much to him. He'd never found an answer.

Rosemary was worried about him. He was so much quieter than usual, more introspective. She wondered if he was praying. She worried that he might feel she had pushed him into leaving Julia, rushed him. Yet when she said this, he dismissed it.

What Theo was actually feeling was a deep stillness, an intense, inexpressible anticipation. This must be what it's like to discover a religious vocation, he thought. The future seemed very clear and simple and certain. Rosemary was only partly responsible for this. It was good to have a lover who was an ally. Rosemary had a knack of making everything seem straightforward, so that even those ambitions which he had so closely and secretly guarded became with her simple, even obtainable desires. For the first time in his life his mental picture of himself was not of a solitary figure.

Yet he felt she would be shocked if she knew the depth of his passion to own that house. She enjoyed houses but in the end they were only bricks and mortar. She would be just as happy with some other grand house. He couldn't explain to her why it had to be Raymond's house. He doubted whether anyone other than Raymond himself would understand.

Rosemary rang Sally on Saturday morning and asked if she and Theo could come up to Glaston for lunch. She'd been waiting for an invitation; it was more than a week since she'd told Sally the news. When she invited herself, Sally sounded delighted: 'Don't just come for lunch – stay the night.'

For Theo it was an opportunity to confer with Duane, to pursue their *folie à deux*. And of course to see Joan. The Rolls was almost out of petrol when they arrived in Glaston so Theo pulled into the first service station he saw. As he stepped out of the car, he found himself staring straight into the eyes of Raymond, on the other side of the bowser, filling up Brutus's tank.

'Oh. Raymond,' he said, starting.

Raymond glared at him then muttered, 'Hello Theo,' and began fiddling with his petrol cap.

Rosemary got out of the car and called across to him. 'Hi Raymond, we're just on our way to Sally's.'

Now it was Raymond's turn to look stunned. He said nothing but kept on looking at her.

'Are you okay, Raymond?' she asked.

He turned to Theo. 'I thought you'd be here to see Joan.' He almost spat it out.

Theo had regained his composure. 'I'll be seeing her, too. But mainly we've come up to stay with Sally and Titus.'

Theo was surprised by Raymond's appearance. He was so changed. He'd lost a lot of weight and his skin was blotchy. Not a good colour. 'You don't look well, Raymond,' he said.

'I'm all right!' Raymond snapped. Without another word, he turned towards the driver's door, got into Brutus, started the engine and drove away. He hadn't paid.

A man sauntered out of the office. 'That was Mr Tyler. He'll fix me up next time. Nice car,' he said, looking at the Rolls.

The lunch with Sally and Titus would have been more successful if they hadn't mentioned meeting Raymond. Sally's face immediately took on a worried frown, which irritated Rosemary. It was the same frown she'd worn when she had tried to restrain Rosemary's aberrant teenage behaviour. It was a frown that made you feel responsible for having made her frown.

'Raymond's been having a terrible time,' Sally said. 'I'm worried about him. He really needs to get away for a break.'

'I don't suppose he's thinking of selling the house, is he?' Rosemary asked brightly.

Theo immediately changed the subject by asking Titus if he could recall the best meal he had ever eaten. This was a subject that could be sustained indefinitely.

After lunch Theo went into Glaston. His main plan with Joan was, for the moment, to stall her. The meeting with Duane would be more delicate.

Rather than park out the front of Duane's shop, Theo went around to the lane at the rear and came in the back door. Duane was with a customer but saw him and raised an eyebrow. When the customer had gone he turned to Theo, who said, 'I thought we should have a little chat.'

Joan was not entirely satisfied with her own little chat with Theo. He advised caution. 'No need to frighten the locals,' he said. 'Let them get used to the idea.'

But Joan knew the locals; she knew the longer you gave them, the more arguments they would muster against her plans. Some of her former colleagues on the Trust would rather see the buildings fall down than have them redeveloped for 'inappropriate' purposes. And there was Raymond, going around town stirring up trouble, wanting to stymie her, for no reason that she could see except sheer contrariness.

'I don't like the idea of having Raymond offside,' Theo told her. Joan nearly exploded. Why should Raymond's opinion matter so much?

'Are you going off the idea?'

'Remember that's all it is at the moment, Joan – an idea. Take things quietly, let all this concern die down and probably in eighteen months you'll be able to do whatever you like.'

Joan scowled, 'Only if Raymond leaves town.'

Theo looked at her curiously. 'I thought you two were friends?'

Joan sniffed but didn't answer. It embarrassed her to remember the hours and hours she'd spent with Raymond after Norma's death. She recoiled from thinking about how she'd been then: so weak, so pathetic, so vulnerable. She must have been vulnerable to let bloody Raymond near her. She hated him seeing her like that. She didn't want anyone to see her like that.

14.

Raymond woke suddenly in the middle of the night. He held his breath, wondering what it was that had disturbed him. He could just make out the distant sound of a car. That was nothing to worry about. He sometimes heard the occasional car or truck if it was a quiet night. But there was something else as well. Shouts? He listened hard but heard nothing. He began to breathe more easily. Once, in the early days here, he had lain awake one deep, still night, suffused with contentment. His limbs light, his mind unclouded. Such a wonderful feeling. He'd lain quietly in the dark listening unperturbed to the noises of the night. At peace. It was a long time since he'd felt that way.

All his anxieties marched towards him. He tried to ignore them by visualising how Glastonbridge would look when it was complete. He took a mental walk from room to room. He would consult Sally on curtains for the breakfast room – something fresh and friendly. Then he remembered Sally's disloyalty. Her sister and Theo. She'd kept it secret from him – how could she? He twisted in his bed and thought about the drawing room instead. But that made him think of Titus; Titus standing on a ladder jovially holding a painting. That was the afternoon of the first power cut. At least they seemed to have stopped. There hadn't been one for a fortnight. He reached over and turned on his bedside lamp, just to be sure.

Two days later, on the morning of his sixtieth birthday, Raymond was woken by the sound of breaking glass. He was already half out of bed before his eyes were properly open. Then he stopped, trembling, trying to focus. What was it? Was he dreaming? He crouched on the edge of his bed, clutching his pyjama pants, the fly still gaping open from where he'd fumbled with himself before dropping off to sleep. His bony feet were cold on the stone floor. He held his breath, listening hard. In the distance, the sound of a car driving away.

Dawn was just breaking as he crept through the house. The deep crimsons in the eastern sky lightened and faded to pale pink then turned golden. The first light advanced across the drawing room floor as he entered. He didn't see the hole in the window until he trod on some broken glass. He cursed and hobbled over to a chair, leaving drops of blood in a trail behind him. He sat on the chair and looked at the high broken windowpane, at the glass on the floor and the large rock lying among it.

He sat like that, his handkerchief wound around his foot, until it was light enough to safely walk around the broken glass. While he waited in that deep-shadowed, high-ceilinged room, he thought about the time he got into a fight at school and Billy Sheldon hit him on the nose. The way it bled! He'd had to sit in the headmaster's office with a snotty, bloody handkerchief to stop the bleeding until his mother came and got him. He'd been terrified of Billy Sheldon after that, terrified, but knew he couldn't show it. He had to brazen it out. It was his first lesson in bravura. Could he muster it again?

Philip rang just after breakfast to wish him happy birthday. 'Are you going over to Sally and Titus's for dinner?'

'No. No,' said Raymond. 'They asked but...'

'You're not still punishing them because of Rosemary and Theo, are you?'

Raymond didn't answer.

'That's really silly, and mean, of you. It's not Sally's fault. She wanted to tell you herself but never got the chance.'

'I can't help it,' Raymond said. 'I just can't feel the same as I did. It's – it's...Oh, it's just too complicated.'

'Raymond,' said Philip wearily. 'When are you coming to Sydney? I'll take you out for a meal.'

'I can't.'

'Can't?'

'I can't leave the house.'

'Why on earth not? You've left it plenty of times before.'

He noticed that Raymond was breathing heavily.

'I just can't,' said Raymond.

Now Philip waited.

'I can't because someone's after me. I'm afraid they might burn the house down.' Was he afraid for the house? Or of the house? He couldn't decide.

'Raymond, I think you need a break. Come and stay with us for a few days.'

But Raymond made excuses and hung up.

He told no one about the rock through the window. He cleaned up the broken glass. When Clover and Bob noticed the hole in the window, he said a stone had flown up while he was mowing the terrace.

The best thing with tormentors was to ignore them. That's what his mother had told him when he was little.

'They only do it to get a reaction,' Lady Tyler had said to him, tucking his shirt into his shorts and pulling them up so violently that he was almost lifted off the ground. 'If you don't react, they'll stop.'

That's what he was trying to do now. Trying to pretend it wasn't happening. Trying to carry on as normal. He didn't want to speak of it. He didn't want to acknowledge it. Yet when he was on his own he thought of little else. He never asked himself why, why him? The answer was obvious, so obvious there was no point in asking it. He did ask himself, once, who he could turn to for help. Faces appeared before him. At each one he shook his head. Perhaps Philip? But Philip was too far away. He'd probably think he was mad.

'Raymond.' Clover was standing at the door. She moved restlessly from foot to foot, working her heels. 'I wondered whether you might like me to stay over in the house for a few nights.'

He stared at her from under his eyebrows. His eyebrows seemed bushier because his face had grown so thin.

'No need, no need,' he said, continuing to stare.

'Only, you seem a bit worried lately.' She ran her hands through her hair. 'I thought you might like the company.'

He shook his head. 'Thank you Clover.'

'It's a while since you went to Sydney. Maybe a break away...'

He shook his head vigorously.

So much pressing in on him, it was impossible to sleep. Most nights now he stayed up, sitting at the refectory table in the library with his books and papers around him. When he tried to lie down the pressure on his chest made it hard to breathe. He'd sit up panting, ears straining to hear. Listening for he knew not what.

How the old place creaked and groaned. Drafts blew through it, doors slammed, panes rattled. Yet he had always thought of it as so solid – indestructible. Now it was as though a puff of wind might blow the house away. The house, or him. So much he wanted to do with the place. So much still to be done. He wondered sometimes whether Berge was conspiring against him. Whether, never having finished the house himself, he refused to let anyone else finish it. Raymond was determined that it would be finished. He wanted to leave it restored, furnished, complete. Not to Lillian. No point in leaving it to her. She hated the place. Titus had said it would need a trust to manage it. The thought of how this might be achieved wearied him. He could visualise what the place would look like. But the mechanics of a trust were beyond him.

As he sat in the library through those mild October nights, with nothing else to do but with the weight of Glastonbridge upon him, he began to write, unsure what it was he was writing. Notes? Instructions? A will? He began to sketch his dream in concrete words. His hopes for the house, what it meant to him and what it could come to mean to others.

Scribbling in his notebooks, he sometimes, for company and to keep the silence and the fear at bay, opened the double doors to the adjoining sitting room, the clock room. The multitude of ticks and tocks, discordant, out of step, carried him through the darkest stretches of the night and bore him, with the striking of one hour and the next, towards the dawn.

*

'We probably should go over and see Raymond,' Sally said as she placed the last spray of wattle in the big arrangement she was making.

'I don't know why you bother doing that – it'll be dead by tomorrow,' Titus said. 'And there's not a lot of point in going to see Raymond. He obviously doesn't want to see us.'

'I'm sure he'll get over it. Don't be so crabby, darling.'

Sally carried the vase into the lounge room and put it on the piano, then leaned against it absently.

That's where I found her. She seemed embarrassed to be found loitering.

'Maybe you should go away for a bit,' I said. 'Do some painting. Away from this life.'

'We're all too comfortable, aren't we? Well, all except Raymond. Raymond's hardly comfortable.'

'Raymond's grandly uncomfortable,' I said.

She laughed. Then, after a silence, 'Where would I go?'

'I don't know. Where would you like to go?'

'Somewhere on my own – just for a while.' She shot me a quick guilty glance.

'Titus takes up too much of your attention.'

'Titus and...everything. Oh but I can't. Maybe later. What of you? Will you settle here, do you think?'

I shrugged.

Shrugs were all that were left to me. All the things I had left unspoken were catching me in the throat. It had become too hard for me to talk of staying, to talk of leaving. These friendships had protected me. Their fellowship held back the darkness. But that fellowship was fracturing. Like travellers gathered round a campfire, we'd all been cocooned in the lamplight, in the glow from one another's faces. Isn't this what human beings do? We build a circle of light. Hunched together, intent on whatever myth it is that we are building, we keep our backs to the darkness. And in the daylight we go about our lives as if there's no such thing as night.

*

At the Friends of the Library meeting, William found himself standing beside Joan at the supper table.

'It's good to see you out and about again Joan,' he said, to make conversation.

'And why shouldn't I be?' asked Joan.

'Well, I just meant...picking up the reins again.'

Joan scowled at him but said nothing.

As William was trying to think of something else to say, Brenda approached. She had only recently joined the committee and was proving a most energetic member. William smiled at her warmly. Brenda Watkins was a much more confident and forthright young woman than he had previously thought. It was good to have the local newspaper involved.

Brenda, too, was surprised at her newfound sense of resolution. Such a tumultuous year for her: Duane and Hogarth's and poetry, then

Norma dying. She felt as strengthened by the griefs as by the joys. Only now, fronting up to Joan, did her resolution slip. Yet she was determined to speak.

'I'm glad to find you both here,' she said, 'because I've had an idea that I want to discuss with you.'

Joan looked at her, her brown eyes steady, holding Brenda's gaze.

'I thought it might be nice,' Brenda said, just a little nervously, 'if one of the school prizes was named after Norma. I mean, there's her contribution through the bookshop. But also the Sells are an old Glaston family. Or rather, were – there's none of them left.'

'I am aware of that Brenda.'

'Yes, of course.'

Brenda watched Joan anxiously. But Joan was looking at her toes.

William, too, was waiting for a cue before venturing an opinion. But as the silence lengthened uncomfortably, he dared to mumble, 'I think it's a marvellous idea. It should be one of the bigger prizes. Perhaps the Year Ten history prize?'

'Not history,' said Joan shortly. 'Norma didn't care for history.'

She glanced sideways at Brenda. 'It's a very nice idea, Brenda. Thank you for thinking of it.' Her face was like stone and it was hard to tell if she was pleased, annoyed or upset.

Brenda generously interpreted it as reawakened grief. 'I hope you don't mind me mentioning it Joan. Perhaps I should have waited. But the end of the year is not far off and...and I really think we should honour Norma. She was such a good person.' Tears started in Brenda's eyes. She pushed them back with the knuckle of her index finger. William reached forward and squeezed her arm.

'Yes,' said Joan dully, 'very appropriate.' Then she put down her teacup and turned and walked away.

'Oh dear, I shouldn't have mentioned history,' William said. 'I fear it's a sore point with Joan these days. What with the Trust sidelining her and now this stoush with Raymond about the old buildings. Oh dear.'

'Maybe Mr Tyler would sponsor a history prize?' suggested Brenda.

'Well, he might.' William was doubtful. 'But I don't think we should ask him just yet. He's got a lot on his mind at the moment. And anyway, it will only provoke Joan more.'

*

Theo was having his morning coffee in Macleay Street when Duane called him on his mobile. He went and stood out on the pavement to better hear what Duane was saying. He couldn't quite believe it. Raymond had gone. Duane was sure of it.

'He's either gone or he's gone bust,' Duane said.

Raymond had been seen leaving Glastonbridge, following behind a removalist's truck. Clover had gone to investigate. The best of the furniture was missing and so was Raymond.

'You sure it was Raymond?' asked Theo.

'Well, it was his car. I reckon he's shot through.'

Theo almost floated back to his table. He sat down and put the sleeve of his white jacket into a puddle of spilt coffee. He didn't notice. When the waiter brought him his second cup and set it down before him, Theo didn't even acknowledge it. When he finally saw it, he drank the coffee in great greedy gulps. Then he stood up and tossed a twenty dollar note on the table.

He was halfway to Greenknowe Avenue before he realised he had left the Rolls in the other direction. He retraced his steps, walking with such jauntiness and such a beaming face that passers-by noticed and smiled, too.

He drove home, barely noticing the traffic, and spent the rest of the afternoon reviewing his financial affairs, now both complicated and simplified by the split from Julia. Simplified, because at least he need not justify his purchases any more. Not to Julia anyway. And to Rosemary? She had yet to take on the role of censoring spouse. Nonetheless he was glad that he wasn't seeing her tonight. He wanted the evening to himself.

*

Raymond had spoken to no one of his plan. He sent Bob and Clover home in the morning, before the truck was due to arrive. When it came he directed the men towards only the most valuable and transportable pieces. He was not leaving for good, only temporarily. He would give the best pieces to Philip to mind then decide what to do next. He wasn't really thinking too far ahead. He almost rang William then decided against it.

On the outskirts of Sydney, he stopped and rang Philip. By mistake he rang Philip's home number and got the answering machine. He wasn't going to leave a message. But he hung on to the phone, breathing heavily. Then, without meaning to, he began to speak:

'I-I'm sending some furniture down to you.' He stopped. 'I-I just had to get out of the house...' his voice was cracking. 'You don't know what it's been like. The stuff will be safe with you, won't it? I hope you've got room in the warehouse.

'I'm not even sure where I'm going. I suppose to Lil's...' His voice was suddenly weary. 'Although I don't really want to.

'I'd come to you, only I don't want to be a burden...Dear boy. The things I've sent – well, you'll see for yourself. It's the best stuff. A lot of pieces that we chose together. Huh, gosh we had some fun, didn't we?

'I want you to take care of it. You will take care of it all, won't you?'

His voice was cut off by the click of the answering machine, the tape running out. He stood in the phone box a while, wondering what to do next. Should he warn Lillian he was coming? She'd been at him for weeks to have what she called 'a business meeting'. She'd even threatened to drive up to Glaston to have it. He didn't think he was up to that tonight. All he wanted was a safe place to lie down and sleep. He thought longingly of the guest bedroom at Lillian's, with its pale blue walls and soft pillows and clean white sheets. He would even put up with a lecture if he could reach that safe place.

'You're in,' he said when she opened the door.

'Where else would I be?' she snapped. 'You look dreadful. What's the matter with you?'

'Nothing, nothing,' he said and shuffled down the hallway towards her living room.

'For God's sake, have a shower,' she said. She grabbed his arm to stop him sitting on one of her cream brocade sofas. 'You look like a tramp.'

He allowed himself to be directed towards the guest suite.

'I'll get you a cup of tea if you like,' she said grudgingly.

'That'd be nice.'

Showered and dressed in clean clothes that he'd left there last time, he sat on a stool in the kitchen, drinking his tea. Lillian was on the telephone and he could hear snippets of her conversation.

'How have you been, Lil?' he asked when she came into the kitchen.

'Never better.'

There was something ferocious in the way she said it. He had to admit he'd never seen her looking so robust. He almost asked if she was taking something. She moved her body confidently and her cheeks glowed. But there was a glint in her eye that he didn't like the look of. If only she would leave him be.

'I should go and see Philip shortly.' He didn't really feel up to going anywhere. 'But I'll be back. You don't mind if I stay?'

Lillian's fist lay clenched across her breast.

'That'd be right,' she said bitterly, 'just use my place as a hotel.' She stalked out of the kitchen.

Wearily, Raymond followed her. 'I thought later, maybe tomorrow, we could have that chat you've been wanting us to have.'

Lillian remained with her back turned to him. 'Of course you can always delay a meeting with your sister.' She gazed unseeing through the wide glass windows. The last glow of sunset could be seen beyond the dark curve of the bridge and lights were coming on around the harbour.

Raymond sighed, giving in. 'What is it this time, Lil?'

A truck stopped outside Philip Dexter Antiques, blocking half of Queen Street and hemming in one Jaguar and two BMWs. Philip was still at his desk at the rear of the half-lit showroom when the front door buzzer went. That was unusual at this hour. Before he opened the door, he peered out. The truck certainly wasn't one he knew, with its dusty green cabin and battered red sides. The driver, in singlet and shorts, was mouthing something at him through the plate glass. Philip reluctantly opened the door.

'Sorry,' the man said. 'I was meant to be here earlier. Flat tyre. Bloody nuisance.'

'Excuse me, where are you from?'

'Glaston. Got some stuff here for you...' he checked his paperwork, 'from a Mr Tyler.'

'I think you had better bring the truck around the back,' Philip said, 'so I can see what you've got in there.'

Lillian stirred Raymond's gin and tonic and handed it to him. She must control herself. She must say nothing to alarm him. They must discuss this calmly. Raymond must remain calm, must remain seated there in the best chair, must drink his drink and hear her out. To ensure this, she herself must remain calm. Nonetheless her hand trembled as she put down the gin bottle.

'Something has to be done Raymond. You must see that. I can't afford paying you that ridiculous amount each month. I've got the car to pay off now, too.'

Raymond had been expecting this. Nonetheless, when it came, a great weight of weariness fell across him like a heavy sheet. He struggled to push it aside. He took a sip of his gin and tonic to fortify himself. He could at this moment have been having a nice little drink with Philip. Dear boy. He'd seen too little of him lately. Why was it one always saw too little of those who mattered most? If he could just get this business of Lillian's over with, he would be free to go. He tried to concentrate. What was it she had said?

'Are you listening to me?' Lillian asked.

Listen. Yes, he must listen. Oh dear, how much more must he listen! The weight on his shoulders was pushing down on him, pinning him to the chair. Trying to speak, he cleared his throat. It tasted thick and unpleasant and he swallowed hard. A piercing pain hit him in the chest. He tried to move his arm, to pick up his drink. But he didn't have the strength. His wrist was limp, rubbery. It refused to respond. He leaned his head back and closed his eyes. Lillian was speaking again. What was it she was saying this time? He couldn't follow it. If only she would shut up.

Once, when they were children, he had gone into her room to play with her dolls. He'd heard her coming along the passage and had to hide in the cupboard. He had sat in that dark cupboard for what seemed like hours. All the time, Lillian sat on her bed playing with her dolls, talking to them, singing to them, scolding them. Talking on and on and on, while he crouched in the black cupboard, the blackness growing ever more oppressive, Lillian's voice going on and on.

Lillian's voice was going on and on and the blackness was pressing in on him again. He opened his mouth to speak, to scream, but no sound came. Just more blackness, pouring into him, pouring out of him. Then, at the end of it, light. A glorious light, a burnished golden light spreading across an unfamiliar, yet oh-so-familiar landscape. And there was Glastonbridge. Not Glastonbridge as he had last seen it in all its darkness and gloom. But a glorious, bewitching Glastonbridge, glowing in the sunlight as he rushed towards it.

Lillian was trying to explain to Raymond all her recent miseries. He was listening quietly, which made a change. She wanted him to understand how hard it was for her. How hard it was for her here, all on her own, and that being poor just made it impossible. She was glad he wasn't interrupting as he usually did. It was important that he listen to her and understand. There were so many bad times between them, so many arguments. And she knew it had sometimes been her fault. She wanted to tell him that. She didn't want it to be like that, she truly didn't. And she was sorry that she had said so many cruel things, particularly lately. That's why it was so important that he stay home with her this evening and hear her out, and stay calm and quiet. Calm and quiet, just as he was now.

'You do understand, don't you?' she said to him, looking at him for the first time in some minutes.

Raymond appeared to be asleep. 'Oh Raymond, you haven't been listening, have you!'

She went towards him. 'Raymond?' She touched his shoulder. Then she shook him. His head slumped forward. She took two quick steps backwards and fell into an armchair. Her fingers dug into a cushion and she picked it up and jammed it into her mouth. She didn't scream. She just stared and stared at Raymond.

Was it ten minutes, half an hour, an hour later that she stood up and went to the telephone to call an ambulance? While she waited for them to arrive, she moved around the room, tidying it, humming a repetitive little tune. She took the glasses and the ashtray into the kitchen and washed them up, then went into her bedroom to powder her nose. She saw a throw rug on the chair and a thought occurred to her: perhaps she should cover him, keep him warm? If people were in shock, they should be kept warm. Perhaps Raymond was in shock. She took the blanket out to the living room and laid it across him. Then the paramedics were ringing the doorbell.

'Should I come with him?' she asked them as they lifted Raymond's body onto a stretcher.

One of them looked up at her. 'You can if you like. Are you his wife?'

'No, his sister.'

She seemed so calm, so he said, 'You know, he's dead.'

'Oh.' After a pause, Lillian said, 'I suppose there's no need for me to come with you then.'

It was about an hour afterwards that Philip called. He had just got home and heard Raymond's strange message on the answering machine.

'I'm sorry Philip, Raymond can't come to the phone.'

'I only want to speak to him for a moment, Lillian.'

'No, I'm sorry Philip, it's not possible.'

'Lillian...'

'Goodnight Philip.'

She put the phone down and said to herself what she hadn't said to Philip: 'Raymond is dead.' She said it again. 'Raymond is dead.' She sat down to better think about it. But she couldn't get her mind around it. Until she thought of his will.

This sent her into an immediate frenzy. She rushed into his bedroom and looked about her as if expecting to find the will propped up on the dressing table. They had never spoken of his will. What if there was no will? What if he had left it all to charity? She had heard him once make some absurd remark about leaving Glastonbridge to the National Estate. She didn't believe he would do it. It wasn't the sort of thing a Tyler would do. But then Raymond always was strange. If there was a will, she must find it.

Pausing only to collect Raymond's keys, Lillian picked up her jacket and handbag and caught the lift down to the garage.

Shortly after ten o'clock that night, Theo stepped jauntily down the Astor's marble stairs and set off for a brief stroll to clear his head. The anticipation had been building all evening so that he almost couldn't control himself. He hummed a little tune, round and round, like a child's skipping song:

'Raymond's fled, Raymond's fled

And Glastonbridge will soon be mine.'

Occasionally he doubted. Perhaps Duane was mistaken? Could there be another explanation for Raymond's sudden departure – with a removalist's van? No, it must be true. Then the little tune would start up again: 'Raymond's fled, Raymond's fled. And Glastonbridge will soon be mine.' Theo gave a little skip as he ambled along Macquarie Street. He veered off down St Mary's Road and decided to do a circuit around Woolloomooloo. It was still early and he was far too excited to sleep. A long walk would tire him and calm him. It was a cool night. A light mist lay hazily in the hollows of the city, silhouetting the Moreton Bay figs on the edge of the park, surrounding the sodium lights with an orange glow.

As he walked, Theo composed his announcement to Rosemary. She probably wouldn't be surprised. Rosemary had a disconcerting way of accepting the most extraordinary things matter of factly. Theo gave a short laugh. He imagined her saying, 'I knew we'd get it eventually'. He shouldn't have too much trouble talking her out of that silly idea of turning the house into a hotel.

Then his thoughts reverted to the house itself and its contents. He hoped Raymond hadn't taken the Sly bookcases with him. He would insist on having those. Hadn't Philip Dexter told him they'd been made specifically for Glastonbridge?

Theo stopped at a pedestrian crossing in Sir John Young Crescent and waited for the lights to change. His eyes dwelt idly on a car that was also waiting for the lights. Then he drew back in consternation. There, in her powder-blue Mercedes, was Lillian Tyler-Watson. It seemed inevitable that she would see him so Theo waved. Lillian looked as if she'd seen an apparition. Her body fell forward on the steering wheel and, not waiting for the lights to change, the engine roared and she accelerated across the intersection, only just missing a derelict drunk who was weaving his way towards the centre island.

Theo gazed after her then went to help the drunk who had flopped into the gutter. Theo set him on his feet and saw him safely to the other side.

The mist was heavy in Glaston when Lillian arrived in the dead hours of the early morning. The streets were deserted, damp. Quiet in the eerie way of a small town whose few thousand souls are absent in sleep. No one noticed the blue Mercedes as it traversed the main street and went down the Old West Road, across the river and up to the Glastonbridge gate.

Lillian's purpose, by the time she reached the house, was clear. It was to find the will, if it should exist, to secure the more valuable and transportable items, and to leave the house as safely locked as possible. She knew the house, she knew her brother's habits. But several times in the first hour or two her spirit nearly failed her. She had never been here alone before, had never contemplated that she might have to be here on such a purpose. Several times she started at a noise. A creak, a groan. She tried to ignore it and worked steadily from room to room, searching, sorting. By daylight she had done what needed to be done.

The rain began as she was preparing to leave the house. She had found the keys to the largest cupboards and had locked away the best of the silver, all that would fit, when the first clap of thunder struck overhead. Lillian's knees almost buckled. She sank into a chair in the front hall and decided to wait the storm out. Rather than abating, its ferocity grew. Wind and rain slammed into the tall windows, making them shake so she thought they would shatter. The branches of trees bowed down, scraping and banging against the gutters. It grew as dark as night again and when she switched some lights on they flickered ominously, so that she had visions of power lines blowing down, of the house surrounded by live wires. The force of the wind, in great blasts, shook the doors and she heard tearing sounds, as of roofs being ripped off like the lids from tins.

Finally, it stopped.

Lillian stepped out into the still aftermath of a maelstrom. The roof had come off the coach house and lay on its side in the paddock beyond. Timber and slate from the porch was scattered around its base. Lillian stepped gingerly towards her car. It was covered in wet leaves and small branches but was otherwise unharmed. Relieved, she got in and started down the drive. A fallen tree blocked her path. Panicking, she put the car in reverse. The wheels spun and then the car stopped with a jolt and the sound of crunching metal. She had backed into a tree stump. Going forward, she managed to manoeuvre around the fallen tree and continue down the track.

As she drove through Glaston, the damaged rear bumper bar hanging dangerously low, Lillian noticed that the storm seemed to have passed by the town. The streets were dry, tidy, unscarred.

The telephone rang at Philip's shop a little after ten-thirty. Jules was in the showroom and answered it. It was Lillian.

'Philip is not 'ere Lillian. But he will be back in a little while. Can I help you?...The name of Raymond's solicitor? No, I am afraid I do not know it. Why not ask Raymond?'

A few minutes later, Philip arrived and was told about the call. He was immediately alarmed.

'What's going on Lillian?' he asked as soon as she answered the phone.

'Raymond is dead.'

'My God! My God, Lillian, what do you mean?...When? How?'

'Last night. I don't know how,' she said impatiently. 'He just is.'

'When last night?' Philip was asking questions without thinking. He couldn't take it in. But her reply focused his attention.

'Around seven,' she said.

'But I spoke to you at nine!'

'Yes, yes, I know. I couldn't tell you then. It was important no one knew. There was that house up there – all wide open. Anyone could have walked in and taken anything.'

'Lillian, what are you talking about?' The shock of Raymond's death was beginning to hit Philip. Shaking, he said, 'I-I can't talk now. I'll have to talk to you later.'

'Philip, don't you tell anyone. I have to talk to the solicitor first...'

But he had already hung up.

Theo arrived at Rosemary's house that evening with a bottle of Bollinger. Rosemary said, looking at the bottle, 'Well, that's nice. But I don't know how appropriate it is. Some awful news. Sad news.'

'Oh?'

'Raymond's dead.'

The bottle slipped from Theo's hand and crashed to the floor. He looked stricken. 'Dead?'

Rosemary jumped away from the splinters of glass and grabbed a dish cloth.

'Leave it! Leave it!' Theo said. 'Tell me what happened.'

'I don't know. It was last night. He was at his sister's apparently.'

'But I saw Lillian last night,' Theo blurted. 'She did behave rather strangely…My God,' he said half to himself, 'Raymond dead.' Then suddenly, 'What of?'

'No one is sure,' said Rosemary, crouching down and picking up pieces of broken bottle. 'They think a heart attack. Sally is terribly upset.'

Theo's own heart was thumping heavily in his chest. He pulled out a stool and sat down, resting his large head in his hands. He stayed like that for some time.

'Darling,' said Rosemary when she noticed. 'Are you all right? What's the matter?'

Theo remained bent over, his shoulders slumped. At last he held up his head and, shaking it, said, 'This is quite a shock.'

Rosemary looked at him curiously. 'I had no idea you were so fond of Raymond.'

'Fond?' He supposed he was in a way. But that wasn't the cause of his distress.

15.

When Raymond died I realised there were things I should have told
him. But I had only just made the connections myself. And now it was
too late.

Or perhaps it wasn't.

Raymond's body was brought back from Sydney and laid out at the
undertakers in Glaston in a quiet, bare room. He was dressed in his
favourite pale-grey Gieves and Hawkes suit. (Robbie said that Glaston
had never seen him looking so fine.) He actually looked much better
than he had in recent months, except for his colour: neither white, nor
grey, nor yellow, but somewhere in between.

There was no one in the room but me. I went up to him and stood
there a while, looking down. Then I said, 'I want to tell you a story.' I
felt foolish as I began but after a while I got used to it. I remembered
how Raymond had taken his mother to Scone after she died. Perhaps
his spirit could hear me.

I said to him, 'I've discovered that I can trace my family line back to
the puntman's daughter, Kathleen. And that she had a son, Sam. Sam
was the son of Kathleen and of William Berge.'

Poor Kathleen's bastard son, given up to the Harknesses.

'And Sam's son was Tom Harkness, the Tom who bought Glastonbridge. You knew about the Harknesses. But you never knew about Kathleen.'

*

It gnawed at Sally that she had in some way failed Raymond. She had thought him more difficult than usual because he was angry at her over the Rosemary and Theo business. But there had been a deeper malaise and she had missed it. Even the trouble with the power being cut off repeatedly had not concerned her as much as it should have. Titus had often teased her about being overly solicitous of Raymond, but she had not been solicitous enough.

'None of us could have done anything,' Titus told her, trying to reassure her. 'How can one predict a heart attack?'

'Clover did.'

'How do you mean?'

'Not a heart attack exactly – but she knew something was going to happen. She was the only one of us who wasn't shocked.'

'There's the phone,' said Titus and went to answer it.

When Sally followed him into the kitchen, having wiped away a fresh set of tears, she could tell he was talking to Philip.

'Funny, the one who is really taking it hard is Bob,' said Titus into the phone. 'Clover said she went out to the house and found him sobbing in the kitchen…yes, Lillian thinks the house is all locked up but she's forgotten that Clover and Bob have keys…they know the house better than anyone else. We can ask them to have a look. Hang on, I'll put Sal on.'

He passed the phone to Sally. 'Philip wants Clover and Bob to search the house, see if there's another will anywhere.'

'What's this about a will?' Sally asked Philip. 'Oh, surely not...Raymond always said he wouldn't let Lillian get her hands on it...1972! Surely he made another will since then. What about his talk of leaving Glastonbridge to a trust?...Heavens yes, we'll turn the place upside down. Wait a minute, Titus wants another word – yes, everything's organised for tomorrow. I persuaded the minister to let Raymond have a plot in the old churchyard. They're not burying people there any more but I knew he'd hate it in the new cemetery.' She started to cry again and handed the phone back to Titus.

Titus asked Philip, 'Have you checked all the pieces he sent down to you, all the drawers? Nothing there?...Ah, just a thought. Okay, see you tomorrow...Bye.'

Titus put his arm around Sally's shoulder and squeezed her. 'Well, at least we've stymied bloody Lillian. She thought that if the funeral was up here no one would come, but all Raymond's mates are coming, all his society friends, Philip says – Lady Regan, the Contessa, the Forsters, the Lloyd-Jenkinses and half of bloody Queen Street. That'll show her.'

William ran his pen down the foolscap paper. Had he thought of everything? He had checked the order of service with Sally but was still nervous he might have forgotten something. He'd just run through it one more time then take it down to the printers. Really, this should have been Lillian's job. He didn't like funerals. But at least they'd give Raymond a nice one, much nicer than Lillian would have.

William was going to play the organ himself, at least for the main pieces. He'd start with selections from Handel's concerto in D minor as people were coming into the church. That would give them plenty of time to settle. Oh dear, he did hope everyone would approve.

Robbie stood in the doorway, frowning. 'I just drove past Duane's shop,' he said. 'There are two cop cars outside it.'

'What can that be about?'

'Dunno. Think I'll ring him.' A minute later Robbie came back into the room and said, 'He's not answering.'

*

St Aidan's was on one of the low hills on the western side of Glaston. A rough gravel path led steeply from the iron gates through a tangle of trees and shrubs, boulders and tussocky hillocks to the stone church. On one side a new housing estate had crept almost to the churchyard, but behind was open country, a clear view across the river and flat farmland. If you looked closely, you could just glimpse the roof of Glastonbridge behind its screen of trees.

Sally had chosen the plot for Raymond so that his view would be uninterrupted, at the end of a row where the ground fell away beyond the low hedge. As people were arriving at the church for the service, she went around the back to make sure the gravediggers had dug the right plot.

The church was filling fast and it looked as if not everyone would fit inside. Titus was talking to the minister on the doorstep. Could a speaker be put outside, so that those who couldn't get in could still hear the service? The street was full of an incongruous mixture of cars: Jaguars and farm utes, BMWs and ancient Valiants, expensive four-wheel-drives and tradesmen's vans. Inside the church, their owners had clumped themselves into immediately identifiable groups. The antique dealers – fey and fresh faced or scruffily eccentric – on one side; on the other, the Glaston tradesmen and shopkeepers who had been won over by Raymond's peculiar charm. The businessmen, in serious black, sat at the back; the Contessa and her cronies, decked out in hats and elegantly subdued suits, at the front. In the very front row sat Lillian with an assortment of second and third cousins no one had ever seen before. Across the aisle from her were Philip, Jules, Sally, Titus and Robbie. William was at the organ, playing the Handel in D with a steady hand.

The minister had just begun his opening address when Rosemary and Theo arrived, Rosemary muttering 'Family, family' to ensure their admittance as they squeezed through the crowd at the door. Theo had insisted on coming and she had reluctantly agreed. It had meant missing an important meeting. They found room to stand at the back. Theo nodded at Joan Beaverstoke, who stood a couple of metres away. Joan wore the dark purple dress she'd bought for Norma's funeral. She hadn't expected to wear it again so soon. Theo thought it made her look like Queen Victoria.

As the minister launched into a reading from Ephesians 5, Theo sank again into that state of reverie that had become habitual to him in recent days. To look at him, he seemed at peace, but behind the trim beard, behind his steel-rimmed spectacles, his mind danced a tortuous dance. 'Put away lying,' the minister was saying, 'speak every man truth with his neighbour.'

I don't lie, thought Theo. Perhaps I dissemble, perhaps I haven't been straightforward, but I don't lie.

'Let no corrupt communication proceed out of your mouth,' said the minister.

Ah. Theo grimaced. Yes. He remembered that last conversation with Duane.

'Let all bitterness, and wrath, and anger, and clamour, and evil speaking, be put away from you, with all malice.'

Yes, I felt all of that about Raymond, Theo thought: envy and evil, jealousy and malice.

A few rows in front of him, Bob Pitts crouched, wondering if the minister was speaking to him directly:

'Let him that stole steal no more, but rather let him labour, working with his hands the thing which is good.'

I've only taken a few things, Bob thought. Ray wouldn't have minded. I worked for him for years for a pittance. Why should I leave everything for that bitch?

Brenda Watkins sat on the end of a pew with her notebook on her knees. She had scanned the crowd when she arrived but knew he wasn't here. Her stomach was a hollow pain. Duane had gone, left town without telling her. She wasn't sure what she felt. Anger? Grief? Hatred? Love?

'Be ye kind to one another,' the minister said, 'tender-hearted, forgiving one another.'

Could she ever forgive Duane? What he had done to her, what he might have done to Raymond?

The people around her were singing *The Lord is my shepherd*. Brenda tried to join in but the words wouldn't come. She was glad when the voices subsided and the church choir began *O little one sweet, O little one mild*. She pulled out her handkerchief.

As the choir concluded, Philip stood and went to the lectern to give the eulogy. He had sat up in bed last night composing it. What could one say about Raymond?

'Raymond has been the most important influence on my life,' he began. The society ladies scrabbled in their handbags for tissues. How handsome Philip was! How well he spoke.

'Without him my life would have been so different, so much poorer, that I find it hard to even imagine. He treated me like a son, took me under his wing and taught me all he knew.' Here Philip's voice cracked slightly. 'He was an extraordinarily knowledgeable man, and very generous with that knowledge. He wasn't always easy. In fact, he was often infuriating but that was because he had his own vision that he was following, and it wasn't always easy for the rest of us to understand what it entailed and what lengths it drove him to. Those who only knew Raymond in the latter years of his life saw him in his most eccentric phase.' There was a humorous murmur from the congregation. 'But Raymond was always an original. It was because of his originality, the originality of his vision, of his view of the world, that he was able to inspire such affection and such loyalty – as is demonstrated here today.'

Sally's shoulders shook; the Contessa wept openly, wiping her cheeks with a hanky, leaving pale streaks through her rouge. Lillian sat in the front row, upright and stony faced. Since Raymond's death she'd been angry and relieved. Angry because he'd slipped out from under her yet again; relieved because it seemed that she was at last free of him. But sitting in the church she had the first pang of grief. She had a sudden glimpse of her future life without him. Without him, or her mother, or her father, or Harold. Emptiness yawned before her; fear immobilised her.

As Philip spoke, people fumbled in their pockets, bowed their heads. But Lillian stared straight ahead, hollowed out.

'So,' Philip, concluded, 'Raymond seemed at times a lonely, almost pathetic figure, but he touched so many lives in so many areas of life. He was...' Philip's voice almost broke, 'very human.'

Joan Beaverstoke had been feeling worse and worse the more Philip spoke. When Titus stood up to sing a Bach cantata, the combination of Philip's words and the deep, resonant chords and Titus's wonderful bass brought a rush of tears to her eyes. She fought them back, fought them back so that they ran down the back of her throat. She felt like she was drowning. Then Norma's face swam towards her, how she'd been at the end with the spittle running from the corner of her mouth.

Joan clung to the back of the pew in front of her. She looked so awful that Theo moved across to stand beside her and took her elbow.

Joan barely noticed. How she had profaned Norma's memory! All those wonderful years together and instead of treasuring them she'd thrown anger and bitterness at her, cursing her in her grave. 'Let not the sun go down upon thy wrath,' the minister had said. Joan's hands shook on the rail. She was a wicked woman! She lashed out without cause. Look how she had treated Raymond, and after he had been so kind to her. She gave a small sound that was both whimper and groan, and Theo clutched her elbow tighter.

Clover sat on the edge of her pew, gazing up at Titus with the calm and concentrated gaze of a madonna. It was a beautiful service. It would have been terrible if Raymond's funeral had been ugly or ordinary. She would miss Raymond of course, and she dreaded what might become of Glastonbridge and all the work she'd done there. But she couldn't be sorry the way the others were, the way Sally was. No one could have changed how things had happened. It was simply the way it was meant to be.

Brenda was sitting just in front of her. She'd been crying quietly almost since the service began. Weren't people strange! thought Clover. She'd hardly known Raymond.

It was true that at first Brenda's tears were not for Raymond but for Duane, and herself. But she, too, was moved by Philip's eulogy. She wished now that she had known Raymond better. Clearly he was a very special man. She would devote a column to him in the *Gazette*. No, not a column; perhaps a poem. A poem of Wordsworth's that she had learnt by heart came to mind. She would put a special heading on it: 'In Memory of Raymond Tyler'. She glanced down at the program she was clutching, '5/10/1936 – 21/10/1996', and recited the lines silently to herself:

> Our birth is but a sleep and a forgetting:
> The Soul that rises with us, our life's Star,

Has had elsewhere its setting,
And cometh from afar:
Not in entire forgetfulness,
And not in utter nakedness,
But trailing clouds of glory do we come
From God, who is our home:
Heaven lies about us in our infancy!

As the minister came to the end of a reading from Luke 7, a mobile phone began ringing up the back, among the pews of businessmen. One of them scrabbled in his briefcase to find and silence it as the minister led the congregation into the opening bars of *Praise to the Lord*. This time Brenda joined in the singing, all her frustrated passion in her voice.

Meanwhile, Rosemary was wondering if it would be possible for her and Theo to buy Glastonbridge. She dearly wanted to discuss it with him. She had tried the morning before, when they were lying entwined in bed together. But he didn't seem to want to talk about it. He'd been behaving so strangely. Rosemary had heard that Lillian had got everything, but she didn't think she would want to keep the house. Rosemary imagined her life transformed. She would be an entrepreneur; she would turn Glastonbridge into the finest country house hotel in Australia. She was quite determined about it. She and Theo might or might not live there. Theo seemed to prefer Sydney anyway. They could turn the coach house into an apartment, as a weekender. She glanced across at him. Why on earth was he hanging on to that huge woman in purple?

Theo had resisted thinking of Glastonbridge but as he heard Philip speak about Raymond's passion and vision, another thought occurred to him. Couldn't he repay the debt he owed to Raymond by completing his great work? No one understood the house as he did. No one else could preserve the spirit of the place as he would. Was there anyone else who could bring Raymond's dream to fruition? He had admired Raymond. Perhaps he had even loved him. Then a shudder ran through Theo, such a shudder that he had to let go of Joan's arm and grab the pew for support. How his envy had run away with him! He'd been covetous. And suddenly he knew Glastonbridge could never be his. He gripped the pew with both hands and bowed his head. His whole body was wracked with guilt and anguish. He couldn't do it! He couldn't step into Raymond's shoes.

It was only towards the end of the service that William stopped worrying about how it was going and allowed himself to be affected by the ceremony. As the prayers began he moved his mouth as though following the words, but really he was thinking about all the years he had known Raymond. Was it thirty? Was that possible? He'd never noticed that they were aging. If Raymond could drop dead from a heart attack then he could, too. What a strange thought. He still couldn't quite believe that tomorrow he wouldn't see him, that he wouldn't call around with Miffy or chance to drop by just on dinner time. William smiled. Touching his face, he noticed that it was wet.

The choir was beginning to sing *Never weather beaten sail*. It would be his turn again soon. He should prepare himself. That song described Raymond, really. He always seemed to be buffeted but one never knew by what. Yes, he had been a complainer but never about the things that really mattered. What was he thinking, at the end?

William had chosen for the last piece of music, while the coffin was being carried out, Handel's *The cuckoo and the nightingale*. He didn't believe in being too maudlin at the end of a funeral. He thought Raymond would approve. He knew, anyway, that Raymond had liked the piece.

On this thought, William made his way to the organ. As he played he remembered the last time he had played for Raymond; remembered how, at his best, there'd been a reckless joyousness about him. And it was in this spirit that William played so that as the pallbearers – Philip and Jules, Titus and Robbie – carried the coffin down the aisle, there was more spring in their step than was strictly seemly, while their eyes were blinded by tears.

This was how Raymond Tyler went towards his grave. As the mourners followed the coffin out, William blazed away at the organ, head up, cheeks wet. As they shuffled up the aisle everyone was smiling and sniffling, clasping hands, kissing cheeks. All except Lillian. Lillian was left standing alone and silent in the front pew as the mourners moved away from her. Only when the assistant minister came and took her arm did she move forward and follow the rest towards the gravesite.

Epilogue

Theo has gone off to Russia on the trail of icons and was last seen lurking in the Church of the Assumption in Smolensk.

Sally, too, is in Europe. She is spending the northern winter at an art school in Florence. 'Something just for myself,' she told me, surprise in her eyes. She has promised Titus she will be back in time for the grape harvest.

Rosemary was left behind when Theo went off to Russia. When I asked Sally, she shrugged, 'I think it's over.' So Rosemary has been unlucky in love yet again.

We can live our lives on endless repeat or we can push for a different kind of future. Sometimes you just have to forge ahead, regardless. That is what I am trying to do. I never thought my future would be in Glaston. But I've found I'm rather fond of it. My cottage came up for sale so I've decided to buy it. I have friends here who care for me and I care for them. And links to a past I never even knew about.

Clover and I have been spending a lot of time together. I'm going to need her help with the house – there is so much wood to be restored she may even need to move in. Of course her work at Glastonbridge is over.

Glastonbridge has been abandoned on its hillside. It's locked and empty. Lillian cleared it out and sent everything to be auctioned once it became clear that Theo Roth would not be calling. She couldn't believe that he didn't even want the Sly bookcases. The house is for sale but no one yet has been brave enough, or mad enough, to take it on.

About Upswell

Upswell Publishing was established in
2021 by Terri-ann White as a not-for-profit
press. A perceived gap in the market for
distinctive literary works in fiction, poetry
and narrative non-fiction was the motivation.
In her years as a bookseller, writer and then
publisher, Terri-ann has maintained a watch
on literary books and the way they insinuate
themselves into a cultural space and are
then located within our literary and cultural
inheritance. She is interested in making books
to last: books with the potential to still be
noticed, and noted, after decades and thus
be ripe to influence new literary histories.

About this typeface

Book designer Becky Chilcott chose
Foundry Origin not only as a strong,
carefully considered, and dependable
typeface, but also to honour her late
friend and mentor, type designer Freda
Sack, who oversaw the project. Designed
by Freda's long-standing colleague,
Stuart de Rozario, much like Upswell
Publishing, Foundry Origin was created
out of the desire to say something new.